SACRAMENTO PUBLIC LIBRARY
828 "I" Street
Sacramento, CA 95814
01/19

D0462734

FEARLESS

By Sarah Tarkoff

Sinless
Fearless

FEARLESS

EYE OF THE BEHOLDER

BOOK 2

sarah tarkoff

HARPER Voyager
An Imprint of HarperCollins Publishers

This is a work of fiction. Names, characters, places, and incidents are products of the author's imagination or are used fictitiously and are not to be construed as real. Any resemblance to actual events, locales, organizations, or persons, living or dead, is entirely coincidental.

FEARLESS. Copyright © 2019 by Sarah Tarkoff. All rights reserved. Printed in the United States of America. No part of this book may be used or reproduced in any manner whatsoever without written permission except in the case of brief quotations embodied in critical articles and reviews. For information, address HarperCollins Publishers, 195 Broadway, New York, NY 10007.

HarperCollins books may be purchased for educational, business, or sales promotional use. For information, please email the Special Markets Department at SPsales@harpercollins.com.

Harper Voyager and design are trademarks of HarperCollins Publishers LLC.

FIRST EDITION

Designed by Paula Russell Szafranski

Library of Congress Cataloging-in-Publication Data has been applied for.

ISBN 978-0-06-245640-3

19 20 21 22 23   LSC   10 9 8 7 6 5 4 3 2 1

For Ari

FEARLESS

I want to start by saying thank you. I know my words chronicle a painful time for many of you, and I will be forever grateful for your willingness to read.

Up until this point, I've put off recounting many of the events that might seem mandatory material for an autobiography about Grace Luther. I wanted to take the time to set the stage, to help you understand how I got to where I am now. Luckily, I can reassure you, this next chapter will include many of the moments you've all been waiting for: the true, untold story of the fateful night that started it all, for better or worse.

I'm sure that some of you disagree with me politically, religiously, morally—and there is nothing I could say to convince you that I'm not evil, that I'm not a heretic, that the consequences of what I did were worth it in the end. All I can offer you is a promise that whatever viciousness you might level at me, I will never return it in kind. I aspire to forgive the way Great Spirit forgives—completely and unconditionally. To forgive my enemies, and to forgive myself.

Thank you all over again for lending me your ears and your hearts.

With all the love of Great Spirit,
Grace Luther
c/o Arlington Federal Prison

BOOK
ONE

This time, it was my hair running a dangerous mission.

The sparkly clip restraining my kinky, curly locks held a powerful recording device, one sensitive enough to pick up the sound of keys clacking on a keyboard, to see fingers typing from across the room. All our previous attempts to hack into Prophet Joshua's server had failed, and this was our last, best chance to infiltrate his computer network. If we succeeded, we might finally create some chink in Joshua's otherwise impenetrable armor and get some idea of how to take him down for good.

Dawn had been quite clear about what to expect if the recording device was discovered and my cover within Joshua's organization was blown—interrogation, torture, death. Joshua and the other prophets knew a worldwide resistance was out there—and they were desperate to stop us however they could.

With that weighing on my mind, I pasted on an innocent smile for the benefit of Guru Samuel Jenkins, the prophet's right-hand man. He'd never particularly liked me, and his words always seemed laced with a hint of suspicion. "Tell me what you've been up to lately, Grace."

His coy smirk made my stomach flip-flop. And I began to lie my ass off.

2

won't lie to *you*. I was not born to be a double agent. After getting Punished for the first lie I attempted post-Revelation (telling the babysitter I was allowed to stay up past 9:00), I'd never told another. That is, until I stumbled upon the truth at the age of seventeen, the truth about what was really happening in our world, and my whole life became a house of cards poised to fall at any moment.

And indeed, during the six months I'd spent as a double agent for Dawn, the precariousness of our situation was driving me toward paranoia. The prophets held all the power, while we were struggling just to survive, to avoid being discovered, captured, killed. Though we tried to keep hope alive, the futility of our situation was obvious. Even if we managed to reveal the truth, the simple act of revealing that truth would likely cause the death of anyone who *heard* it. Guilt at questioning the word of the prophets . . . that was all it took to cause a lethal Punishment. Just about every human being on Earth believed these people were direct mouthpieces to Great Spirit, believed that mankind's very survival relied on following their Proclamations.

And to a certain extent, weren't they right? Mankind was thriving under their leadership. With the world united under one ideology, we'd finally been able to put aside our differences and live in peace. Now that crime itself carried a swift and sometimes deadly Punishment, the world had not witnessed war, or large-scale violence of any kind, in a decade.

But unlike the rest of the world, most of whom still believed what they were told about the origins of this phenomenon, I'd eventually learned it wasn't judgment from on high causing our Punishments—it was the chemicals in our brains associated with guilt. I'd learned that there was a network of tiny machines whirring beneath my skull—nanotech. These machines monitored everything we felt, and when they sensed guilt, they caused the physical changes we referred to as Punishment—making their host uglier, sicklier, sometimes even monstrous-looking.

Our seeming utopia wasn't the work of Great Spirit, but the sinister creation of humans.

I never would have believed any of this until I saw it with my own eyes. And once that happened, and especially once I started working with the resistance movement trying to expose the truth, lies became my daily means of survival, a routine I fell into: eating breakfast with my dad every morning, walking to class with my best friend, Macy, chattering away as if nothing had changed.

But it had, everything had. And the strain of it all was changing *me*, sometimes in ways I didn't like. By the time I made it to my high school graduation, I already felt like an impostor in my own life. These kids I'd once thought were my best friends were already strangers, their happiness so alien to me. My goal to take down the prophets filled every fiber of my being, consumed my thoughts, but I still felt lost, adrift somehow. Back when I'd believed my sole purpose on this planet was to glorify Great Spirit, my task seemed simple enough. All I had to do was live my own life with courage and conscience.

But what I was doing now? The sheer size of our undertaking overwhelmed me. I couldn't imagine my actions making a dent in the problem at hand. As important as I knew our goal was, it felt impossible. Doomed.

Maybe if we'd had leadership I trusted more, things would have been better . . . but ever since the disastrous op in West Virginia, one that had left dozens of innocent scientists dead, I was wary of Dawn's motives, wary of her methods. As if I needed any more people to be wary of.

She'd promised to keep me in the loop about our strategy if I helped her, and at first she made good on that promise. But after I graduated from high school and started at NYU, Dawn went radio silent. Based on the messages she sent through intermediaries, I got the sense that she was in some kind of trouble. While I worried for her, I also felt stranded . . . and more and more like I'd made a terrible mistake signing up for all this.

The only person I knew for sure I could trust was Jude, my childhood next-door neighbor and first love. Dawn had saved his life after a nearly fatal Punishment, and in return, he'd given up his identity to help her cause, to help her save others. I hadn't seen him since we'd made our plan to run away together six months ago . . . because rather than running away, I decided to stay and help the resistance. It was a decision I questioned every single day, every time I wondered what he was doing, what he thought of me.

Did he hate me for abandoning him, for choosing to stay behind and help Dawn instead of escaping into a life of safety and happiness together? Or was he proud that I was taking up the mantle of his cause?

Against my will, as the months wore on, my time with Jude began to feel more and more like a dream. Because no matter what we'd experienced, our romance had been brief, and in the same way that time dulls pain, it dulls happiness, too. I tried to remember, tried to keep the details of his face in mind when I closed my eyes. But the vast sea of weeks during which I'd thought him dead, and the ocean of days that followed after, when I wasn't allowed to see him—all that time began to dwarf the little island of lovely hours we'd shared. The kisses goodbye, our work for the resistance, even the night he'd saved my life. It was all getting further and further away, no matter how I tried to hold those moments in my mind; tried to keep him with me, even if only in my memory.

I certainly wished Jude could have been with me when I was sitting across from Samuel Jenkins, whose discerning eyes took note of my every movement.

"I've been doing as you and the prophet instruct me," I told him obediently. Six months of experience had made me more confident in my deception at Walden Manor, though no less terrified of failure.

"Have you encountered any heretics?" he asked casually.

"Heretics?" I feigned innocence, letting a horrified expression fall over my face.

"Those who worship in the old ways, who defile the name of Great Spirit?"

"I don't think so . . ." *Well, unless you counted every member of Dawn's organization . . .*

He leaned very close to me, conspiratorial. "Because we've heard rumors. It's been a decade since the Revelations, and the sad truth is, people tend to get complacent as tragedies become more remote."

"I haven't seen anyone getting complacent," I said honestly. I tried to stay focused on my mission—I needed to convince Samuel to log on to his computer, so that the camera in my hair clip could record his password. "But there is one thing I saw the other day. A video that was a little offensive."

Samuel's ears perked up. "Where?"

"It's on YouTube. I can show you." I gestured to his computer, and he obliged, signing on with a flurry of keystrokes. Instinctively I grabbed at the hair clip, hoping it was positioned correctly to see what Samuel had typed. I directed him to a video of a worship center play filled with silly jokes that only the most conservative folks at Walden Manor might find scandalous. He nodded politely, turning it off before it was over—clearly not interested in seeing the rest. "Thank you for showing that to me."

"You're welcome." I smiled piously.

His fierce gaze drifted away from me as he busied himself with files on his desk, and I hoped that meant I'd fooled him.

"Well, I think we're going to give you something a little more interesting to do," he said so offhandedly, it took me a moment to realize . . . Had I finally managed to earn Samuel's trust?

I remembered to beam proudly, though my stomach flip-flopped again. I had no desire to do anything remotely interesting for him. "Whatever the prophet requires of me."

He handed me a green metal square, a little thicker than a credit card. It had my name and picture on one side, and the prophet's symbol on the back—a bald eagle entwined with a dove. "What's this?" I asked.

"Something to identify you're with us," he said. "We may put you in touch with other friends of Great Spirit in New York, so don't lose it." I tried to read into his intonation, his expressions, but I couldn't get a sense of whether this was a test, so I simply nodded as he handed me a thick folder. "It might be helpful for this."

I opened the folder to discover a dossier: background information on a theology professor at NYU, Irene Hernandez. "You want me to investigate her?" I asked, and Samuel nodded.

"We don't want to make our inquiries too public, and worry the general populace. So Joshua occasionally asks trusted representatives to observe and report back on those who might be spiritually endangering our world."

As I scanned the file, I felt sick. Snapshots clipped to her bio showed a lively woman walking her dog around the city, laughing with friends. I hated that to help the resistance, I had to play my part by helping Samuel, too. If this woman's actions were deemed a threat to our peaceful utopia, she might be imprisoned—put away with everyone else whose work questioned the word of the prophets. Even if I managed to protect her from Joshua's reach, the resistance would still have to whisk her away from her life and family and force her to live in hiding like Dr. Marko.

But Samuel showed no concern, no remorse. "I've taken the liberty of changing your schedule at NYU. Her class will count toward your major, don't worry."

I'd decided to major in theology when I was nine, and unfortunately, changing that plan now might endanger my cover. Which meant I was in for four torturous years of lectures extolling the many fictional victories of Great Spirit.

"It's already a couple weeks into the semester . . ." I said, trying to find an excuse to let this probably innocent woman off the hook. Though, I remembered, Samuel must have a million other bright-eyed recruits like me. Even if I didn't investigate Professor Hernandez, someone else would.

But Samuel didn't bite. "You're smart, I'm sure you'll catch up." He never let his eyes stray from my face, ever watchful for any twinge, psychological or spiritual. But I remained calm, stone-faced. Until I knew more about this woman, all I could do was keep my cover and agree to investigate her. I thanked him and exited his office as quickly as I could.

Adrenaline pumping, I was on a high. *I'd survived.* But little did I know, this one small task was about to set off the chain of events that would change everything, forever.

As soon as I was outside, well away from the prying eyes around Walden Manor, I took a deep breath. As far as I knew, my cover was safe. As long as the recording device inside my hair clip had worked properly, my mission for the resistance had gone off without a hitch. And Dr. Hernandez . . . I'd have to handle that when the time came. Maybe I could even help— better me looking into her than one of Joshua's true believers, right?

And if I couldn't help? That was the anxiety I couldn't shake. I could accept risking my own life; that was the choice I'd made, to stay behind and work with Dawn. But the thought that at any moment, with one wrong move, I could ruin someone else's life—that was harder to grapple with. Over the course of six months, that constant fear had started to wear on me. I wanted to shrug it off, let it go, but I couldn't. Part of me knew that as overwhelming as the fear was, to some extent, it was helping to keep me and my friends safe: if I was always on high alert, I knew I could fool Samuel, at least.

I headed around the corner, where an identical hair clip was hidden within a false brick in the alley. I quickly pulled out the brick and exchanged the clip, glad to be clear of the incriminating evidence, and hoped that whoever came to retrieve it would be able to pass it to Dawn safely.

My relief was short-lived. I had barely taken two steps out of the alley when I heard a deep voice that made me jump.

"Grace?"

Zack. Macy's brother. My childhood crush turned . . . I wasn't sure what.

Dawn had told me Zack was monitoring me on Joshua's behalf, and I'd pieced together a bit more from the few details Zack had inadvertently revealed. He seemed to be employed by some larger organization, maybe government run. After we'd worked together to save his sister six months ago, he'd promised to protect me as much as he could . . . but he was still so secretive, and he still hadn't come clean about the simple fact that he'd been asked to watch me. Bottom line, I knew he wasn't someone I wanted to trust.

I put on another big smile, trying not to show that his presence was sending my adrenaline rushing. "Zack! I can't believe you're here."

I could, obviously.

"Yeah, I stop by for work sometimes." His tone was casual, friendly.

"That's right! I forgot." It was a game of chicken, same as

always. Neither one of us wanted to be the one to break the spell, to give up the lie. "It's almost like you're following me," I couldn't help but joke. I desperately hoped he hadn't seen my accessories swap in the alley.

If he had, he was playing it perfectly cool. "Are you heading back to New York? I'll take the train with you."

I pretended to be thrilled by the idea. "Sounds great!" Inside, the dread began to build. One interrogation down, one to go.

So this was my life. Instead of relaxing with Jude at some picturesque hideaway in Nova Scotia, I was a prisoner on a train to Penn Station, enduring Zack's endless stream of probing questions about my day. "What were you doing at Walden Manor?" "How are your classes going?" It was a dance we both knew well, and the steps never changed.

The one person who wasn't playing our game was Zack's sister, Macy. After my first week at NYU, she'd called me; no pleasantries, no "How's college?," just straight to the accusatory, "What's going on with you and my brother?"

"Nothing," I said, as innocently as I could muster.

Macy was not appeased. "Why are you always hanging out? Every day, he posts another picture of you guys at some coffee shop in the Village or something." Indeed, not long after I'd graduated, Zack had told me he was moving to New York, to an apartment a few blocks from NYU. *For work*, he'd said. What he hadn't said was what I already knew—his "work" was keeping tabs on me.

With Macy, I played dumb. "I thought he was trying to be a good big brother to you, being nice to your friends."

I could practically hear Macy's eyes roll through the phone.

"Trust me, Zack has never once worried about being a good big brother to me."

"That's not true!" I insisted, knowing just how wrong she was.

"I'm just saying, I'm not the one he's getting ice cream in Central Park with."

I wondered how Zack had explained our strange relationship. "Did you ask him about it?"

"He was weird about it, too!" she said, accusatory.

"I'm not being weird about it." I was totally being weird about it.

"You're totally being weird about it!" And then, with the kind of disgust only Macy could manage, she asked, "Do you have, like, a thing for him or something?"

"No," I said definitively. "No way. There is no way I would ever date your brother."

Which was . . . mostly true. I knew what he was. I knew why he hovered around me. I assumed he wasn't actually interested in what I had to say, beyond sifting for clues that might interest Prophet Joshua.

But . . . in the same way time was forcing Jude to slip away from me, it was pushing me toward Zack. While consciously I could never be interested in someone who was so obviously my adversary, the more we hung out, the more it just felt . . . easy. We both loved the same ramen spot downtown; he liked teasing me when I was frustrated waiting for the train; I knew exactly which faces of mine would make him laugh. And even though I couldn't truly be myself around him, I was growing comfortable with the role I was being forced to play. If I had to be Boring Pious Grace all the time anyway, I somehow didn't mind being her around him.

Which was lucky, since the ride back to New York City was a long one. "How's your dad doing?" Zack asked, as he always did. Apparently, Joshua had an interest in checking on his clerics as well.

"Good." I tried to keep my answers as short as I could.

"Still dating Evil Stepmother?" he teased.

I smiled a little. "She's not *evil*." In the decade since my mother had died, my dad had never dated seriously. But now, all of a sudden, this Samantha woman was everywhere. She ate breakfast in our kitchen; she sat next to me at our worship center on Sundays. I'd been excited to escape many people by going to college, and Samantha was at the top of the list.

It wasn't that there was anything wrong with her, at least not outwardly. But something about her just rubbed me the wrong way. My mother had been fiercely witty, captivating, wickedly smart. And Samantha was . . . fine. She was nice, in a perky way, but she was entirely bland. She lacked my mother's empathy, her depth, her insightfulness. And while it bugged me that my father would settle for someone so obviously inferior, there was also something about Samantha's bland cheerfulness that seemed . . . sinister, somehow.

Though when I related all this to Zack, it was that last bit he seized on. "Sinister?" he teased.

"You know what I mean," I grumbled. "She's just so happy all the time. No one's like that in real life. She's putting on an act, and at some point, the facade's gonna lift, and my dad's gonna get hurt. And he doesn't deserve that."

Zack seemed touched by that. "It's sweet that you care about your dad that much."

"He's all I've got," I said honestly.

"You're going with him to Johannesburg next month, right?" My father had been selected to speak at a theological conference in South Africa, the most important religious gathering of the year. Prophets and gurus from all over the world, giving sermons to a stadium packed full of the most devout of believers. This was where Proclamations and Prohibitions were made, where religious policies were set. It was the biggest honor my father would likely ever receive. And I was skipping it.

"I haven't decided yet," I evaded. "I want to, but I'm worried about getting behind in my classes. And, you know, my extra-curriculars." I tried to hint that it might be work for the prophet keeping me away. But the truth was, it had been heartbreaking just listening to my dad's sermons at our worship center every week, knowing what I knew. Surrounded by a whole stadium full of blissful ignorance, I was certain I'd blurt every secret I held out of sheer frustration.

"But you have to go," Zack protested, echoing what my father had said a thousand times. "I'm sure he needs your support."

I shook my head. "Your sister's going with him, as a cleric-in-training. She'll carry around his notes and stuff." Since her near-death Punishment last year, Macy had tagged along with my father and his junior clerics everywhere, devoting herself to being devout.

Zack, however, was not assuaged. "My sister? She's an organizational nightmare. You should go just to keep her *away* from your father's notes."

"Macy'll do fine," I said, laughing.

Zack grew concerned—for once, it seemed, not as a monitor, but as a friend. "Seriously, Grace. This is a once-in-a-lifetime thing. He'll be devastated if you miss it."

"I know," I relented. He was right. "I'll try." *I'll drag my feet until the tickets are too expensive*, that was really my plan.

"You're lucky to have him. A parent who's, you know, wise and stuff."

I thought of Zack and Macy's parents, who were lovely in their own dotty way. "You mean your parents aren't wise?" I teased him.

"My mom's sermons about why she's always right and my dad's always wrong would be . . . enlightening in their own way, I guess?"

We both smiled at the thought. I wondered what my own mother's sermons might have been like, if she'd ever been able to give one. Somehow in my gut, I'd always assumed she would have handled this strange new world better than my dad. That like Dawn, she would have figured out the truth and been strong enough to fight against it with me. Thoughts like that made her absence feel even starker.

"Your dad, though . . . he's the real deal," Zack insisted. "It always feels like he knows the right thing to do."

I'd once thought the same thing. My father had always been my source of all knowledge about right and wrong. I knew if I followed his advice, I could solve any problem. At least, until six months ago, when I first encountered a whole mess of problems he had no idea how to handle. And now I was navigating without a compass, hopelessly lost.

But I couldn't tell Zack that. "I wish there *was* someone who always knew the right thing to do," I lamented.

"Besides the prophets, you mean," Zack said, a challenge in his voice.

"Of course," I said, catching myself. "I mean, you know, normal people. People you could talk to in real life."

"Me, too," he said. Then, after a moment of consideration, he joked, "I guess you'll have to become better friends with Prophet Joshua."

The thought chilled me, but I laughed. "Dinner parties with the prophet?"

"I bet they're a riot."

I searched for a subject change. "Or who knows, maybe *you'll* be the next prophet after Joshua. Great Spirit could pick anyone, right?"

Zack snorted. "I'm pretty sure Great Spirit's got better options."

When Zack and I emerged at Penn Station, I stopped to marvel at the skyscrapers—I still wasn't used to how tall New York was, how small yet alive I felt here. I hadn't spent much time in big cities before college, and it was exciting to hear all the strangers around me chattering away in unfamiliar melodic languages, moving like a river in an impressionist painting—each person a colorful dot that added up to a breathtaking whole. Even trapped here with Zack, this city made me feel free.

Over the next few weeks, I tried to focus on school, on keeping my cover, and on catching up with my new class: History of Native American Religion with Professor Irene Hernandez. A small lecture, just two dozen students in a musty classroom, leaning in to hear the professor's low voice over the rumble of traffic outside.

I initially expected it to be the same rote, Universal Theology drivel. But as Professor Hernandez spoke, I was intrigued by her lecture on the etymology of the term "Great Spirit," and whether its current usage as a catchall for the spiritual force behind all religions was respectful, given its original meaning as a more subtle, ethereal, decidedly *not* Judeo-Christian higher power. The whole discussion was fascinating: dissecting the meaning behind religion intellectually, rather than blindly reciting what we were told. But I had a feeling it all would sound heretical to Prophet Joshua. I could tell why I'd been asked to investigate this woman, at least.

After my third class, I decided to stop by Professor Hernandez' office and try to learn more about her. I wanted to get her alone—whatever I discovered, I needed to keep it to myself, so I could decide what information to pass along to the prophet. I walked a few steps behind her, watching her trade jokes with an upperclassman, looking for some kind of easy entry to the conversation and finding none.

As he peeled off and she headed into her office, I braced myself. This was my moment. But before I reached her door, I was cut off by a girl I recognized as another student from class—a tiny thing with frizzy brown hair and a pink ZTB sorority bag slung over her shoulder. "Professor Hernandez?" Her voice had a slight accent I couldn't quite place.

Professor Hernandez looked up, recognizing her. "You're

the girl with all the questions in my . . . Native American Religion class, right?"

"Yes," she said. "Aviva."

The professor gave the girl a warm smile. "Aviva, right. You have *more* questions, I imagine?"

The fast-talking, intense Aviva certainly did. "The Universal Theology says that all religions are equally valid ways of accessing the divine. I don't see how using the term 'Great Spirit' negates any of the validity of the religion it came from. Me thinking that 'Great Spirit' means one thing doesn't prevent someone else from believing it means something else."

Professor Hernandez nodded thoughtfully. "Of course it doesn't. But if, say, the word 'Yahweh' was used to describe a completely different kind of higher power, a kind that contradicted the historical Jewish tradition, I think former Jews might have some similar concerns."

"I disagree," the girl said. As she argued her point, I lurked in the doorway, trying not to draw attention to myself. It was then that I noticed something sitting on the desk right behind Professor Hernandez: a picture. *A wedding picture*, of two smiling women in poofy white wedding dresses. One was the professor, of course. But her arm was wrapped around someone I knew well.

This wasn't just any random educator. Professor Irene Hernandez was Dawn's wife.

4

I realized I'd never given much thought to Dawn's personal life. She'd never offered details, and like the self-absorbed teenager I was, I'd never asked. But here, apparently, was her wife—and it was my job to investigate this woman for Joshua? My heart began to race as panicked thoughts swirled through my mind. If Joshua suspected Irene, that meant he might soon be onto Dawn as well. And Jude. And even me—the stakes were suddenly sky-high to protect this woman.

"I've heard that former Muslims consider it an honor that words from their culture have moved into wider use," Aviva rattled on. "'Cleric,' 'prophet' . . . why would 'Great Spirit' be any different?"

"It has to do with the way those words are used," Irene told her. "'Cleric' and 'prophet' didn't fundamentally change their meanings when incorporated into the lexicon of the Universal Theology. 'Great Spirit' did."

"It's meaning didn't change, it just expanded . . ." Aviva insisted, but the professor interrupted before she could finish.

"Why don't you come by during my office hours tomorrow and we can discuss some more?" Professor Hernandez was impossibly polite as she told this girl to get lost.

Aviva put on a smile so broad it could only be fake. "Sounds great."

She turned to leave but seemed surprised to see me waiting a few feet behind her. Disconcerted, Aviva took a step back, knocking a pile of papers and notebooks off the professor's cluttered desk. "I'm so sorry!" she cried out, and the three of us stooped to pick them up.

"I hate to toss you girls out, but I have work to do," Professor Hernandez said, doing her best to hide her annoyance.

"I understand," Aviva answered apologetically. She turned to leave, and I realized I had no choice but to follow her out, immensely frustrated that this girl's chattiness and clumsiness had cost me my moment to confer with Dawn's wife.

I dragged my feet, trailing behind Aviva as we exited the building. Once the girl was out of sight, I doubled back to Professor Hernandez' office, where this time, she was less polite about brushing me off. "I'm sorry, I really don't have time . . ."

"Are you married to Dawn?" I asked her bluntly, my voice hurried and hushed.

She was suddenly on guard. "How do you know Dawn?"

I stepped into her office, and she closed us both safely inside. "I work with her. And . . ." I pulled the green square from my pocket, the one to identify I was with the prophet.

"You work with Joshua." Her voice held a deep well of fear.

"I was sent to investigate you. They've heard about the kinds of things you say in your classes."

A rueful smile spread across her face. "Dawn will just love this."

"Excuse me?" I asked, suddenly realizing how stupid I'd just been. Walking up to this woman and admitting who I was, outright. What if Professor Hernandez was a plant I'd been led to by Joshua? An elaborate ruse to trick me into outing myself? If so, I'd just given myself away as a double agent. Panic surged through me.

"She's warned me a thousand times to be more careful," Irene continued, and I breathed a sigh of relief as she went on a tirade against Dawn. "But I told her, my lectures have always been like this, even before I met her, even before I knew the truth. No one ever complained, even after the Revelations. Wouldn't it be more suspicious to change my entire teaching style at the drop of a hat? Wouldn't holding myself back be a clear sign to the prophets that I suddenly have something to hide?"

"It'll be okay," I tried to reassure her. "I'll tell Joshua whatever Dawn wants me to tell him. You'll be safe. She'll make sure you end up somewhere safe." I was certain Dawn would protect her own wife, at least.

Irene seemed less certain about that, as she moved around her office, packing things up. "She's barely able to protect herself lately." Irene's pointed words left my legs feeling wobbly; her fear was bringing my own right to the surface.

I jumped as Irene started tossing the contents of her desk on the floor, frantically searching for something. "SHIT."

I so rarely heard anyone swear, the word itself rattled me. "What's wrong?" I asked nervously.

Irene was tearing the place apart. "There was a purple folder here, with all my lectures. Transcripts, going back years. I swear, it was just here. Have you seen it?"

I scanned the room as she searched, but I saw no sign of the folder. And I was pierced by a horrifying realization. "What if I wasn't the only one sent to investigate you?"

Irene quickly put it together, too. "You mean that other girl . . ."

"Aviva. What if she's working for Joshua, too?" Or with that accent, more likely a prophet from some other country. And it looked like she'd already stolen what she needed to arrest Professor Hernandez. I was too late.

5

W hat do we do?" I asked Irene, but Irene was busy panicking, pacing the room in despair.

"Dawn is going to *kill* me . . ."

"She's going to save you, it'll be fine," I said, trying to calm her down, and trying to calm the dread swelling inside my own stomach. If Aviva reported Professor Hernandez' heresy, and I reported nothing was amiss, would Joshua suspect me of being a double agent?

"What if Dawn *can't* save me? We've had so many friends disappear . . ." Her words hinted at a kind of danger Dawn had been shielding me from.

I thought fast. Could I steal back whatever information Aviva had before she turned it in? Watching Irene frantically pawing through her desk drawers, I had a feeling she wasn't the type who would stand up well to torture. If she was taken, it might be only a matter of time before Dawn and everyone working for her fell, too.

"Call Dawn, tell her what happened. She'll make a plan to get you to safety." Professor Hernandez nodded, clearly relieved that someone else was giving her direct instructions. "I'll find that girl, I'll get your lectures back, and we'll figure out the next steps from there."

Having a plan seemed to reassure her, at least. But as Irene and I parted ways, I realized I knew very little about this Aviva person. I could find her on social media, but it's not like her Instagram account would list her dorm room or class schedule. And waiting until Dr. Hernandez' next class would be too late. Unless . . . I'd seen Aviva carrying that pink sorority bag. Could I track her down in sorority housing?

With a little help from the online campus directory, I found the building that held ZTB. It was just one floor in a massive skyscraper, nothing like the sorority houses I'd seen in the movies. With a glance up at the ZTB banner hanging from the tenth-floor windows, I slipped in behind a pizza delivery guy.

The walls on the tenth floor were plastered with pictures of smiling young women doing fun, pious activities. My heart ached a little as I passed them: this was exactly the life I'd always imagined for myself at college—being part of the perfect clique of pretty people. These happy, carefree sorority girls reminded me of who I used to be, the kind of person I could never be again. But, I reminded myself, they weren't who I wanted to be anymore.

I asked around until I found the right door to knock on, and Aviva answered. It took her a moment to recognize me. "You're from one of my classes, right?" she asked, clearly puzzled by my out-of-the-blue appearance on her doorstep.

"That's right," I said, feeling very silly.

"Why are you here?"

I took a breath—*here goes nothing*—and whipped out my little green card. "I think we have something in common."

Her eyebrows furrowed as she took it. "What's this?"

My gamble hadn't worked. Maybe whichever prophet she worked for didn't use the same identification system as Joshua? "I'm working with the prophet," I told her. "Like you are, right?" I hoped I hadn't completely misjudged her. Panic sprinted through me. What if Irene had merely misplaced her files? What if I'd outed myself to this random girl for no reason?

But then a smile came over her face. "Oh! No one told me I would find another friend of Great Spirit here. Come in."

I breathed a sigh of relief as she let me in. "Thanks."

I desperately scanned her undecorated apartment for the folder, but I didn't see it anywhere. I wondered if she was even really a student or, given the state of this place, just posing as one temporarily.

"Sorry, I'm still moving in. Can I get you anything to drink?"

"No, thanks," I said. I definitely didn't trust her enough to eat or drink anything she had to offer.

"You're here for Professor Hernandez, too?" she guessed.

"Yeah. I thought maybe we could compare notes, work together. Two heads are better than one, right?" I was playing my best sorority girl, smiling brightly, trying to channel the women I'd seen lining the walls.

Aviva seemed intrigued. "What have you found out so far?"

That Irene's married to the leader of an organization that's actively opposing the prophets. That she's onto you and currently plotting her escape out of town. "Well, that class sure was something," I said. "And you asked great follow-up questions in her office."

"Thank you." She preened a little. "Apparently all her classes are like that. From what I hear, she's been getting more and more off book every year. Really radical stuff." So Irene *hadn't* always asked her students to think deeply and critically about the world around them——the kind of teaching that scared the prophets. Knowing the truth from Dawn had likely affected Irene's lectures, whether she'd realized it or not.

My persistent scanning of the room finally turned up a bright purple folder sitting under a newspaper in the corner. But before I could make a move for it, a knock sounded at the door.

Aviva looked at me. "Did you come with anyone?"

I shook my head no, but the moment she opened the door, I realized it had been a lie.

Zack was standing in the doorway.

had to hold my hand to my mouth to keep from audibly gasping. But Zack ignored me completely, focused entirely on Aviva. "Hey! I'm Zack."

He stuck out his hand, and Aviva shook it with a polite smile. "Aviva."

It was then I noticed the NYU T-shirt Zack was wearing. This diversion was planned. "I'm new in the building. I wanted to invite you girls to a party we're having tonight."

"Are you a freshman?" Aviva asked skeptically.

"Senior. It's not gonna be a big thing, just chilling with my buddies from ADPi. If you're interested."

Based on her reaction, Zack had done his research, and girls from ZTB liked boys from ADPi. Why he'd done that research, I had no idea, but as long as he was here, he was distracting Aviva, which was exactly what I needed.

I drifted to the other end of the room as quietly and casually as I could, watching Aviva carefully. But her gaze was fixed completely on Zack, as he ran his fingers through his tousled hair. "What time are you guys starting?" she asked.

"About ten? We should be going pretty late." Zack winked at Aviva in a way that, if I were capable of being jealous over him, would have made me tear my hair out. With all our history, and all the secrets I knew about him, I sometimes forgot just how desirable Zack appeared to the outside female world.

Aviva played coy. "Maybe I can stop by at some point? I already RSVP'd to a couple other things."

"No pressure. Just trying to be neighborly." Zack grinned. I tore my eyes away from their flirting to grab the folder, silently shoving it in my bag. My heart was racing, but it didn't need to—Zack and Aviva were ignoring me completely.

I knew that the risk of Aviva discovering my crime increased the longer I stayed in her room, so I made a beeline for the exit. "Hey, I gotta go," I interjected.

Her eyes flicked to me in surprise; she'd forgotten I was even there. "Oh, yeah. See you later," she said, clearly glad I was leaving her alone to flirt with Zack.

As I slipped out, I expected Zack to follow me, but he stayed at the door, consumed by Aviva.

"Can I text you, to find out if the party's still going?" Aviva was asking.

"Sure," I heard Zack say. "Let me give you my number." At that, I felt another dumb pang of jealousy I had to push down. *He is your enemy*, I reminded myself. *No matter how dazzling his smile is.*

I was already downstairs, hurrying away from the building, when the owner of said dazzling smile called after me, "You okay?"

I turned around. It had always felt like the smart choice to ignore the way Zack coincidentally appeared wherever I happened to be. Any prolonged discussion of why he was following me would no doubt end poorly. But him showing up in a stranger's dorm room, pretending to be someone else, without even acknowledging he knew me . . . I would be blowing my cover if I *didn't* point out just how weird it was. "I'm fine. What was that all about? What are you doing here?"

"You know what I'm doing here," he said evenly.

"I *know*? What am I supposed to know?" I asked, trying to force him to be the one to come clean.

And he did. "The prophet. He asked me to follow you."

I hadn't expected him to be quite so honest, so it wasn't hard to feign surprise. "Follow me?"

"Because you're new."

"Did I do something wrong?" I asked carefully.

"I don't think so. But he's still vetting you."

My anxiety surged. "What do you mean?"

"He does it with everybody, I think. You know, all the new recruits."

He still wasn't saying it out loud. "So you know . . ."

Zack only hesitated a moment before admitting, "That all the 'errands' you've been running have been for Prophet Joshua? Yeah, I know."

I took a deep breath. As long as he didn't know I was working with Dawn, maybe talking more openly about our arrangement would make everything simpler. I stayed as nonchalant as I possibly could. "I thought it was weird that you kept popping up, but that explains it. I kinda suspected, I guess."

Zack laughed. "Did you have any other working theories?"

"Not really. Macy thought you had a crush on me." I chuckled, making sure he knew I was joking.

He grinned at that. "Yeah, that must've been weird, if you didn't know. You really didn't know?" He was acting concerned now, as though he actually cared what I was thinking or feeling.

I answered truthfully, drawing on my own frustration and general mistrust. "Samuel never told me. Why did you wait this long to mention it?"

"They told me not to," he said with a shrug.

"Who is 'they'?" I asked.

"His people, my bosses," Zack said vaguely, giving me no new information. "Please don't tell anyone I said anything, okay?"

He seemed nervous, and I nodded, trying to reassure him. "I won't, of course. But why are you telling me now?"

"The way you act around me," he said. "Lately you've seemed edgy or something." Like I said, I was never born to be a double agent.

"Maybe I was edgy around everyone?" I suggested. "Since I was keeping secrets all the time. I'm not very good at that— I guess that's clear by now."

"Pretty clear." He always enjoyed finding an excuse to tease me about something.

Remembering my initial mistake with Professor Hernandez, I realized this, too, could be a ploy: maybe Joshua had told him to confide in me like this, to gain my trust. If that was true, I knew better than to fall for it. And I saw an opportunity to use this ploy to my advantage. "What do you tell Joshua about me?" I asked, genuinely curious.

"That you're perfectly pious," he said. I flushed a little at his use of the word "pious," knowing what it meant to him.

"Thanks," I mumbled as we began ambling down the street. I'm not sure either of us had a particular destination in mind, but there was a strange comfort in being with him, now that at least some of the truth was out in the open.

At least until he said, "What was in that file?"

"Hmm?" I kept my mouth shut, waiting for him to force an answer out of me.

"In that girl's apartment. I saw you grab something. What was it?" he repeated patiently.

"Am I allowed to tell you? Isn't that confidential?" I asked, hoping to protect Dr. Hernandez as long as I could.

He smiled, amused again. "Keep your secrets if you want. Since you're so good at it."

I smiled back, playing along. "Hey, I could be good at keeping secrets. Maybe I'm fooling you right now." The minute I said it, I kicked myself—if the thought hadn't occurred to him before, it certainly would now.

"Sure you are," he said, destroying me with a wink. "Hey, are you hungry?" He pointed to a deli, and I nodded, relieved for the change in conversation topic.

"Starving." My stomach grumbled, not just with hunger, but with excitement—for once, I realized with dismay, I was actually looking forward to my interrogation.

7

It was funny how much it felt like any dinner with an old friend. Now that things were out in the open, I was reminded of all the reasons I'd always liked Zack—he was engaging, and made the ordinary seem fun. As we settled at a table with a couple of corned beef sandwiches, he took note of all the NYU students. "I definitely did not expect to be back at college so soon," Zack said, stifling a laugh.

"Didn't you like college?" I asked. Zack seemed like the kind of smart, extroverted person who would have thrived on campus.

"I liked it fine. But I wanted to get out into the world. Do something meaningful with my life."

His words gave me pause. They seemed genuine enough; it wasn't the kind of sentiment I thought he'd bother to make up. And it even made a certain kind of sense—people with a feeling of social responsibility *would* be more likely to work for powerful, charismatic leaders who promised to do good things for the world. Zack probably didn't know who Joshua really was, at least not when he signed up. It's easy to enlist for the army—it's a stroke of luck whether you end up on the "right" side. As I thought this, I wondered if I was lucky enough to be fighting for the good guys. Or if there *was* any such thing as the "good guys" in this particular war.

"Do you feel like you did it?" I asked. "Something meaningful with your life?"

Zack thought long and hard about that. "That's a lot of pressure. I've still got some time to get around to the meaningful stuff, right?"

"I don't know, you seem pretty old to me," I joked back.

When the food came, Zack made a big show of protecting his plate, declaring I was a food stealer, before doing what he usually did and depositing half his fries on my plate. As we ate, Zack grew contemplative. At one point he asked, "Do you think you'd believe in Great Spirit if you didn't have the proof?"

The question immediately set me on edge again. In any case, I certainly knew my answer: "Yeah," I said, "I would."

"Why?"

"Because if I didn't have proof Great Spirit existed, I'd have to prove Great Spirit didn't exist. And proving that seems even harder."

"But why?" Zack pressed. "Wouldn't you just assume that Great Spirit was something we made up? If you can't prove something's there, doesn't that mean it probably isn't?"

One look at his face and I realized—this wasn't a test or a trick. Zack had a suspicion that this hypothetical world he was describing was the real one. He'd used the "magic" pills, so he knew that Punishments weren't the work of Great Spirit, but of chemicals. And he knew I'd used those pills, too, and therefore was aware that our world wasn't entirely what it seemed. He must've felt as isolated as I did, keeping his own secrets. That might even be his reason for confessing he was following me, despite all the risks that entailed—he just needed to talk to someone else who understood.

I felt a pang of real sympathy for him, and I tried to offer an answer I thought might make him feel better: "We had to prove electricity existed," I pointed out. "And atoms, and evolution, and all kinds of other things we now accept as fact. Maybe even if we had no evidence of Great Spirit causing Punishments, we'd find Great Spirit somewhere else."

Zack nodded. "Or maybe there is no such thing as proof," he mused. Though his words might have felt run-of-the-mill before the Revelations, in that climate they felt explosive, inflammatory. "I just wonder, you know, if there were no Great Spirit . . . and I don't know, even if there is . . . Sure we know there's some higher power, but that just kicks the can down the road. Where did Great Spirit come from? Where did the universe come from? And why does any of it exist at all? Everyone thinks we have it all answered now, but we don't really. We're no closer than we were before."

"I know what you mean," I said slowly. I hadn't anticipated that Zack, of all people, would be knee-deep in a crisis of faith. But I'd been thinking about all this recently, too. When your entire worldview is ripped to pieces, you have to try and find your own answers to stitch it back together. But at that moment, I still hadn't found any. I still believed in the Great Spirit, but

I wasn't sure what that even meant anymore. Working with the resistance had given my individual actions a sense of purpose—but it hadn't given any meaning to the larger whole. Once this battle was over, would Great Spirit send me down some new path? Or would I have to invent some imaginary purpose and convince myself that it had cosmic significance?

"What if the Punishments just stopped one day?" Zack continued. "Do you think people would go back to being, you know, evil? Do you think they'd stop believing?"

"Believing, no. I think people would still believe—I think people *need* to believe—in something. But the bad parts of humanity . . ." I thought of Dawn, I thought of Joshua. The things I'd seen them do, unconstrained by Punishments. "I think evil would come back." It scared me to consider: that was the world I was fighting for, the world I was willing to die to bring back. To give mankind back its freedom, I had to give every human on Earth the power to kill each other again.

"Well then, it's good Great Spirit's got our backs," Zack said, breaking me out of my reverie.

"Yeah, good thing," I said, watching him closely. I wished I could get inside his head, know what he was thinking at that moment. Zack's affability was the perfect mask—I could never quite see what was beneath it.

And maybe I never would. Zack's whole job was to hide his true feelings, and he was good at it. I was relieved when he headed to the bathroom, giving me a moment to gather my thoughts.

It was then I noticed a woman in a wheelchair staring directly at me. Unnerved, I looked away, but a moment later she rolled up to me. "Did you get the lectures?" she asked, without preamble.

I should have been expecting a message from Dawn. I nodded, tentatively.

The woman dropped a piece of paper into my hands and wheeled herself outside without another word.

The note didn't say much—just a street corner, Sixth and Waverly, and a time, 10 P.M.

I crumpled up the message and shoved it in my pocket as Zack returned to our table, no sign he'd witnessed anything unusual. "Ready to go?"

I'd let myself forget for a moment that I had a job to do, an enemy to fight. I steeled myself against Zack's charms. "I'm ready."

8

As we stepped outside, Zack glanced around, taking in the possibilities. "So? What should we do now?"

"Hmm?" I said, surprised. Usually he asked his probing questions and then left me alone. But tonight, he strolled along next to me, with no seeming ulterior motive. As though we really were friends.

"Come on, the night's young. You haven't really explored much New York City nightlife yet." It was true; I was as reluctant to lie to strangers in dance halls as I was to lie to the girls in my dorm. Fear had turned me into a homebody.

"Don't you have a party to host?" I reminded him. "Your 'frat brothers' at ADPi will be *superbummed* if you stand them up."

Zack laughed. "Don't worry, I already handled it."

He showed me his phone, a text to Aviva, which I read out loud in a mocking, flirty voice. "Bad news, party's off. Maybe we can grab coffee Friday night instead?" I tossed the phone back to him. "Subtle."

"I gotta check out the people you're hanging out with. Make sure they're on the up-and-up, make sure you aren't getting into any trouble."

He nudged me in the arm, a joke. Coupled with the way he was hitting on Aviva, I was starting to find his platonic playfulness annoying, in spite of myself. "I promise you, I'm nice and boring."

"Well then, I guess this is just for fun." He gave me a sidelong glance. "Your friend Aviva's cute."

In a weird way, Aviva seemed perfect for Zack—pious and employed by a prophet, just like him. I hated how unhappy their potential happiness made me. "She's not my friend, just a girl I met in class," I insisted.

"Well, maybe Friday night she'll be *my* friend." He winked, clearly enjoying himself. I wondered if he was trying to make me jealous or, worse somehow, not trying at all.

Either way, I wasn't going to let him get to me. "Good luck with that," I said.

A silence settled in, and I couldn't help but imagine how that date with Aviva might go. I knew I'd lived a somewhat sheltered life, even by the standards of our pious, buttoned-up society, but I did have a sense of what people did on dates. I found myself wondering—had Zack had sex before? The moment I thought it, I kicked myself . . . of course he had. He was twenty-three, good-looking, plenty charming. Before, I might have judged him—though Prophet Joshua had explicitly sanctioned premarital sex, I'd still grown up in a community that looked down on promiscuity.

But now that I knew none of that really mattered, that Great

Spirit wasn't going to judge me the way I expected? I'd started allowing myself to think about those things. Started pushing past the shame and embarrassment I felt, and imagining, wondering what it might be like to experience them myself. But Jude was no longer in my life, and as cute as Zack was, I couldn't bring myself to think about him like that.

But someone new? The possibility was intriguing. That is, if I could figure out how to get close enough to anyone new, to form any kind of a relationship when I held all these secrets.

As if he was reading my mind, Zack started goading me on. "So come on, where are we going? You've got a whole city full of people to meet."

Was he really just trying to hang out with me? The prospect seemed impossible, and even if I'd wanted to, I had an appointment to get to. "I'm going to bed," I said politely.

"You're no fun."

"Bed sounds plenty fun to me," I said, then felt my face run hot when I saw his smirk. "That wasn't an invitation," I added quickly.

My embarrassment seemed to deeply amuse him. "Noted," he replied.

When we arrived at my dorm, I made a show of heading upstairs, watching from the window to make sure he was gone. As authentic as our conversation in the diner had seemed, I had to stay vigilant. Zack was not my *friend*. I left my cell phone in my room, just in case he was tracking my location. Checking again to make sure he wasn't anywhere outside, I quickly slipped out of the dorm.

When I arrived on the appointed street corner, I eyed all the passersby, looking for whomever I might be meeting. I couldn't believe how many people were out on the street so late at night. As I examined my options, the answer became obvious: that same woman in the wheelchair was headed straight for me, rolling down the sidewalk with a bit of momentum. Apparently, my meeting was with her.

I was about to say hello, when BAM—without a word, she slammed right into me, the wheel of her chair connecting hard against my shin and bumping me backward into the street, into traffic.

I heard the squeal of tires as I stumbled onto the asphalt, off-balance, trying to regain my footing. But not fast enough.

I spun around to see a taxi coming straight for me, its brakes screeching wildly. I had only a split second to realize what was happening, before the taxi's bumper made contact; pain shot through my legs, and I found my feet flying out from under me. As my skull slammed into the cold pavement, the world went dark.

9

From the darkness behind my eyelids, I heard voices heading toward me. Felt a hand grab my wrist, take my pulse. In the distance, one car horn, then two, then six.

As I opened my eyes, the outside world seemed black, too, until my vision started to focus, and I saw the half-dozen faces crowding around me. "Are you okay?" "Move your eyes back and forth."

Was I okay? Though my bruised limbs ached against the rough asphalt, I couldn't find any other injuries. I was shaking something fierce, but I'd miraculously avoided serious damage or death.

A few feet away, I could hear the taxi driver screaming into a phone. "She just stepped in front of my car!"

I craned my neck, trying to find the woman who'd pushed me into the street—who was she? Who would want me dead? And then I saw her, a few feet away, tears streaming down her face, being comforted by another pedestrian. "You didn't see her, you couldn't have stopped it."

She knew I hadn't died. And if she'd tried to kill me once, she probably would again. I needed to get away from here, get to safety somewhere.

I tried to stand up, but those Good Samaritans swarmed me, gently pushing me back to the ground. "Just wait here, an ambulance is on the way," a friendly-looking man said. All these annoyingly pious people, hoping Great Spirit would reward them for doing a good deed I didn't want done . . .

"I feel fine," I said, trying to escape, but I couldn't overpower all of them. I waited helplessly, watching the woman in the wheelchair out of the corner of my eye, terrified of what she might do next. I tried to calm myself: *She can't hurt you while you're surrounded by all these people.* Sirens wailed closer to us, and I breathed a sigh of relief—the EMTs would keep me safe.

I hadn't been near an ambulance since Jude's accident, almost three years ago. I'd held Jude dying in my arms, and the same loud wail had burned my eardrums as the EMTs pulled me away from him. As *Dawn* pulled me away from him, I remembered, letting her cohorts drive him to safety—not to the hospital, but to a new life. That was how she'd built her resistance network, by rescuing people and recruiting them to her cause.

As an EMT loaded me onto a stretcher, it suddenly hit me what was really happening. They rolled me inside the ambulance, and I almost said her name before I saw her, standing with an IV in hand, staring back at me with her familiar, stoic gaze. Dawn.

10

It had been so long since I'd seen Dawn in the flesh, I almost didn't believe it, even when she was standing right in front of me. She was wearing an EMT uniform, just as she had been when I first met her at the site of Jude's accident. She didn't acknowledge she knew me, just continued with her duties, shining a light in my eyes. "Pupils look okay," she said to her colleagues.

"A few scrapes and bruises, nothing serious," another EMT told her.

As the ambulance doors closed, her demeanor changed, loosened. "Good. Grace, do you feel okay?"

I sat up. "What on earth is going on?" I demanded. The shock of being hit by a taxi overwhelmed any relief I had at finally seeing her face-to-face again.

"As you might have guessed, I'm under some scrutiny right now, because of Irene. This was the best way to talk to you," she said unapologetically.

"To throw me into the street and run me over with a car?" I asked, incredulous.

Dawn remained unfazed. "The taxi driver was one of ours, we had people monitoring from every angle to make sure you were okay." All those Good Samaritans who'd surrounded me, preventing me from leaving—they all worked for Dawn.

"Is Irene okay?" I remembered to ask.

"Yes. I've arranged for her to get on a plane overseas tonight—she should be safely out of harm's way even if Aviva does make her report."

This was all good news, but I could hear the anxiety in her voice. There was something she wasn't saying. "You didn't run me over just to let me know Irene's safe, did you?"

Dawn sat next to me, putting her words together carefully. "Remember the nanotechnology Dr. Marko told you about?" she asked. "The *new* technology that was being developed in West Virginia before we stepped in?"

"Right. The research you killed a bunch of scientists to prevent from being finished, how could I forget?" I didn't hide my contempt about that particular incident.

Dawn's voice was tense. "Not prevent, delay. Dr. Marko said our actions delayed development by about six months."

"That's it?" I asked, incredulous. All those lives lost, and we had only bought ourselves six months. And then I realized: "It's been more than six months already."

Dawn nodded. "Once we gained access to the prophet's computer system with your help—thanks, by the way—we were able to find the blueprints and confirm that the tech is already in production. And now we know exactly what the little bots do." I wasn't sure I wanted to know, but Dawn was going to tell me anyway. "The nanotech that's running through your head right now, it senses your natural feelings of guilt, and in response, it changes physical features of your body—disincentivizing you from taking the action that caused the guilt."

"Right . . ."

"Well, what if I told you Prophet Joshua could go one step further and actually put *new* thoughts into your brain?"

The very idea sent a chill through me. "What kind of thoughts?"

"For a start, he could change your motivations, the things you think and feel. Change your perception of reality. These little bugs are so advanced, they can read your thoughts and respond with whatever fits Joshua's agenda at the moment."

"Well, that would be bad," I quipped, grappling with the possibility. It was terrifying to imagine what Joshua might do with that kind of power.

"Yeah, it would be. It would destroy everything we've been working for; it would crush every last bit of rebellion and give the prophets complete and total power over all of us. Joshua's already got a test batch, ready to target people he knows are members of the resistance. A trial run, before releasing it on the public. On the whole world. Airborne, the way we were all infected the first time during the Revelations. You'd never know anything was different."

Punishments were enough mental manipulation for me, thank you very much. "We have to destroy the new technology, before he can use it—that's what you're saying, right?" She nodded. "Where is it?"

"A research facility attached to Regent's Hospital."

I noticed one of the other EMTs entering my information into a computer—except that it wasn't my information at all. Dawn had made me a fake ID, with a fake name. This whole ambulance ride would be nearly impossible to trace back to me. Which was good, since I imagined Zack would be on high alert if "Grace Luther" checked herself into the ER.

"You have a choice," Dawn said. "Where we go next is entirely up to you. The tech is hidden in a walled-off area below the ER—originally it was a Cold War–era bomb shelter, but it's been closed up for decades, purchased by the government for storage. Top secret, very difficult to access. I tried getting in there myself, but I couldn't get past security," she explained. "I've sent in dozens of people since, but no one's been able to get close enough."

"But you think I can?" Why on earth did Dawn think I could pull off this mission when she herself hadn't been able to?

"You have one thing no one else on my team has," she said.

It took me a moment to realize what she meant. "The ID I got from the prophet," I said slowly.

"It's our last shot. Flash it, and there's a good chance they'll let you in—that card proves you report directly to the prophet himself, and people are afraid to contradict his orders."

"Cool," I said, surprised to hear I wielded so much power.

Dawn was not so enthused. "There's one problem with this plan. Joshua hasn't authorized you to enter the storage facility."

I read between the lines. "You're saying they'll let me in,

because they're afraid of Prophet Joshua. But when they check on me later, they'll know I was lying, and my cover's blown." The prospect left me shaking with fear.

"Most likely, yes. Now, I know you were a somewhat reluctant participant in this whole movement to begin with. So maybe this plan kills two birds with one stone for you. This is the most important mission we could possibly task you with. Complete it, and you're done. We'll try our best to move you underground before Joshua realizes what's happened. As long as you make it out of the hospital without being detected, you should be able to leave the country tonight, on the same plane as Irene. But it's up to you. I won't force you to put yourself in danger like that."

I could tell from her voice just how much Dawn, and all of us, had riding on me saying yes. Which is why I felt selfish that I hadn't said yes yet. As much as I wanted to help, as much as I'd sworn I was willing to risk my life . . . now that it was time to take that risk, I found myself hesitating. "There's no one else who can do it?"

"No one," Dawn said, voice hoarse.

My head spun. How could I possibly make a decision this huge so quickly? To never see my father, my friends, ever again. But Dawn's expectant gaze left me searching for a way to accept, a way to convince myself to do it. "If I agree, it's the last mission I ever have to go on?"

"That's right."

If I did this, I could finally stop living this horrible double agent life. Maybe I could even carry out my plan from six months ago—living a simple life in some idyllic small town. Only . . . the person I'd wanted to live that simple life with was gone. "Where's Jude?" I asked hesitantly.

"He's out of the country right now," she said, a little evasive, "working with some of our international partners."

"How is he doing? Is he . . ." Safe? Healthy? Furious at me for abandoning him?

"He's doing just fine," she said. "I'm sure he'd be glad to hear you're doing well, too."

I wanted to ask if Jude could join me when I defected from Joshua's army, but I was too ashamed. Who knew if Jude would even want that after the way I'd treated him? And I didn't want Dawn to think my willingness to help depended on a boy. In truth, it didn't. I might not fully trust Dawn, but I was committed enough to her cause to risk just about anything. I worked up my courage and finally spat out, "I'll do it."

She watched me for a moment. "Before you go in there, I need you to know—once your cover's blown, your life will change completely. Joshua will be gunning for you like never before. You'll be subject to extreme scrutiny at every border crossing. Even if you leave the country, there's nowhere on Earth you'll ever truly be out of his reach."

"So you're saying this is dangerous?" I deadpanned, even as my fear threatened to choke me.

Dawn nodded, not in a joking mood. "I won't think less of you if you choose not to go through with it. Neither would anyone else."

A thousand thoughts rattled around in my mind. Would this

be a repeat of West Virginia, where there was a secret cost to our mission, innocent lives lost because of Dawn's dishonesty? Or might this be the rare opportunity to shift the tide of this war? I couldn't reconcile all my doubts, but I knew what my answer had to be.

"Tell me what I have to do."

11

The plan was relatively simple: I had to gain access to the underground shelter and destroy Joshua's stockpile of nano-technology.

I stared at the ceiling warily as the EMTs wheeled me into the hospital, counting the fluorescent lights as they whipped by above me, trying to calm myself. One last mission, one last big risk, and then I could be done. I repeated it to myself like a mantra, hoping that if I thought it enough, it would come true.

The EMTs met with a nurse at the ER entrance, who jotted down facts about my incident. "Hit by a car, potential concussion . . ." It all passed in a blur until the nurse leaned down and touched my hands, which I realized were shaking wildly with fear.

"Potential tremor," the nurse said as she scribbled on her pad. "Should run some neurological tests."

The EMTs bumpily settled my stretcher behind a set of rolling blue curtains, nodding a farewell. And the unspoken: *Good luck.*

I eyed the nurse as she took my vitals. I'd have to wait for her to walk off, so I could slip away. From here, I'd have to navigate the winding hospital halls to the shelter entrance deep within the building, relying on only my memories of a map Dawn had shown me for five minutes during the ambulance ride. Meanwhile, Dawn's allies would launch a coordinated cyberattack on the prophet's online files, destroying every copy of the technology's blueprints that existed in digital form. If everything went according to plan, we would destroy every hard copy of the tech as well as every offline copy of the instructions needed to create it. Joshua would lose everything and be forced to start over from scratch. *If* everything went according to plan.

While the nurse was distracted at her station, I hopped off the stretcher and tiptoed behind the blue curtain, slipping through double doors into the main part of the hospital. I wove through hallway after hallway with my practiced look of innocence. No one stopped me; everyone assumed that with my pious face I couldn't be up to anything nefarious.

Finally, in a secluded area, I slipped into a seldom-used janitor's closet, and deep within it I found a giant silver door. Well, *I* knew it was a door. From the point of view of a doctor walking these halls, it looked more like decoration, an odd and dated bit of wallpaper or something. It had no handles, no way of getting inside. This was the secret entrance that hid the modified bomb shelter beneath. I retrieved a silver key card Dawn had given me, which had been stolen from some high-up person at this hospital, or maybe a government official even. All I knew was that more than one person had died so that the resistance could get their hands on it—the weight of that not lost on me.

Once I made sure the coast was clear, I brushed the key card along the edges of the door until I heard a click, and it opened, revealing a staircase. So far, so good. I stepped in and quickly closed the door behind me. The others who had tried this before had also managed this part easily. From here it was uncharted territory—my stomach flip-flopped at the thought.

When I reached the basement level, I found a massive hall-way, eerily lit with an orangey glow. Down the corridor, a guard was stationed, and my anxiety spiked when I saw the size of the assault rifle hanging at his hip. He turned to scrutinize me, his blond eyebrows furrowed with suspicion—on edge perhaps because of all the previous intruders.

Despite my nerves, I approached confidently. "Hey there, sorry to bother you. Prophet Joshua sent me." I flashed my green card for inspection.

"No one told me to expect you." He remained polite, but he wasn't stepping out of my way.

I smiled, unfazed. "Last-minute request. I just got the call a few hours ago. I was the closest one to the area." I still had trouble concocting lies, but at least I was getting better at repeating ones that were crafted for me by Dawn.

The guard nodded, verifying the validity of the card, then pulled out his phone. "Let me call my supervisor."

"Of course," I said.

I watched him closely. From his reaction, it seemed that the call had gone to voice mail—the phone lines jammed by Dawn. He tried a second time, then a third. "I can't reach her."

"It's time sensitive . . ." I added, turning up the pressure.

After a moment of indecision, he weighed his options, then reluctantly entered a code on a biometric keypad. "This way."

"Thanks." I tried to conceal my excitement as he led me inside—the plan had worked! Now, I just had to face whatever new obstacles might be waiting for me up ahead.

"What are you looking for?" he asked, casually inquisitive.

"I need to see the storage facility," I said, following Dawn's script. "Joshua wants a second opinion on the count."

The guard nodded again, seemingly satisfied.

I followed behind him, heart beating wildly. As he picked up the pace, I reached into my purse to steady the sharp, wiry device that was hanging heavy inside it. I took a deep breath. All I had to do now was set off this bomb.

12

Abomb?" I'd asked Dawn in the ambulance, incredulous. "I don't know how to wire a bomb."

She seemed unmoved. "It's easy, I'll show you."

I'd agreed to this mission without knowing all the details, and now I deeply regretted it. "I don't know if this is a good idea . . ."

Dawn knew me well enough to guess the root cause of my concern. "The bunker you need to infiltrate is sectioned off from the rest of the hospital. You won't cause any casualties."

"How is that possible? I'm setting off a *bomb*."

"The storage facility is fireproof, and usually empty, I promise. Get in and out, and everything will be fine."

She'd lied to me about things like this before. I was filled with desperate fear—fear that something would go wrong, fear that I'd make a mistake. But I had to pick someone to trust, and in that moment, I chose Dawn and popped a pill—whatever guilt I might feel, I couldn't let it show on my face.

Now, walking through the bunker, I could feel the nervous sweat trickling down my neck; I stayed a few feet behind the guard, hoping he wouldn't smell the stink of guilt on me. As he led me through a maze of hallways, I tried to memorize every turn, knowing I'd have to find my way back through them quickly once the bomb was set. I tried to push all my worries out of my mind . . . I couldn't risk doubting my mission, even for a moment.

But I couldn't help it. The fear overcame me, nearly immobilized me. It took everything I had just to keep putting one foot in front of the other, keep moving down that hall. All I could think of was the massive fireball that was about to consume this place . . . and me, if I wasn't careful.

As we walked through a heavy vault door and down a second set of steps, I felt a jolt of adrenaline. This was it. The inner sanctum. Concrete walls, high ceilings, a feeling of dust and disrepair. I suspected the cobwebs in the corner had been spun by spiders dead for decades.

As I took in my surroundings, I saw the guard eyeing me closely. "You don't have a notepad or anything?" he asked.

"Hmm?"

"To write numbers on. If you're counting boxes."

I pulled one out of my back pocket. Dawn had thought of everything. "Right here."

The guard nodded and led me past a glass wall, behind which I could see massive machinery churning. This was the manufacturing area, where right at this moment, new little bugs were being created—the mind-control nanotech. When the bomb went off, it'd have to be strong enough to destroy all this equipment.

The guard led me into an underground warehouse, and I nearly gasped aloud. The space was huge, wall to wall with boxes, twenty feet deep on either side. And their contents? I knew that nanotech was microscopic. The sheer quantity of ammunition in this room . . . no wonder Dawn was worried they could strike any day. "Everything okay?" the guard asked. Clearly I hadn't done enough to mask my horror.

"Yeah, I, uh, didn't think there'd be so many to count. It's all good, thanks," I reassured him, moving deeper inside. As I wove through boxes, stacked as high as my chest, I pulled a little spray bottle from my purse, filled with an odorless, extremely flammable liquid. I needed to hit as many of them as I could, as strategically as I could, to make the ensuing fire as massive as possible.

Again, I had to push out of my mind the fearful image of that fireball, consuming and charring my corpse. *Follow orders*, I told myself. *Get out of here alive.*

Moving as far as I could from the guard, I made notes on my pad every so often, trying to appear thoughtful and focused, covertly spraying as I went. By the time I'd run through the contents of my bottle, the guard lost interest in watching me work. With a breath of relief, I slipped into a gap between the rows and dug into my purse, pulling out the bomb.

It was tiny, palm-sized, but delicate and powerful. There were two pieces: the blasting cap, which would set off the initial explosion, and a block of grayish high-explosive putty, which, once set off by the blasting cap, would make sure all that flammable liquid caught fire. I'd never imagined I'd learn how a bomb worked, but . . . well, here I was.

My hands shook as I followed Dawn's instructions, pushing the blasting cap into the putty, and I winced as they made contact . . . *please don't explode yet!* But after a few seconds of panic, settling into echoey silence, it seemed I'd been successful.

I'd managed not to blow myself up yet, at least.

I took a deep breath. Was I really going to activate this thing? Was I really capable of setting off a bomb? I'd kept my cool this long, but as I fiddled with the timer, terror set in. I had five minutes before the blasting cap ignited, and then this entire shelter would be on fire, along with everything and everyone in it.

"Grace?" My head snapped up. The guard was walking toward me. Startled, I turned to attention, and in my haste, my arm knocked against the bomb, sending it off its purchase on top of the boxes. I watched in horror as it tumbled to the ground, flipping over and over in the air. I couldn't catch it, I could only watch it fall and brace myself, waiting for it to hit the ground and explode . . .

It impacted on the concrete with a tinny smack, and then . . . nothing.

I was alive. The bomb hadn't gone off. I let out a shaky breath and glanced down.

The device was in pieces at my feet. Two small wires had come out of the blasting cap, and the shell had cracked in two.

The bomb was broken.

stared at it, in shock.

Was it going to go off any second? Never? The guard was mere feet away from me now. He couldn't see the bomb, but I also couldn't pick it up without drawing his attention to it.

"Everything okay?" he asked.

"Are there any other storage facilities in this building?" I stalled, trying to appear nonchalant despite the desperate pounding in my chest.

"This is it," he said. "How much longer do you think you'll need?"

"Just a few more minutes," I squeaked out. The look he returned was far from reassuring, but he accepted my answer, walking back the way he came.

The moment his eyes were elsewhere, I quickly stooped to pick up the bomb, which felt like it could crumble further with each movement of my hands. I fumbled with the blasting cap, fingers unsteady. I didn't know how to put it back together without setting it off.

I wanted to abandon all pretext and book it the heck out of there, but I forced myself to stay put, stay focused. I couldn't leave unless I knew for certain this bomb was armed.

Ducking behind the boxes, I examined the blasting cap more closely and found what I thought was a solution. I could see where the wires used to be connected; I tried to twist them back into place, but the wires kept slipping. I listened for the guard's footsteps, hoping desperately that he wouldn't pick this moment to notice how absolutely freaked out I was.

Finally, despite my hands quaking violently, I managed to secure the wires to the blasting cap. This was the best I could do. Maybe by dropping it I'd broken it completely, but if not, I only had a very short time to get out of there.

I left the blasting cap inside its broken shell and hid the bomb deep within the stack of boxes, next to the remains of that bottle of flammable liquid, walking quickly back to the guard. "All done!" I said brightly. "I'm ready to go."

He frowned, noting my sudden shift in demeanor. "You in some kind of hurry?"

"I'm running a little late for something. Do you mind taking me back?" I asked, attempting breezy.

I could tell he was definitely suspicious now, but I couldn't worry about that. I'd gone into this planning to blow my cover—I just needed to get out alive.

We retraced our path, me walking a frantic step or two ahead of him. "Why did the prophet want a count?" he asked, trying to keep up with me.

"I don't know. I just do what they tell me to do," I said, smiling over my shoulder.

The guard seemed confused. "He didn't give you any reason?"

I struggled to think of an acceptable answer. "I assume it has to do with time of deployment?"

"Deployment?"

I improvised, "You know, when it's time to use the tech."

I glanced behind me and saw his startled expression. "Tech?"

I immediately realized that I'd said too much; the contents of the boxes must be a more closely guarded secret than I'd anticipated. But I kept walking ahead, eyes fixed on the exit. "Just what I was told."

He didn't respond. When I looked back; he was gone, his feet pounding toward the storage room.

I only hesitated a moment before sprinting after him, kicking myself the whole time. My carelessness had tipped him off, put his life in danger, and bungled the mission to boot.

I hurtled into the storage room and saw the guard digging through boxes. How could I stop him, how could I save him? "What are you doing?" I called to him.

"Trying to figure out why you're really here," he snapped.

I wasn't going to convince him of my innocence, no matter what I did. Whatever horrors Joshua might inflict once this guard detained me—that was a foregone conclusion. Now I just had to save both our lives.

"Look, I'm sorry, you're right, I lied to you." The guard looked up at me, listening. My voice trembled, knowing what a risky play this was, but I pushed forward. "I came here to sabotage this facility. This technology is dangerous."

The guard pointed his gun at me. I felt a surge of terror, realizing for the first time that he might be willing to shoot, to kill, in the name of his prophet. "Don't you dare move," he barked.

"There's a bomb that's going to go off any second," I told him as calmly as I could, afraid of alarming him further. "You can't stop it. We have to go, now, or we'll both die." The guilt was coursing through me—this was the outcome I'd most feared, that I was about to directly endanger the life of another human being.

He was unmoved. "You're not going anywhere."

I added a little more urgency to my tone. "You can shoot me if you want, but if you don't get out of here right now, you're going to die. Do you understand me?"

He hesitated. Would he really be willing to do it, commit murder? He was angry, he wanted to stop me in my tracks . . . but he couldn't. The Universal Theology, his fear of Punishments, were too powerfully ingrained. Still, he aimed the gun at my chest, shaking as he asked, "Who are you working for?"

"Please," I begged, "we don't have time for this."

Frustrated, he accepted his inability to take a human life and holstered his gun so he could resume tearing through the boxes.

"You're not going to find it in time," I tried to convince him. "Please, just come with me, save yourself."

"It's my job to protect this area," he said, growing more desperate. I saw in his face something familiar—a willingness to die for his cause. The same willingness I had to die for mine. He might not be able to kill, but there was one life that was his own to give, and he'd clearly given it to the prophet long ago.

He was as staunch a believer in the prophet's message as my father was . . .

I couldn't convince him.

With a pang of deep guilt, I realized that if I couldn't save this guard, I had to try to save myself. I took one last look at him, then bolted back toward the vault door. It occurred to me that I hadn't looked at my watch after setting the bomb's timer. Had it been five minutes yet? It seemed like it must have been.

As I ran up the steps, a new, sickening thought occurred to me. What if I'd simply disarmed the bomb when I dropped it? Then I'd fail my objective, lose my cover, get arrested— and it all would have been for nothing. As the moments ticked by, my dread increased. Why had I thought I could repair the blasting cap?

But as I raced around the final corner, exit in sight, there it was—the explosive boom, as I felt my feet lose touch with the concrete beneath me. The force of the explosion knocked me forward, whacking my ribs hard into the ground. I gulped in deep breaths of thick smoke, clinging to the ground for any wisp of fresh air as my ears were overcome by a cacophonous clanging, and a raging heat lapped at the soles of my feet. I'd succeeded after all. If I could survive this.

I just had to get to the doors. I could crawl there, I could make it.

The smoke surged around me, and my whole body ached from the impact of hitting the floor. Inch by painful inch I edged toward the door, calling on every last reserve of strength . . .

You're not going to make it, a voice in my head told me. My muscles were drained, I was too weak, I was overcome by the lack of oxygen. My fear subsided into a kind of acceptance . . . *this is the end.*

As I lay there, dazed, a pair of high heels stepped into my line of vision, cutting off my path to freedom. A woman in a sharp blazer was coming toward me in a haze of dust, her legs ashen with smoke. Her face was covered by a gas mask, so I couldn't make out who it was. Could it be Dawn? Had she come back to save me?

"Come on." I heard the woman's voice as if from under water as she pulled me to my feet, supporting me as I lurched to the exit.

"There's a guard back there, too," I rasped. "He needs help."

She didn't reply. Propping me against the wall, she managed to pry open the vault doors, and I felt the cool breeze of the outside air wash over me. The oxygen fanned the flames behind us as she pulled me back to my feet. "Go, quickly," the woman said, and I stumbled out into the hallway, collapsing onto the cement floor.

As she pulled off her gas mask, she released a thick mane of dark, wild curls. Through the wafting smoky haze, familiar brown eyes pierced mine. This was a face I'd memorized, a face I'd idolized.

The woman who'd just saved my life was my mother.

BOOK
TWO

1

It's funny how memories work. Immediately after my mother died, I could recall every intimate detail about her. Her smell, her laugh. I could predict how she might have responded; imagine the way she would've jumped to my defense against a bully, the soothing words she might say when I was feeling down. As I grew older, it wasn't that my memories of her were lost—I simply began to remember the stories about my memories better than the memories themselves. My experiences of my mother were condensed into anecdotes, and she became more of a legend than a person. Over the years, as my father filled in more details about her life and history, things I'd never known when she was alive, those new details shaded the pieces of her still lodged in my brain. Eventually, it was hard to know what was memory and what was myth. Given all that, at the age of eighteen, this is what I knew about the late Valerie Luther.

She'd graduated top in her class from her inner-city D.C.

high school, gotten a degree in social work from Yale, and she'd met my father while running a battered women's shelter in Washington, D.C.——before the Revelations, mind you, when volunteer work was solely done for idealistic reasons, rather than as a calculated attempt to improve one's appearance. Everything I remembered about her, everyone I'd talked to, painted her as the kindest, most thoughtful woman there could be. So when she was struck down in the American Revelation, I'd never figured out why. I'd never understood what she'd done that Great Spirit would have Punished her so drastically for.

Of course, later I'd realized her murderer hadn't been Great Spirit after all——it was her own guilt. She must have done something that weighed on her so heavily it ultimately killed her. If my father knew what it was, he'd never told me.

I'd been to her funeral, that was true. But it had been closed casket——common practice in cases of lethal Punishment.

Now I wondered; could she have survived somehow, escaped? In the bomb shelter, her voice sounded different——stronger, clearer. But maybe that was how she sounded in person: all I remembered at this point was her voice on our home movies.

In my bleary, disoriented state, I tried to get out a question, or words of any kind, but my vocal cords failed me. My eyes slid shut, stinging and watering from the smoke, and when they opened again, the woman was gone, vanished into the haze. I called out, "Mom?" But there was no answer. There was no trace of her, not even the faint clacking of her heels——as though she'd never existed at all. And quickly I found myself wondering . . . maybe she hadn't.

I pulled myself to my feet and limped up and down the underground hallway, looking for her, trying to figure out where she might have gone. "Mom?" I creaked out again. After a few minutes of searching, I found no entrances or exits. If she'd left this hallway, she must have gone out through the silver door upstairs.

I staggered back that way as quickly as I could, with two competing imperatives drumming inside my head: first, I needed to get out of here before I was caught, and second, I needed, more than anything, to figure out where my mother had gone. I emerged back into the janitor's closet, in that secluded hallway of the main hospital; I was back where I'd started. I looked around, but there was no sign of her, no sooty footsteps walking one way or the other. There was also no sign that a bomb had gone off directly under the building.

You need to get out of here, I reminded myself, overriding my foolish desire to comb these halls searching for her.

I walked quickly toward the exit, my ribs twinging with every step, certain some hospital administrator was going to stop and question me at any moment. My grimy clothes and hair got a few odd looks from other patients as I passed, but I found my way back to the ER, where my stretcher was still waiting, empty. I realized I hadn't been gone that long—my whole expedition into the bunker had only taken about fifteen minutes.

The doors to the outside were in sight, I was almost there . . . until that nurse walked up and intercepted me, annoyed. "There you are. Where on earth did you go?"

"Sorry, I had to use the bathroom," I explained innocently. "I think my mom's outside, I need to go find her . . ."

"Your mom can find you in here," she said and blocked my path until I reluctantly plopped back down on my stretcher for my medical exam. I'd tried to wipe off the smoke and grime from the explosion with my sleeves, but there was nothing I could do to hide the lacerations all over my arms and legs.

"You were in a car accident?" she asked, perplexed.

"Yep," I said. "I feel fine, but someone called an ambulance."

"You don't look fine."

I peered past her, inspecting every passerby, hoping to see even a wisp of my mother's familiar dark hair. "Have you seen someone who looks like she could be my mother?" I asked the nurse. "A little taller than me, wearing a suit jacket with a skirt? I don't have my phone so I don't know if she'll be able to find me back here . . ."

"Someone out front will be able to direct her to you, don't worry."

As new nurses and doctors came over to check on me in quick succession, my unease intensified. Was this building in any danger? No alarms were going off, and none of these people seemed to know an inferno was raging below us. Dawn had promised the shelter's seal was airtight, and it seemed that promise must have been real—I couldn't think of any other explanation for the normalcy all around me.

While I waited to be diagnosed, I found my mind drifting over and over the facts I knew about my mother's death, trying to organize them into something that made sense. When I was a little kid, my father had lied to me initially about my mother's disappearance, saying she'd fallen ill on the day of the American Revelation. Even once I suspected that her illness wasn't some coincidence, I'd never confronted him about my suspicions that she'd been Punished; I'd never known how.

But what if I'd been wrong in my conclusions? What if my father's lie was bigger than I'd ever imagined, and he was actually hiding the fact that she was still alive?

But why lie at all? And if he knew she was alive, why wouldn't he have given his desperately grieving daughter some kind of hope? My head pounded. None of it made any sense. All I knew was, I had to find that woman, I had to get some answers.

I was finally discharged with a few stitches and a diagnosis of bruised ribs and booked it out of the hospital. Bandaged and numb from all the painkillers, I looked around the busy street outside the building. Dawn had told me to wait outside until I could hail taxi number 532, which pulled up a few minutes later.

When I plopped in the back, I noticed it was empty. This was a driverless taxi, a technology invested in heavily since the Revelations—a way to prevent accidents like Jude's, save more lives. As we inched through the parade of tourists and club-goers, Dawn's face popped up on a screen on the back of the front seat. "Well?" she asked me.

I was beyond relieved to see her. "It worked. I blew up the vault."

Relief swept across Dawn's face. "Wonderful. This taxi will take you to a safe house—you'll get a new passport, and we'll get you into hiding."

"Wait," I said, desperate for some answers. "There's something else. There was this woman . . ."

"Someone saw you?" Dawn's voice sharpened.

"This woman saved me from the explosion. And . . ." It was harder than I expected to say the words out loud. They sounded so absurd. "She really looked like my mother."

Dawn seemed confused. "I thought you told me your mother died in the Revelations."

"She did! Or I thought she did. But just now, this woman . . . She pulled me out of the vault just in time. I swear it was her."

"She pulled you out, and then . . . ?"

"She left." It sounded stupid and strange to me, too. Why *had* she left so quickly?

"What did you say your mother's name was again?"

"Valerie. Valerie Luther. Cooper was her maiden name."

My hopes were dashed as Dawn shook her head. "I'm sorry. I don't know anyone by that name."

I pushed harder. "But it's possible, isn't it? I thought Jude was dead, but he's alive. And Ciaran, he turned up in that cell in West Virginia. Why not my mother, too?"

"I guess it's not impossible," Dawn said hesitantly. "But before I recruited you, we checked into your background pretty thoroughly. I have a lot of connections, I don't know why it wouldn't have come up—"

I interrupted her. "What if she's living under some other name? She could be hiding, like Jude is. Don't people call him Ben sometimes?"

"I gave Jude that secret identity. If I'd given your mother one, I think I'd know." Dawn must have seen the distrust bubbling up on my face. "Grace, I'm trying to help you, I promise."

I was growing more and more suspicious the more she

tried to convince me not to be. "You hit me with a car today," I pointed out, not hiding my anger. "You killed all those people in West Virginia. You asked me to help you, and I have been helping you. But in return, I want the truth."

"I'm telling you the truth. I'll look into this for you, I swear I will," she said. But something about the way she said it . . . A little voice in my head kept echoing all the sins she'd committed. All the reasons I shouldn't have trusted her six months ago, all the reasons I shouldn't trust her now. She tried to shift the subject, saying, "You did a good thing today, let's focus on that."

But suddenly I didn't care. The resistance, the fate of the world, they all paled in comparison to the possibility of reuniting with my mother.

The obsession must have been written all over my face, because Dawn delicately added, "And . . . you should be prepared for the likely possibility that this woman, if she even exists, is not your mother."

"If she even exists?" I repeated, dumbfounded.

She spoke quickly, "You were in a traumatic situation. Your memories may not be entirely accurate. And, correct me if I'm wrong, but doesn't your dad have a new girlfriend you don't like very much? It just seems possible that, in a moment when you were afraid, when you needed comfort, you imagined the person you've been missing a lot lately."

At that moment, I deeply regretted whining about Samantha to Dawn. "I know what I saw," I snapped. "Why are you trying to convince me that I'm imagining this?" *Unless there was something she wasn't telling me?*

"I'm not trying to convince you of anything," she protested, but her voice seemed strained. Something was wrong. Dawn clearly didn't want me digging into whoever this woman might be.

And then I realized there was a more pressing problem— even if my mother *was* alive, I would still never get to see her again. I had chosen this moment to go into hiding forever. Maybe we'd win this war in six months, six years—but by then, the trail would be cold.

I couldn't do it. I had to find her. I *knew*, deep in my bones, that this was something I needed to do. And if Dawn wasn't going to help me, I would have to stay and look for her myself. "I'm not ready to leave New York yet," I said, steeling my resolve.

Dawn was flabbergasted. "What do you mean? Grace, you need to leave right now, you're in danger."

"I don't care. I have to find my mother." I knew it sounded insanely stupid. But I'd spent every day since I was nine years old wishing that I could see my mom again, dying to hear her say she loved me just one more time. I'd risk just about anything if there was a real chance I could do that.

"Grace, you don't understand what you're saying." Dawn begged me.

I held firm. "Explain what I saw then. Tell me where to find her."

Dawn was getting angry now. "I *can't*. As far as I know, your mother is dead. You can't give up your only chance to save your life on the minuscule possibility that someone who supposedly died a decade ago might have instead gotten amnesia and found her way, unnoticed, to work in a hospital in New York City."

Everything she said was logical. But I felt myself opening the taxi door before I even realized what was happening. I could see the pavement gliding along beneath us. With all the traffic, we weren't going faster than about ten miles per hour.

"Yes, I can," I said, and I jumped out. My feet stung at the shock of hitting the ground, even at such a slow speed, and it took me a moment to catch my breath.

"Grace!" I could hear Dawn shouting from the screen as I ran off, down the street. My lungs burned, and every bit of my body ached, but it didn't matter. I was giddy with possibility, electrified by this new goal. By the only thing in the world that mattered to me at that moment.

My mother was alive, and she was in New York. I was going to find her.

2

After a few blocks, once I was safely away from Dawn's cab, I slowed and considered my destination. My adrenaline rush was wearing off a little, and now I had to try and think logically. While I knew my mother was somewhere in New York, I wasn't stupid enough to go back to the hospital and ask about her, the way that voice in my head was begging me to.

So instead, I returned to my dorm, quietly borrowed my sleeping roommate's phone (I doubted Zack would be tracking her browser history), and began digging. No references to any-one named Valerie on the hospital's website, no Valerie Luthers or Coopers in New York that could have been her. What else did I know about her? What other trails could I follow?

As I reached digital dead end after dead end, it hit me just how rashly I'd acted, jumping out of that taxi. But it was too late; I couldn't go back now. This was the path Great Spirit had chosen for me, and I had to believe it was the right one. I had to follow the clue trail I *did* have, and my next, safest lead was the one I'd had all along, the last person I was sure had seen her alive—my own father.

And so, in the middle of the night, I hopped on a train back to Tutelo, Virginia. On the way into New York, public transit had felt freeing—each person next to me a potential new adventure, signs of a big wide world to explore. But on the way home, their stares felt oppressive. Any of those people could be working with Joshua, could be here to arrest me. Any moment now, someone would pull up video footage of me at that hospital, and I'd be done for. I had to get home to my father before that happened. Once I had some answers, I could focus on getting out of town, to safety.

As wisps of fall foliage whipped by out the window, I let my mind drift, to imagine the scant possibility of actually finding my mother. Where would she be? What would she be doing? Would she be happy to see me? Why *hadn't* she wanted to see me all these years?

Asking those questions made me nervous. Sure, there was the possibility that my mother had gotten amnesia or something, that she didn't even remember me. But more likely, she did . . . and for some reason, she'd chosen to stay away. Was she in some kind of trouble, a trouble I couldn't even imagine? The kind of trouble even Dawn wouldn't know how to solve? Or worse . . . was she completely fine? What if she'd taken the Revelations as an opportunity to escape to a new life? What if she'd simply wanted to ditch my father and me? What if I found her and she was . . . disappointed?

Lost in thought, it took me a moment to register the glimpse of a figure approaching in the window's reflection. I didn't even turn my head; I knew I had no hope of running, of evading whoever was after me on this moving train. As my pursuer sat next to me, I finally hazarded a glance.

"What are you doing, Grace?" Zack asked me quietly. His voice was simple and curious—I searched it for a threat and found none. Yet still I knew a threat was there—Zack's mere presence was threat enough.

Did he already know about my involvement in the bombing? The fact that he was here told me he might. "Heading home," I said, keeping my expression level.

"So that's it, a few weeks and you're over college?" he teased, as casual as he had been just a few hours ago. Could he really not know what I'd done?

I kept playing my part. "My most important job is to get information for the prophet. I want to deliver what I found to Samuel in D.C. as soon as possible."

Knowing Irene was safe, I handed him the purple folder I'd stolen from Aviva, and he paged through it, curious. "That's very . . . devout of you."

"I guess. I figured I can skip a few classes."

"Sure." He glanced over at me, a wry look on his face. "You realize no one actually goes to college for the classes, right?"

"That's what everyone keeps telling me," I said. "An older friend of mine said all she did in college was smoke weed." I didn't mention that the "friend" who'd told me that was Dawn.

Thankfully, Zack didn't press for details, he just grinned. "Yeah, I hear college was more fun before the Revelations. Still though . . . you don't want to make friends? Even without Prohibited substances, you can still have a pretty good time."

I shrugged. "I've tried. I say I'm a cleric's daughter, and then they want to talk about religion, but I can't talk about Prophet Joshua because it's this giant lie of omission . . . So I'll probably never make another friend again."

"I get it," Zack said, and I could tell he actually did. He offered me a smile. "I'll be your friend." *Whether you want me to be or not*, I finished for him.

Instead, I found a different way to bite back. "I thought you were busy being Aviva's friend." The words came out harsher than I'd intended them . . . as though I actually *was* jealous.

Zack thankfully didn't seem to notice the unintended venom. "I'm a social guy," he quipped back. "I can have more than one friend."

"I'm sure you can," I said, voice full of disdain. I hated the way he talked to me, half flirty, and the way that, against my will, it made me feel special. I hated knowing that, objectively, I wasn't, because this was just the way he acted with women, the way he got what he wanted. And I knew just how dangerous that could be.

"C'mon, I'm serious," he said. "It bums me out that you're just hanging out alone all the time. I'll take you out, I'll introduce you to some people."

It was almost like he was asking me on a date, except we both knew he wasn't. "You don't have to take pity on me," I said.

"But I love taking pity on you. It's fun." He grinned again.

I tried to ignore his bluster, focusing on my problem at

hand. "Earlier tonight, after we split up, did you enjoy that New York City nightlife?" I asked, fishing to find out if he'd been near the hospital. "Or were you too busy doing your important work for the prophet, following around an eighteen-year-old girl?"

He laughed a little, but avoided giving too much away. "A *little* nightlife. I saw your cell signal leave the dorm an hour ago. Kinda cut the night short."

He'd just admitted to tracking my cell phone . . . another revelation. Another sign he trusted me? Maybe he really didn't know about the hospital yet. He'd find out soon enough though. Any moment they'd pin me to the bombing, Zack would get a text about it, and that would be it. "Is everything okay?" he asked, brow furrowing.

Clearly I wasn't doing a great job at hiding the anxieties that were constantly running through my mind.

"Hmm?"

"You just seem a little . . . I don't know. Frazzled."

"I'm just sleepy," I said.

"Take a nap. You can lean on me." Zack patted his shoulder. After a moment, I leaned into it. It was comfortable, and I worried about being lulled into a false sense of complacency. But . . . for the moment, that complacency felt too nice to turn down. "Sweet dreams," he said, brushing my hair away from my face, and the skin on my cheek tingled as his fingers made contact.

I was sure I'd never fall asleep—I was wound too tight with anxiety. But the next thing I knew, the train was chugging into the Tutelo station in the early light of dawn. Zack had also fallen asleep, his head resting on top of mine.

"We're here," I said, nudging him to wake him up.

Zack stirred, scrubbing a hand over his face as he glanced around. "Wow. I was out."

"Me, too. Your shoulder's comfortable."

"Hey, didn't you want to get off in D.C.?" he remembered. The train had left D.C. more than an hour ago.

"I need to go home first and see my dad," I said quickly, hoping I was lying well enough to fool him. "I'll go back into D.C. later today."

Zack nodded, seeming to buy my excuse. He glanced at his phone, scrolling through something on it, and panic surged through me. Was he finally reading that inevitable incriminating text, linking me to the attack on the hospital? But he seemed unmoved by whatever was in his inbox, and we exited the train.

I took a cab home, then headed into my silent house, where my father was still asleep. I wanted to stay up so I could question him the moment he woke, but I was too exhausted. *Sleep*, my brain was telling me, *you have to sleep.* As if under its spell, I crawled into bed and immediately passed out.

When I blinked open my eyes, it was almost noon. I sat up with a start. *Stupid*, I thought, *you have Prophet Joshua's entire organization gunning for you, and you take a big long nap?*

I could hear my father moving around in his office, and I summoned my courage. "Dad?" I called out, heading inside— only to see that Samantha was there, too, laughing uproariously at something my father was saying. They seemed surprised to see me enter.

"Grace!" My father wrapped me in his arms. "What are you doing here?"

I said quietly, "I wanted to talk to you." *But I can't, because Samantha's here,* I tried to convey. It hit me then, what should have hit me months ago—Samantha's timing was incredibly suspicious. She'd appeared in my father's life right after I'd started working with the prophet. After years of my father keeping his relationships private, coincidentally now he decides to let this woman into our home? She must be a plant, by the prophet or by Dawn. There was no other explanation.

"Is everything okay?" Samantha asked, frustratingly cheery as usual.

"Yeah, I'm fine," I muttered back, wishing she'd get that stupid nice smile out of my house.

But that stupid smile finally said something useful for a change. "I'll give you two a minute."

As she left, my father looked after her. "She's so sweet, isn't she? I'm thinking of taking her to the conference in Johannesburg. What do you think?"

That you're making a terrible mistake? "That's great," I said, wondering if she was listening at the door. Ultimately, my father's questionable romantic decisions were the least of my problems right now. I lowered my voice to continue, "I was actually wondering . . . can I ask you some questions about Mom?"

My dad nodded through his confusion. "Of course."

Nervous, I tried to broach the subject as delicately as possible. "Is there anything I don't know about her? Anything you haven't told me?"

He seemed puzzled by that. "Why are you asking?"

"You saw her, right? Before she died?"

"I did . . ."

I took a deep breath, asking him the question I wished I'd been brave enough to ask years ago. "And she looked . . . normal?"

He finally realized what conversation we were having. "You mean was she an Outcast?"

"Yeah."

He looked at the ground, fresh pain washing over him. "Yes. She was an Outcast."

"Are you sure it was her?" I asked him. "There's no way it was a different Outcast you saw in the hospital? Is there any chance she could be alive, somewhere?"

The anguish was all over my father's face. He'd lied to me many times, but I couldn't imagine he was lying now. "I was there, I held her hand while she died. It was the single worst moment of my entire life."

Hearing the confirmation stung worse than I'd expected. "Why didn't you tell me?" I asked him.

"I wanted you to remember the good parts of her. Whatever it was she did . . . I knew it didn't change who she was. But as a little kid . . . I wasn't sure if you'd see it the same way. I should have known you'd figure out the truth eventually." His pride was muted by a sad smile.

"You don't know what she did? Why she was Punished?" I pushed.

"I don't, I'm sorry." But he looked away from me as he spoke.

His avoidance was frustrating. "Dad, I'm eighteen. Whatever it is, you can tell me."

He turned back to me, and he seemed torn. "I don't know anything for sure."

"I won't look at her differently, I promise," I said, hoping not to provoke any feelings of guilt. "You can tell me."

He sat down, trying to find the right words. "In the months before the American Revelation, I was working a lot. Prophet Joshua had asked for my help, and there was nothing more important to me than serving Great Spirit. But your mother might have felt . . . ignored? In any case, she started coming home later and later. She wasn't acting like herself. She was evasive, she wouldn't tell me who she'd been meeting with."

My breath caught in my throat. "You think she was having an affair?"

My father shook his head, still unable to verbalize his suspicions. "I never would have suspected it. That wasn't the woman I thought I knew. But after she died, after she was Punished . . . it made a certain amount of sense . . ."

It did. The mother I knew would have felt guilty for hurting my father. My mind spun, trying to figure out if it could possibly be true. "You never found out who it was?"

My father let out a chuckle at that. "No. Although years later, I learned the rumor going around in our worship center before the Revelations was it was Prophet Joshua."

His tone was light, happy he could finally find something to laugh about amid all this darkness, but my blood ran cold. My father might think the prophet wasn't capable of such a transgression, but I knew better. I knew who, *what*, Joshua really was.

It could be a baseless rumor, a dead end. Or it could be a new lead, a seed with the potential to grow into the truth. There was only one person who could tell me for sure. But was I willing to walk right up to a man who was probably waiting to torture me, just to find out?

I'd made a decision when I jumped out of that taxi—finding my mother was worth risking everything I had. Was that still true?

Thankfully, that voice inside my head whispered, nudged me: *Don't give up.*

3

The train ride into D.C. was a blur of indecision. Even a few blocks away from Walden Manor itself, I was still trying to talk myself out of this crazy plan. Approaching Prophet Joshua and accusing him of adultery? It was madness. But as I rounded a corner, my destination in sight, a scolding tone stopped me in my tracks. "Grace. We need to talk."

Zack's voice had become my least favorite sound in the world. This time, I didn't have the patience to face him down, to play our stupid little game. Why even bother? I prepared to bolt—if Zack was here to capture me on the prophet's behalf, I would never be able to find my mother. But he grabbed my arm before I could make my escape. "Grace! What the hell is going on?"

I shook my arm, freeing myself. "Stop it. Stop following me around, stop pretending to be my friend." I took a moment to revel in the shocked look on his face. Right now, all I wanted was for him to go away.

But he didn't, and his voice held a warning. "Grace, I'm not an idiot. What's up? Don't lie to me."

I puffed up my chest a little. "Why, so you can run and tattle to the prophet on me?"

Zack seemed genuinely offended. "For the record, I've been *covering* for you all day. Reporting that nothing's out of the ordinary. But sure, yeah, if that's what you really think of me." I knew I should be trying harder to protect what was left of my cover, but I was too angry at him to care. I stayed silent as Zack continued his interrogation, undeterred. "Why are you looking for your mother?"

How did he know that? "My mother's dead," I corrected him.

"What about all the questions you asked your father? About whether he was sure he held the hand of the right dying Outcast? Why would you ask him that?"

A shiver ran down my spine. Our house was bugged. I'd always suspected it, but hearing it was a reality made my skin crawl. "How did you hear all that?" I demanded. Even though I knew the answer, I wanted to force him to say the words.

Zack didn't even flinch. "The prophet asked me to bug your house. Answer the question."

I took a deep breath, trying to find a way to spin this. "In one of my classes at NYU, we were talking about the Revelations . . . it made me stop and think and realize there were so many things I don't know about my mom, how she died."

"But why the urgency?"

"It wasn't urgent," I insisted.

Zack didn't buy it. "You told me you were in some huge

hurry to give that folder to Samuel, but instead you go home to grill your dad?"

"You've never lost anyone, you don't know what it's like," I shot back. Though I was trying to cover, the anger behind my words was all too real.

"I do know," he said, with a quiet sadness I wasn't expecting. "I have." I saw the grief sweep across his face, and for a moment, I had compassion for him. The truth was, I didn't know Zack, not well enough to understand whatever pain and anguish lay deep inside him. And even at my angriest, I still didn't want to hurt him.

"Who was it?" I asked gently, but Zack just shook his head.

"It doesn't matter. What matters is, I know how you think. And right now, you think your mother's alive. The way you talk about her, it's as though there are stakes still." He must have seen on my face the accuracy of his guess.

I tried to remember what I'd said to my dad. "They just found her lying on the ground outside our worship center. Couldn't it have been some other Outcast woman that my mother was mistaken for? How could they prove it was her, how do we really know? And if there *was* some mistake . . . if she's out there . . ."

Zack looked at me with sympathy. "I get it. I do."

"Yeah?"

His voice went quiet. "I've never lost a parent, but . . . I know that feeling. When one moment changes your whole world, and you'd give anything to go back to before, to make sure things turned out differently." Instinctively, I reached out a hand to touch his arm, to offer him some kind of comfort when he looked so sad. "Thanks," he said.

His moment of empathy weakened my defenses, made me feel like I could confide in him, at least about this one thing. "Wouldn't you want to know anything you could, about someone so important, that you lost so young?"

Zack shook his head, immediately on edge. "Not if that meant questioning the morality of a prophet."

"Why? Do you think it's true?" I tested him.

As usual, Zack's expression betrayed nothing. "I have no idea. But if you go in asking questions, he's going to ask some back. Ask me things, ask your friends things. Questions maybe you don't want to answer." Zack's words felt pointed—they hinted he knew what my answers to those questions might be.

"What does it matter to you?" I asked, fishing a little.

"Seriously? You think after all the time we've spent together, I don't care what happens to you?" Despite myself, his words gave me a little shot of adrenaline, a little jolt of pleasure.

But I tried to squelch those feelings. "So now you're pretending we're friends? Whatever friendship we have is based on you *lying to me*, and following me around, and reporting on me to the prophet. That's not healthy, that's not mutual respect. If you really care about me, then stop. Stop doing it. Be on my side, for real."

I could see my words punching a hole right through him. "I am on your side," he swore.

"Seriously? That's the best you've got?" I spat back, realizing how much pent-up anger I had toward him. He was the personification of everything I hated—the prophet, this situation, this whole crappy world. I couldn't help it, couldn't stop myself.

I saw Zack working to restrain whatever comeback he wanted to throw at me. His response was reserved, measured. "You're right. I'm sorry. I haven't been a good friend to you. But I'm trying to be one now. Don't go to Prophet Joshua with this. I promise you, you'll regret it."

But my gut was telling me that Zack was wrong. Though usually the thought of facing down the prophet would have terrified me, in this moment, the prospect didn't scare me one bit. The search for my mother had imbued me with a kind of bravery I'd never experienced before, an eagerness to waltz right into the prophet's office and tell him whatever I needed to in order to find her.

If my mother *was* alive, she was at the center of something big—something both Dawn and Zack were trying to keep me away from. Which meant I needed to find out what it was, as soon as possible.

I allowed my face to slip into an expression of resignation. "Okay. You're right. I'll keep my distance," I promised.

Zack nodded, seemingly placated.

Now, I just had to get a meeting with Joshua.

Once I'd evaded Zack and made my way into that familiar, ornate Walden Manor waiting room filled with desperate Outcasts, paranoia overtook me. Did I really think I could pull this off? But I quieted those anxieties. If I was going to survive this encounter with the prophet, I had to appear calm.

And indeed, a kind of calm did come over me as I entered Samuel's office and faced down his smug smile. After the hospital bombing, Dawn had told me to expect the worst, and the worst hadn't come. And somehow, intuitively, I'd known it wouldn't—some inner knowledge had told me to jump out of that car, that I'd be safe if I did. It was the kind of inner knowledge I'd always attributed to Great Spirit showing me the way.

Basic logic still told me Zack was right, that this was a terrible idea. But after all my hand-wringing, hoping for some kind of sign from the universe about what my purpose might be, here it was: a big flashing neon sign saying, PURPOSE, THIS WAY. I had no idea where Great Spirit might be leading me, but I felt certain of one thing: if I trusted the feeling in my gut, Great Spirit would protect me, would lead me to my mother. And with that brazen confidence, I told Samuel, "I want to talk to Joshua."

Samuel looked at me like I was crazy, which, to be fair, maybe I was. "*Joshua?* I'm sorry, was the president not available?"

I ignored the derision dripping from his voice and stared him straight in the eye. "He was having an affair with my mother. Before she died." It felt incredibly satisfying to catch him off guard.

"Where—where did you hear that?" he stuttered.

"It was the rumor in our worship center, before the Revelations," I said evenly.

I expected him to shut me down. To tell me I was wasting his time. But instead he cast a skeptical eye at me and murmured, "Wait here."

Maybe he was amused by my request. Maybe he knew something I didn't. Or maybe I was wrong about Great Spirit protecting me and my number was finally up. I'd find out soon enough. As he left the room in an officious huff, I tried to maintain my sense of calm. I had to trust that I'd been led here for a reason.

I waited in Samuel's office an interminable amount of time. It would have been so easy to rifle through his drawers, go through his computer, but Samuel struck me as the type who might have a hidden camera. So I sat, and I waited, until an aide finally entered and ushered me toward Joshua's office. I took each step with a sense of calm and purpose—*my plan was working.*

Joshua himself was waiting for me inside, an expression of

deep annoyance on his face, despite his gracious, welcoming words. "Grace, so good to see you again."

"You, too, Prophet," I said, humbled. Standing in his presence, I was reminded of just how much power he wielded. To the rest of the world, this man was divine perfection embodied . . . how could I possibly bring up the affair? It was blasphemous, what I was about to accuse him of. But it was too late. I was going to have to.

His eyes were innocent, curious. "I hear you have a question about your mother?"

My stomach lurched with fear, but I pressed forward. "I heard a rumor, that . . ." I forced myself to say it: "She was having an affair before she died."

His voice betrayed no hint of emotion. "With me." Looking at his handsome face, I understood why my mother might have been tempted.

"Yes," I squeaked out.

His tone was gentle, avoiding any condescension. "And you want to know if it's true?"

It would be easy enough for him to lie, unless I convinced him that I already had the evidence. I straightened my shoulders, steeled my voice, finding a confidence I never knew I had. "I already know it's true. I'm here to ask you why."

My plan had succeeded in throwing him off guard, at least. "Oh?"

I tried to ignore the absurdity of coming to the great prophet with something like this and stood my ground. "I can't ask her. So you're the only one left who can explain what happened."

Joshua seemed strangely impressed by my boldness. His eyes

searched mine, intrigued. "Why not let her rest in peace? Why dig up painful secrets?" It was almost an admission, the way he said it.

I watched him carefully, knowing I was treading on dangerous ground. "Some secrets are more painful buried," I said. "At least for me."

He nodded. "You want to know why she was Punished? You think it was my fault?"

"Do you think it was your fault?" I asked tentatively.

"I think if anyone is responsible for the actions of Great Spirit, it's me," he said in his magnanimous, prophety, meaningless way. "It's my job to guide every human being in this country toward Forgiveness. What kind of prophet would I be, to let that kind of harm come to someone else?" That was the very question I would have asked, if I didn't know the truth about him, the truth about this world.

"Do you feel guilty?" I asked, moments later remembering that he knew as well as I did what it meant to feel guilty in this new world.

"Of course," he said, not missing a beat. "It pains me every day that I was Forgiven for things that so many others weren't. That my sins were washed away while others were Punished."

"Like what happened with my mother." I wasn't going to let this go until he gave me a straight answer.

His voice grew quiet. "Like that, yes. If she was taken, I should have been, too."

There it was. It was true. They had been having an affair. Though I'd come in with such bluffing confidence, the reality of it still blew me away, left me weightless, adrift, reeling. How could I reconcile this newly uncovered sin with the impeccable picture of my mother I'd always held in my mind? I'd idealized her, filled in the gaps in my knowledge of her with wishes instead of facts. But all those stories I'd told myself about her perfection would have to be rewritten now.

"I'm sure Great Spirit had His reasons for taking her," I mumbled, trying to conceal my shock.

Joshua could tell I was upset and softened his tone further. "All I can imagine is that Great Spirit needed me to help lead humankind toward enlightenment, despite my moral failings. Though what human doesn't have those?"

As he spoke, I realized that my trail of clues had reached a dead end. It seemed as far as Prophet Joshua knew, my mother really was dead. Which meant, if he was right, I had a whole new reason to hate him—*he was the one responsible for her death.*

"Why didn't you try to help her?" I couldn't help but ask. "She didn't die right away; you could've sat at her side, like my father did. You help people. You touch them and they're Forgiven." I could hear the accusation in my tone, despite my best attempts to contain it.

"I tried, of course I did," he insisted, with a kind of passion that made me believe him. "I wondered why I couldn't help. But eventually I had to accept that Great Spirit must have had His reasons. I assumed He wanted to free me from all possible distractions."

My stomach curdled with that last sentence. *A distraction.* That was what my mother had been to him? And the way he said that word—"all"—it sounded like my mother wasn't the only *distraction*. A picture was sharpening of the kind of man

Prophet Joshua really was, beneath his holy veneer, and I didn't like it one bit.

Slowly, over the course of our conversation, I'd started to accept that maybe Dawn had been right; maybe my mother really was dead, that the woman I'd seen in the bunker was just some hallucination caused by smoke inhalation. All the hope I'd been holding suddenly felt silly. Prophet Joshua himself thought she was long gone, thought he'd been the reason for her Punishment. Here he was confessing it all, with what appeared to be real remorse. Dawn had never heard of Valerie Luther; if she was alive, surely there would have been some paper trail, some evidence.

Though Joshua was the last person in the world I would have thought to trust, the truth made clear by his admission was unavoidable. My mother was dead. I'd hallucinated her. That was the only explanation that made any sense.

But——Great Spirit had wanted me to end up in this room for some reason, I was sure of it. The calm I felt looking at Prophet Joshua seemed to confirm that theory. I tried to figure out why, what purpose this meeting could have to our larger goal, but I came up short.

Here was this man who had foisted a lie upon all of us. He had killed millions, possibly billions of people, and he didn't care. Not even about the ones he knew intimately. I was seized with a sudden urge to tear him limb from limb——if I couldn't find my mother, I wanted to at least avenge her.

He must have seen that, must have expected what his disclosure might do to me. He looked down, casually spinning a prayer wheel on a nearby table. "I'm telling you all this because I trust you," he said.

And because you know if I catch you in a lie, I might start to guess the truth—that you're evil.

His faux-empathetic eyes bored into mine. "You don't need to tell your father anything we talked about today. Great Spirit won't mind if you keep this secret." He was trying to relieve me of my guilt.

I nodded, and as he placed a hand on my arm, I could feel myself being Forgiven. The beauty bestowed upon me via the prophet's touch was unlike anything I'd felt since the Moment. Instinctively I was awed—there was a reason Joshua was famed for his healing hands.

But then I glanced at the prayer wheel he'd touched right before laying his hands on me. Though it looked perfectly ordinary, I was certain there must be something on it, some sort of drug that worked like Zack's pills, that entered the bloodstream through skin contact. As he let go, the faintest hint of yellow residue on my skin confirmed that suspicion.

"How do you feel?" he asked with a charitable smile.

"Amazing. Thank you," I said, making my voice breathless, remembering I had to play my part.

"You're welcome." It was time for me to leave.

As I exited, the high of Joshua's fake healing touch faded into my very real misery. Any hope of seeing my mother again was dashed, and I was going to have to grieve her all over again, now that I'd learned the truth. I wasn't quite sure what my defiance of Dawn had accomplished, although I remained certain it would prove to be the right decision in the long run. Except that now I had no idea what to do next.

As I exited the building, I felt pinpricks down my spine:

someone was watching me. Certain it must be Zack, I glanced around until my eye eventually caught a tall, shadowy figure—most definitely *not* Zack—leaning against a wall, gaze trailing me.

A lurch of fear went through me—was this it, finally? Had Joshua sent someone to do his dirty work for him? He couldn't have me die in his office, after all.

But when the man lifted his head, I recognized his features—the square jaw, the deep brown eyes, the mess of dark hair. It was Jude.

I t took me a moment to really believe it was him. It had been so long, and I wasn't expecting to see him, especially not here. But the moment I pieced his features together into a face I recognized, the moment I realized that the man I'd been trying to push out of my mind for months was finally standing right in front of me, my heart soared. Jude was alive. He was here, in Washington, D.C. He'd found me. My instinct was to run to him, kiss him, but I restrained myself. We were in public, within yards of Walden Manor.

He made eye contact with me and walked away down the street—a sign he wanted me to follow. I trailed behind him, ease washing over me as I watched his familiar gait. He entered a public library, and I followed him up the stone steps, deep into the racks of books. Finally, he turned to me, full of concern. "Are you okay?"

I was overcome with emotion, hearing his voice. I thought of all the imagined conversations I'd had with him since we were separated . . . now, finally, he was here, and real. Instinctively I moved to embrace him, but he took a step back as I touched his arm. "Sorry," I said, embarrassed.

"Don't worry about it," he said. There was a strange hesitance between us, like an invisible barrier had gone up while Jude was gone, and now I didn't know how to break through again.

"Is everything okay?" I asked. *Are you furious? Do you hate me?*

"Everything's fine," he said gently. "I just think we should leave all that in the past." Despite his careful tone, I could tell something wasn't the same. That my decisions had hurt him, whether he was willing to admit it or not.

"I'm so sorry," I said again. "I wanted to reach out, but I couldn't . . ."

"That's not what I'm here to talk about." His voice stayed businesslike, erasing our history in a way that irked me. "Dawn says your cover's blown, but you refused to go into hiding."

"I just walked into Walden Manor and sat down with Joshua. My cover's fine," I said, defensive.

"Because Dawn had your back," Jude said firmly. "She disabled all the security cameras at the hospital. And since you used a fake name, they haven't traced the incident back to you—yet."

"But eventually they will," I finished for him.

"Eventually. For now, it seems like Zack is covering for you, too. We've hacked their network, we've seen all his correspondence." So Zack had been telling the truth. I thought back on everything Zack had said over the past few days. Letting me know my house was bugged; in retrospect, that was a pretty big admission on his part, a risky play if it wasn't sanctioned by Prophet Joshua.

"Do you know why he covered for me?" I asked.

"Maybe he's in love with you," Jude joked. *A hint of jealousy? Or was I just hoping it was?*

I rolled my eyes. "He's not in love with me. I think he's protecting me so I'll trust him, tell him things."

That seemed to concern Jude. "If that's true, you don't have much time. At some point, he's going to tell Joshua the truth."

I knew that already. Had Jude come here just to scold me? Pick up where Dawn left off? "You think I haven't had this conversation with Dawn already?"

"Dawn told *me* this is all because of your mother. What's going on, she said you saw her?"

Something about hearing the question from Jude gave me strength, no matter how skeptical he sounded. He'd met her, he'd been to her funeral; my mother was a real person to him, in a way she never could be to Dawn.

As I relayed the whole story, I finally felt like someone was listening to me, believing what I'd seen. And the way he nodded, I knew he didn't think I was a crazy person, which was gratifying after Dawn's reaction, and even Zack's.

"But the way Joshua was talking about her . . . don't you think I must've been wrong? She's dead, isn't she?" I finished.

Jude looked at me with sympathy. "I honestly don't know. But I do know that you have friends who care about you. And a massive network of people on your side, who can help you.

But trust me, they won't be inclined to look for your mother if you're running around as a liability to them."

I couldn't hide my disappointment. "Dawn sent you to bring me in, didn't she?" It stung to think that was why he was here, just following Dawn's orders.

Jude's face was pained. "No. She left you for dead. I came myself as soon as I heard."

"You thought I'd listen to you."

"Well, no." He smiled a little bit. "You're not much for listening to anyone. But I wasn't going to sit around and wait for you to die."

He'd risked his life to try and save mine. Again. At that, I couldn't help myself—I gave him a hug. For a moment, he let me, wrapped his arms around me tightly, and it was like coming home; I'd forgotten I could feel so safe.

He tried to stay focused. "I've got a passport for you, under a fake name. We'll get you out of the country, somewhere out of Joshua's reach." He pulled away and looked me in the eye, waiting for a response. "Okay?"

"Okay," I said softly.

"Go home, get ready. I'll send a taxi to your house at eight, it'll take you to the train station. Get in it. And this time— don't get out until you get there?"

I smiled, finally. "I promise."

I reached out and took his hand—he squeezed it, but quickly let me go. I watched him hesitate before finally building up the courage to say, "There's one other thing I should tell you."

My stomach lurched. "What is it?"

"I thought you'd be more likely to get in the cab if you didn't know. But . . . I don't want to lure you somewhere under false pretenses."

"Jude, what is it?" I couldn't handle the suspense.

He said gently, "There's someone else." My heart nearly stopped, but I remained silent as he continued. "We've been dating for about four months, and she means a lot to me. You've been my friend as long as I can remember, and nothing can change that, but . . . I know we'd started down a road, before you had to go radio silent, so . . ."

I felt the pressure of tears beating against my eyelids, but I managed to keep them at bay, keep my face neutral. At least, I hoped so. "I totally understand," I said quickly. "I'm happy for you."

"You're still coming?" Jude looked at me, relief and skepticism warring in his expression.

"I'll get in the cab." I swallowed and plastered a smile on my face.

The tension seemed to drain out of him, finally. "Good. I've been so worried about you."

I know, I wanted to say. *I know you'll always worry about me, even when you love someone else. That's what makes you so wonderful. That's why I'm so heartbroken.*

He gave me instructions on where to go once I got to the station, before leaving me with one final reminder: "Eight P.M. Don't bring anything with you." As he walked away, I stared at his receding form, steeling myself. I couldn't cry until he was out of sight. I was the one who had chosen this road, after all. And I hadn't been lying; I wanted Jude to be happy, more than anything. I loved him. But my insides burned with regret. In that moment, I hated myself for not making it to that meeting point, not running away to Nova Scotia with him.

Don't get in the taxi, was all I could think, as I found myself descending into a fatalistic spiral. *Why even bother?* The moment Jude disappeared into the stacks, I gave in to my despair. Jude might be alive, but he was no longer mine.

I cried as quietly as I could, the cold metal shelves digging into my spine as I collapsed against them. *You had a mission*, I reminded myself. *You gave up your own happiness to try and make a difference.* But nothing I'd done felt worth it. It had all been a waste.

My brain's disparaging voice grew louder as I crumpled into a ball on the library floor. *Why keep running? What's the point now?*

"Grace?" I'd been so caught up in my sadness I hadn't even noticed a figure approach. I sat up and swiftly brushed away my tears, hoping my crying hadn't been too audible.

It was Zack. Of course it was. His voice brimmed with a kind of certainty, a finality. "It's time for you to tell me the truth."

He was sterner than I'd ever seen him before, his usual charm, his friendliness, nowhere to be found. And as much as that charm had annoyed me before, now that it was gone I desperately missed it. "You ignored my advice. You went to Walden Manor, asking questions. And now, Samuel is asking *me* questions. And I can make up a story, I can keep covering for you; I'll do that. But if you don't tell me what's really going on, I'm going to have to tell him the truth sooner or later."

"And what's the truth?" I asked haughtily, calling his bluff.

His tone was deadly serious. "That you pass mysterious notes with strangers. That you conveniently went for medical treatment at a hospital in New York, under a fake name, at the exact same time that a terrorist attack occurred in the basement."

My whole body went numb. He knew everything. "I'm not a terrorist," I stumbled out, my lips dry and trembling.

"You're right, I can't prove it. Because the only person who could have identified you died in the blast."

In my haste to find my mother, I'd forgotten about the guard. No, I corrected myself; I'd intentionally put him out of my mind because on some level, I was afraid of what the truth might be. Afraid of what I might have done, for good reason. I tried to hide my horror, keep my cover, but my guilt was too overwhelming. "Died?" I sputtered.

Zack seemed almost pleased to have finally pierced my armor. "Pronounced dead last night. Proud of yourself?"

No.

I'd been part of the raid on the West Virginia prison-lab where dozens of scientists had perished . . . but that had been Dawn's fault. Dawn's mistake. *This* mistake was mine. Someone else was dead because of me, my actions, my failure.

I was a murderer.

I'd been raised with such black-and-white rules about morality; they were the rules that kept our world safe. I'd always been taught that there was no such thing as killing in the name of a god, or a nation, or an ideology—not even in self-defense, not even to protect those you loved. Killing was wrong, no matter the circumstance. And Punishments proved that: the Punishment for committing murder, for any reason, was always swift and deadly.

In my early childhood, I could remember people justifying

war as something that was for the greater good . . . but that was logic from an archaic time, when mankind was ruled by less civilized principles. Now we knew better—violence only begets violence, that had always been obvious. But here I was, making those same brutish justifications, trying to find some way to make myself feel okay about this. *I was a soldier*, I told myself. *I was following orders. I'd taken one life, but saved millions.* It was the same logic Dawn had used to justify the massacre in West Virginia—the irony was not lost on me.

I felt sick. I'd joined this cause because I'd thought I could do better than Dawn, that I could make her movement better. But instead, Dawn had made me worse.

I'm a murderer. For the rest of my life, I'd be a murderer. The guilt tore at me, left me in shreds.

And as I spiraled, I realized, I hadn't taken a pill since the previous night . . . and I was experiencing a Punishment that fit my crime. The guilt I felt was literally suffocating me.

And I wanted it to. I deserved it, I deserved more than death.

I gasped, my lungs constricting. Just before I passed out, I felt myself falling to the ground, falling into Zack's arms. And then I felt nothing.

When I regained consciousness, I could feel the residual pinprick in my arm; Zack must have shot me up with lifesaving drugs. I could feel them coursing through my veins, easing my feelings of remorse. But not erasing them. Nothing ever could.

I lay with my head in Zack's lap, and my eyes fluttered open to find him staring down at me. No longer angry, no longer judgmental. Just looking at me with an unexpected empathy, and concern.

But I knew he knew. "Let's stop playing games, okay?" he said.

I could think of no way to explain my sudden-onset Punishment, besides admitting to being responsible for the guard's death, so I sat up and nodded. "Okay."

Zack took a deep breath. "I know you're working with the resistance. And I want to help."

That, I wasn't expecting. I tried to gauge whether he was

playing me, whether this was still part of some long con. I hated how much I wanted to trust him. "Help with what?" I could barely contain my disbelief.

"I know what I've been doing, the past couple years, okay? The people I work for . . . I thought they were doing great things, helping the world, but . . . I take one of those pills every single day."

The words slipped out. "Because you feel guilty?"

He seemed confused. "Guilty?"

He didn't know, I realized, what was really causing the Punishments. He had a hunch it wasn't Great Spirit, but no one had ever told him any of the neurochemical specifics. Should I be the one to break the news? If he was looking for answers, it was the safest thing I could think of.

So I tentatively explained what I knew about the nanotech, about the way the pills worked. As I spoke, Zack leaned against the bookcase, overcome. "No one ever told you any of that?" I asked timidly once I'd finished.

"No one trusts *me* with any important secrets," he said, voice bitter.

"The prophet trusts you more than he trusts me," I pointed out.

Zack ignored my jab. "Who told you that thing about the guilt?"

"You think I'm gonna tell you *that*?"

"I just want to know what's going on," he said, slamming a fist against the bookshelf in frustration. "I want to know the truth."

"Then maybe you shouldn't be working with the people who are perpetrating the lies," I shot back, standing to move away.

But Zack followed, right on my tail. "That's why I can help! Like you. You've been a double agent, haven't you? I want to do that, too." My hesitation clearly angered him. "All the time we've spent together recently. You can't look at me and know I'm telling the truth?"

I did look at him. And I couldn't tell. "How would I know?" I asked, matter-of-fact. "All the time we've spent together, you've been lying to me."

"I could say the same to you. But I still feel like I know you." His voice softened. "I still consider you a friend."

Zack's charm was back, and annoying me again. But I wasn't going to let it hoodwink me. "You're threatening to turn me in to Joshua if I don't do exactly what you say. That doesn't sound like much of a friend to me."

I could tell that resonated with him. "You're right. I'm desperate and I'm scared, and I don't know what to do. You think I can just quit? You think Joshua won't kill me if I try to walk away?" So he did know what Joshua was capable of. "I want my freedom," he begged. "And I want you to have yours. Whatever it takes, I'll protect you."

"Unless it gets in the way of protecting *you*," I challenged.

Zack sagged, a little defeated. "I'm sorry," he said. "What I've been doing to you, it's not right. It's not right to do to anyone, and especially not . . ." He paused. "I didn't know you when we first started. Not the way I do now. I thought you were just one of Macy's little friends . . ."

"Thanks." I snorted.

"But now . . . I know you." The way he looked at me when he said it made my heart give a funny little jump.

"What do you know about me?" I couldn't help asking.

"I know you get excited every time we pass a horse in Central Park, because you think the way their tails swish is funny. I know you know way more about coffee than any normal human should. And I know that these past few months have been the first time in so long that I've actually been happy to get up every morning, because it means I get to spend time with you."

"But it was all a lie," I repeated, clinging to the words. There was safety there.

He shook his head, genuinely hurt. "Not our friendship. At least not for me."

In my heart I knew it hadn't been for me either. "I guess you weren't the worst person in the world to have following me," I said, then quickly added, "But definitely not the best."

Zack sighed, hurt. "So that's it? You'll never trust me again, will you? You'll never see me as more than that guy who lied to you."

"How . . . how do you want me to see you?" I asked tentatively.

For a moment, the world beyond the bookshelves disappeared completely. All that existed was that look in Zack's eye, as he tried to gauge what I was thinking. "You really don't know?"

My breath caught in my throat. "No."

He moved closer to me, and I found myself taking a step toward him. "Seriously, you have no idea?"

I had an idea, but it felt more like a hope, an idle fantasy. Until he cupped my cheek in his hand, and he pulled me in for a kiss.

It was a good kiss—a killer kiss. For a moment, I was lost in the smell of his smoky cologne, the taste of his lips, the feel of his fingers snaking into my hair, and I forgot who he was, what he wanted from me. The moment I remembered, I came up for air and took a step back.

Zack was smiling from ear to ear, face flushed. "You okay?"

No, I wasn't. I was full of a thousand conflicting feelings, and I didn't know how to sort through them all quickly enough to answer Zack's question. "Why now?" I asked, getting heated again. "You've had all this time. For months and months, I've seen you every day. And today, you decide to declare your love?"

Alarm washed over Zack's face. "Whoa, hang on. I never said I loved you . . ."

I flushed. "You know what I mean," I muttered. "Why are you kissing me now, when what you want is information?" I'd been caught up in the moment, but what if this was just the culmination of Zack's plan? "You're trying to manipulate me."

Zack began to laugh. "Are you serious?"

"Just like you manipulated Aviva. When's that date again? I bet you'll charm lots of secrets out of her for Prophet Joshua."

He stopped laughing, though he still seemed amused. "Grace, do you hear yourself?"

"I'm just stating facts. You tried one tactic. It didn't work. You moved to another, no luck. Now you're trying to seduce me, because you think I'm some easily manipulated teenage girl, who'll fall head over heels for your stupid pious face."

I started to move away, and he followed me. "Grace! I'm not lying to you, okay? You think I wanted to fall for a freshman in college, who also happens to be the last person in the world I should date? Do you know what Prophet Joshua would do to me if he found out I kissed you?"

"Probably give you a medal." My breath was coming fast, furious, like a wild animal.

His voice was desperate now. "What can I do to convince you?" *Nothing.* "I don't know."

"I'll show you every email I wrote to my supervisor about you. I'll tell you anything you want to know."

At that my interest was piqued. I'd spent all this time trying to get into Zack's head, wondering what he was thinking—and here he was offering me an open invitation. Whether he was on my side or not, I couldn't resist the temptation to at least see what he was offering. "Anything?"

"Anything. Everything. I'm telling the truth. I'm on your side. I want to help you. I think you're the only person in the world who can give my life some kind of meaning again. Not because I love you or whatever," he said hastily. "But because you're the only one who can save me from the hell I got my-self into."

I fought against my instinct to run and stared him square in the eye. "Prove it."

Zack nodded, relieved. "We should move. We can't keep talking like this here."

I reluctantly followed him outside—still worried I was being tricked somehow, still wondering if I could have played this some other way, some better way. I sat nervously in the passenger seat of Zack's car as he drove out of D.C., into a secluded wooded suburb.

As the houses became fewer and farther between, I began to get nervous. What if he wasn't taking me somewhere to tell me secrets? What if he was taking me out into the woods to incapacitate me so he could bring me in, the way he'd done with Ciaran? Would I end up back in that prison in West Virginia, sharing my cell with sociopaths?

I considered trying to get away, but I still had a few hours before I needed to meet Jude's taxi, and I worried if I didn't do as Zack asked, he might go to the prophet before then. And deep down, though I tried to push it aside, some stupid part of me hoped that kiss had been real—that what Zack had to tell me would prove he was on my side, that his feelings were genuine.

We finally ended up in an empty parking lot in the middle of a national park—secluded and empty. I followed Zack to a picnic table, where we sat, each regarding the other warily. "So?" I finally said. "We're here."

He seemed hesitant. "If anyone knew I was telling you any of this . . ."

"You'd be killed, I know." I wanted him to get to the point. "And being here with you could get me killed. But I'm here."

He nodded. "I trust you. Even if you don't trust me, I trust you. Okay? Try not to screw me over, if you can."

I glanced around. I didn't see any of his accomplices waiting to jump me or anything, so I asked, "Why have you been following me?"

Zack didn't miss a beat. "Samuel suspects you. He thought if he had you followed, he could find out who you were working with. I was the best candidate because I already knew you. I never told them we'd talked about the pills, or that you'd tried to help me save Macy. I told them you trusted me, because I thought I owed it to you to protect you, because you saved my sister's life. I know what they're capable of."

"Thanks," I said. I tried not to let my feelings shade how I heard his story. I had to stay objective.

"I wanted to help. At every turn, I tried to do what I thought was best. What I thought Great Spirit would have wanted me to do." I wondered if he was invoking Great Spirit for my benefit, because he knew spirituality was something I still valued.

It wasn't the question I'd intended to ask next, but curiosity got the better of me. "How did you end up working for the prophet in the first place?"

It ended up being a long story.

BOOK
THREE

1

The Revelations changed everything for Zack. In 2024, he was fourteen, ultrabright, the kind of kid who had always known what he wanted to do. His first memories were of a country that had inserted itself into numerous conflicts around the globe, where threats were ever present and immensely complicated. He grasped early on what military and political power could do, and how important it was for them to be wielded well. This helped shape his grand plans—to take on politics and become a diplomat or a congressman. And as he entered his teenage years, this path seemed wiser than ever—rogue states and groups were growing closer to acquiring and developing the kind of weapons that could wipe out life on this planet.

And then, out of nowhere, we entered a world where there were no wars to fight, no laws to be made because the prophet decreed them for us instead. Congress quickly became composed of the religious elite—holy men and women of all creeds—rather than the party leaders of years past.

Everyone heading to college at that time was forced to re-evaluate their plans. Zack considered medicine or business, which suddenly seemed like more practical options, but his drive to serve his country outweighed all other considerations. There was no more military to join—enlistments and officer training programs had been discontinued. But he stubbornly remained true to his goals, and he went to college studying international relations and political science, hoping to find some kind of government job when he graduated.

He finished in three years—eager to get out there and start doing *something*—and he applied for everything with a .gov address. Desk jobs, legal affairs . . . he was willing to push a mop around the Pentagon if it came to it, and eventually he got a job as a low-level desk clerk at the office of Homeland Security. As far as he knew, it was a mostly defunct organization, with a few residual employees. He had only a vague idea of what those people must be doing; they had titles like "Project Manager" and "Analyst," and they described their jobs as "community maintenance." Like many other organizations, Homeland Security seemed to have become a charity of sorts, a group of do-gooders.

However, a few important people did come through the office still, including a tough, no-nonsense middle-aged woman everyone called Esther. Her English was perfect, but because of the burqa she still wore, everyone assumed she'd been born into the former Muslim world. Wild rumors abounded about her early days as an undercover field agent—Zack heard whispers that she'd once strangled an Al-Shabaab lieutenant with her bare hands. And while he was never clear on the specifics of her title, he gauged that whatever secretive program she was running, it must be important. Eager and ambitious, he was extra attentive whenever she stopped by, and with his confident, extroverted personality, he was able to charm her—before long they were on a first-name basis.

"Is this what you want to do?" she asked him one day.

"I've wanted to work at Homeland Security since I was a kid," Zack told her. "But working here doesn't mean quite what it used to."

"You wanted to shoot down terrorists?" she asked, a little coy.

He tried to deflect—by this point, militaristic inclinations were looked down upon even at former military institutions. "I wanted—I want—to make a difference," Zack told her. "Excel at something, use those skills to help my country. I'm not sure what good I'm doing answering a phone."

Her eyes had a teasing glint. "You feel your great talents are being wasted."

"I'm learning lots here," he replied quickly, trying to save face. "I'm grateful for the opportunity. Maybe our country just doesn't need help the way it used to."

"Our world can always use the help. We have jobs open in my department. If you still want to make a difference, you should apply. I think you'd like it."

"I'd love to," he said, before he realized he hadn't asked what the open jobs were, or which department she ran.

It turned out the open job he was applying for was "Agent," no other description available. The application requirements were stringent. A background check and complete psychological profile were step one. A series of rigorous academic tests were step two. And after he'd passed every round of testing, he and every other new recruit had to swear an oath of secrecy to Esther herself:

"Do you swear to keep confidential any information you learn here?"

"Yes."

"Do you swear to keep your occupation confidential from all your family and personal contacts?"

"Yes."

"Are you willing to put yourself at great physical risk on behalf of the United States of America?"

At this, Zack's heart swelled. He was in the right place. "Yes, ma'am, I am."

Excitement swirled around the room, as Esther eyed them all. "Welcome to the CIA."

Zack nearly burst out of his skin with pride as he walked through the doors of the CIA's training headquarters for the first time, surrounded by a dozen other new recruits. They were all on the young side, but he was the youngest. All had résumés much longer than his. Lauded psychiatrists, lawyers, police officers. They'd been recruited off the street, at their jobs, all by current CIA officers. None of them knew why they were there, but they all had guesses.

"We're gonna be spies, right?" This came from a balding former accountant in the back, who had clearly been lured by the drama and mystery of whatever this job might hold for him.

A former NYPD officer, the most physically intimidating in the room, countered that with disdain. "There are no spies anymore."

"How do you know?" The room turned its attention to a tall blonde named Jenna as she spoke. A few of the recruits had heard her bragging that she still hoped to work in her former profession—as a runway model in Milan, a job where the competition was fiercer than ever before.

"Spying involves lying, and liars are Punished," said a social worker definitively.

"Maybe we're going to learn how to lie without being Punished," Jenna suggested, though the room was skeptical.

"Look at the budgets," Zack said, glad to have something to contribute. "Every nation has slashed their budgets for national defense down to basically nothing. I worked for Homeland Security, it's a ghost town."

"They're paying *us* somehow. Maybe they buried the funding in some other program?"

The accountant butted in: "It would actually be easy to do. A national budget is so complex . . ."

He was thankfully not allowed to elaborate on the complexities of national budgets because at that moment, Esther entered. She'd been training recruits since 2024, so her presentation was succinct, entertaining, and, all the recruits eventually realized, completely devoid of any information that would tell them why they were here.

"Thank you all for volunteering for your country," Esther said. "You're taking on a very important role as guardians of our international peace. Over the next few weeks, you'll be trained to identify and eliminate threats to that peace. Your focus and hard work will be crucial to your success in this program."

As he left, Jenna turned to Zack, eyes twinkling. "We're totally gonna be spies."

3

Back in high school, Zack had been kind of pimply and awkward. But despite his lack of traditional "piousness," he was confident, and when he set his mind on courting a girl, he usually won her over. Sadly, it was that same stubbornness that tended to put an end to his relationships, too, even once he hit college and his more traditional good looks kicked in. But in all his years of dating, he'd never had a girl pursue him the way Jenna did.

At first it made sense—they were the two youngest recruits, so they had the most in common. Jenna, who had once sought attention from audiences at packed fashion shows, now sought it from the most eligible bachelor of their recruitment class. She cornered him at lunch on day one.

"How many people do you think will make it?"

"Through training?" Zack considered as he finished chewing. "Everyone but that accountant guy."

"No way. A program like this? They'll take two, three tops."

Zack was intrigued. "Did Esther say that? How do you know?"

Jenna shook her head, her long hair billowing as she moved, accenting every word she spoke. "The way they're talking? How elite we all are? You think because you matched squares and triangles in some intelligence test, you're fit to be . . . whatever it is they're trying to make us?"

Zack hadn't thought about it quite like that. "What do you think they're judging us on?"

"Work ethic, obviously. You saw the number of degrees in that room. Physical fitness, but I'm here, so strength can't be all that important."

"I think you could take down a KGB or two," Zack teased, testing her arm muscle.

"You know what I think will matter most? Street smarts."

Zack grinned. "You think you've got everyone beat on that one, don't you?"

She considered him a moment. "We both do. The way I see it, it's me, you, and maybe that guy." She pointed to the big NYPD officer at another table, who was boisterously telling a war story about taking down a pack of Outcasts.

"Why do you say that?"

"I think he's smarter than he looks. His guard is up. Everyone else is putting on this facade, trying to prove how top of their game they are. He's playing along, but he's watching everyone. He's biding his time."

"Biiiiiding his time," Zack mocked.

She pushed him, playfully. Then, abruptly, changed the subject. "What room are you staying in?"

I've talked before about sex-related Punishments, how it was confusing as a teenager to sort it all out, because some people seemed to be Punished for the most minor sexual deeds, while others could hump unrelentingly, Punishment-free. Of course, what most people didn't know was that this all boiled down to guilt. Those who were conditioned by society to feel guilty about sex were more likely to be Punished for having it.

Jenna, though, was not one to be held back by Great Spirit's wrath, nor was she anything like the girls Zack had met in college. Though I thankfully managed to avoid hearing the details, Zack said he'd never found a girl who was quite so excited to see him behind closed doors, and quite so unwilling to be affectionate with him in public. He assumed, in a group this small, she must not have wanted to appear unprofessional. People could see there was an attraction between them, at least, but for the most part, they shrugged it off as "the kids having fun."

It was a competitive group; when given assignments, everyone worked hard, didn't compare notes. Many of the early assignments favored the psychiatrists, and Zack initially felt overwhelmed: his college Psych 101 was woefully insufficient for the kinds of questions he was being asked. But as the days progressed, he found himself more and more capable of guessing the right answers. He learned to do psychological profiles like the ones they'd each been subjected to. He could predict behavior based on a subject's personal history and evaluate personality on dozens of scales. But that wasn't the end of their training.

Next came activities the lawyers excelled in, especially the younger ones—the minutiae of prophetic law. There were so many variations between countries and cultures, so many conditions that might allow Great Spirit to Punish or Forgive you . . . to remember them all was excruciating. Late at night, Jenna insisted Zack quiz her on these, and he was surprised to see her struggling to remember basic rules even an elementary-schooler would know.

And throughout, there was intense physical training. This is where Zack made the most progress, and Jenna began to despair. When he finished an obstacle course, he'd take a lap back around to encourage her; though in her exhausted state, she often spat back her frustration at her cheerleader. But Zack was undeterred and continued to help Jenna whether she wanted him to or not.

It was when they finally began their weapons training that Jenna truly excelled. She'd done a lot of hunting as a child, she explained, and she'd always had a knack for it—only the NYPD officer beat her at their sharpshooting tests. Most of the others were squeamish around just about any kind of weapon—rarely were guns even available in post-Revelation society. But Zack pushed past his wariness and trained as hard as he could—and soon he could hit nearly any target.

As the program neared its end, he'd fallen hard for Jenna, but he still couldn't tell how she felt about him. He could never quite tell how she felt about anything. That was part of her street smarts, he could only assume. Like the big NYPD officer, she was keeping her emotions under wraps—they were safer that way. At least, he hoped that was the case.

So far, no one had dropped out. No one had been kicked out. If Jenna's prediction was going to come true, whatever lay ahead had to be a doozy. And indeed, Esther promised that their final challenge would pull together everything they'd learned.

"Tomorrow, you will meet ten children," she said. "I want you to tell me which one is a sociopath."

4

As Jenna and Zack lay next to each other that night, he saw a flicker of concern cross her face.

"What's wrong?" he asked. He knew her confidence that she'd be one of the lucky few had started to dwindle.

"I'm getting restless," she said, and he had to agree. Since they'd entered the facility they'd basically been locked up. They ate all their meals there, slept there, screwed there . . . and they'd been allowed no contact with the outside world.

Zack tried to console her. "The program's almost over. Either way, you'll be out of here soon."

"I know, I just . . . it'd be nice to have one night out, you know? Go dancing, get really crazy." She smiled, in that way that normally got her whatever she wanted. "Please? Leave with me."

Her request seemed so strange and out of the blue, it left Zack confused. "I don't know how we could."

"You used to work at Homeland Security. You must know

some way to sneak out of a government facility like this. Some old coworker that could help us?"

Zack honestly didn't. And he was concerned: "If you leave this building, you'd be quitting. So would I. We signed all those forms . . ."

The fire in Jenna's eyes had never burned brighter. "Screw that."

His past few weeks of psychology training made Zack feel confident he could diagnose this problem. He rubbed her back, trying to placate her. "Don't give up. I know it's getting hard, and maybe it feels like an easy excuse if you go out and break the rules and disqualify yourself. But it's better to fail, trying, than to sabotage your chances."

When it became clear she would make no headway with him, she rolled over, annoyed. "I think I'd like to sleep alone tonight, okay?"

It took him a moment to understand what she was saying. "Are you kicking me out?"

She shrugged, and he grabbed his clothes, making one last attempt to mollify her. "I'll be down the hall if you need any-thing." She made no indication she'd heard him, and he left, feeling deeply unsettled but unable to figure out why.

Jenna was still in a mood the next day, and Zack's attempts to bridge the divide between them were met with hostility. It was only then that Zack realized how much time he'd been spending with her. The other recruits had developed a camaraderie with one another that he was not a part of. While Jenna sat off by herself, annoyed, Zack tried to belatedly fit in with the others.

"I don't understand why we bothered to learn all that prophetic law if we're just going to analyze personality disorders," the NYPD officer was grumbling.

"Obviously we're doing more than that. Otherwise you'd all be psychiatrists," one of the psychiatrists said.

"What do we have in common?" the social worker asked. "What are we all qualified to do?"

The NYPD officer suggested something like what Jenna had said to Zack on the first day: that they were chosen for their street smarts.

One of the lawyers chuckled. "You mean we're spies, right? That's still the best theory?"

The conversation quieted as Esther entered, asking them to follow her. They walked to a dimly lit room, where through a pane of one-way glass they could see ten preteen boys, playing with an assortment of provided toys. "You have one hour," she said. "You cannot interact with the children in any way. After that hour, I want to know who the sociopath is. A correct answer will mean you remain in the program."

As soon as she left, Jenna sidled up next to Zack, as though the previous night's fight had never happened. "Who do you think it is?"

Zack was annoyed, but admittedly relieved she was willing to engage with him again. "I'm supposed to tell just by looking? It's probably the ugliest kid, right? He'll have been Punished the most." But even as he said it, he could see that all ten boys were equally handsome.

The psychiatrists were furiously scribbling. Zack watched

the boys, all his training slipping out of his head at this crucial moment. What were the qualifications? Something about being emotionally callous. Manipulative. They were charming, right? Violent tendencies.

The NYPD officer was watching two boys in the corner— Boy 1 was bossing the other around as they built a tower of Legos. The social worker had her eye on a quiet kid, Boy 6, who was scribbling a dark and disturbing crayon masterpiece.

But Zack noticed Jenna was watching Boy 10. All the other boys seemed eager to listen to him, and he invented some kind of game that involved them wrestling each other for treasure— the kind of game where the rules only make sense to the children involved. Soon he grew tired of the game and walked over to the intense crayon boy, whispering in his ear. Boy 6 immediately jumped up and ran over to Boy 1, upset. They started to fight, and Boy 1 shoved him. Boy 6 shoved back. A teacher rushed into the room, separating them.

Zack leaned over to Jenna. "Have you figured it out?" But she didn't respond, just acted like she hadn't heard him.

When the hour ended, Zack handed in his slip—marked Boy 10. He wasn't sure how many more might have seen what he saw, but he soon found out. When the group reassembled, everyone was present except two—both of the lawyers.

"Congratulations," Esther said. "You've made it to the next round." Jenna smiled at Zack—they were both still alive.

The NYPD officer spoke up, confrontational. "I'm sorry, but I think I speak for a lot of people when I ask this. What does any of this have to do with national security?"

"That's an excellent question. A question you're finally ready to learn the answer to. But first, I have my own question for all of you—did anyone notice anything odd about the interactions you just saw?"

The social worker's hand shot up. "No one was Punished. Those kids who fought should have had some kind of physical reaction. Neither one did."

"Does anyone have an idea why that might have been the case?"

Zack thought of his whole stay here. His tryst with Jenna that, he'd been surprised, had earned *him* no Punishments from Great Spirit either, despite a few things he'd thought the Big Man might have disapproved of. He hazarded a guess: "Is this place protected in some way?"

"That's very close. And while we'll come back to that, you should know one other thing. That scene out in the real world? You would have seen Boys 1 and 6 come away from their fight with physical deformities. But Boy 10? He would never have incurred any Punishments. Sociopaths have a very special way to evade Punishment from Great Spirit."

"How?" Jenna asked.

But these recruits would never learn the whole truth, only what Esther wanted them to know. "They are agents of the devil," she said. "Able to carry out horrific acts without Punishment."

Esther then showed them a series of videos detailing grue-some crimes of various sociopaths. Showing the way they could go undetected for years, becoming parasites on the world around them, with no retribution from Great Spirit. When the video ended, she told them, "This is what you've been brought here to do. Learn how to stop these people."

The NYPD officer shouted out, "Are you sure we're not spies?" The group laughed.

Whether Esther cracked a smile under her burqa was unclear. "Now—your first mission. One of you is a sociopath. Figure out who."

Zack knew. Of course he knew. He might have suspected from the beginning.

As soon as Esther had uttered those words, sending shudders down the spines of every person present in the room, they'd been ushered out, ostensibly to their rooms to rest before dinner. But they all lingered, buzzing about who it might be.

Zack overheard the social worker whispering with one of the psychiatrists. "What about Starsky?"

The psychiatrist eyed the physically intimidating NYPD officer across the hall. Perhaps he was afraid to say anything. Or wanted to keep his suspicions to himself. He shrugged. "Could be anyone, I guess."

The social worker nervously asked, "You don't think it's me, do you?"

"Oh, sweetheart," the psychiatrist said, "everyone knows it's not you."

Zack lagged behind with Jenna, who remained eerily silent.

Wouldn't make eye contact. She must have known he'd figured it out. As the group got ahead of them, he pulled her into a corner.

"I'm not in the mood, Zack," Jenna said, but he stopped her from walking away.

"Is it you?"

She seemed crushed. "No! How could you say that to me, after everything? Why would you even think that?" Zack had never seen her like this. They'd been dating nearly a month, and she'd only ever seemed cool, emotionless. All of a sudden she was close to tears. "I think I'm falling in love with you, Zack."

For a moment, he was fooled. And then, he asked the nagging question, "Why are you just saying this to me now?"

"You don't love me, that's fine."

He shook his head. "Jenna, you don't love me."

"Yes, I do." The tears in her eyes looked so real.

"Jenna, this isn't going to work. Do you think I'm an idiot?"

She paused, perhaps formulating her next plan. "Of course I don't. That's why I latched on to you on day one. I think you're smart. The smartest person here."

"Thanks." And then he second-guessed himself—was she just playing him *again*? He doubted every word that fell from her lips.

"I don't know that I'm anything. I'm just me. And maybe I'm not perfect, but it's not like I'm some sick monster. You're the only one who's close enough to me to even suspect anything, so let's just let it lie, okay?"

"You think Esther doesn't know what you are already? After

all those tests they put us through?" And then he realized: "This is why you wanted to go out last night, isn't it? You realized what this program was about, you guessed that this was coming next. You wanted to escape."

"Well? Can you help me or what?" He couldn't shake the pity he felt when he looked at her quivering frame. "Or did that video brainwash you into thinking I'm some evil serial killer?"

"Of course I don't think that."

"So help me. Please. Zack, you know I'd never hurt anyone."

Zack was torn. In all his experience with Jenna, he couldn't imagine her being capable of anything more dastardly than a few snide remarks. He wondered if perhaps he was being tested, to see if he could show mercy. When he'd worked for Homeland Security, he'd heard of similar tests in other government agencies, designed to ferret out the most pious. Maybe, rather than seeing who would report Jenna, the goal was to see who would take the initiative to rescue her.

To Jenna, he simply said, "I'll try to help you."

Unfortunately, he had no idea how to do it.

Zack wandered the halls of the compound in a daze, consumed by his dilemma. As he entered the bathroom, he noticed the accountant at the sink, eyeing him carefully, still on the hunt for who their resident sociopath might be. "So what do you think? 'There's one among us, oooh.' Do you think it's bull?"

Zack had no patience for playing this game. "I think we're all sociopaths."

"Why do you say that?"

"Not one of us has been Punished, right? Isn't that the test?"

The accountant seemed surprised. "I've been Punished. You haven't?"

Suddenly, Zack worried he'd been speaking too freely. He'd never even considered there might be more than one. Or that one of them might be him. *Could he be a sociopath?* He thought he had empathy, and he'd never been a particularly violent kid. He'd certainly been Punished before. But had he been Punished enough? Maybe he only thought he was normal because he knew no other way of being.

"When were you Punished? What did you do?" Zack asked, curious.

The accountant glanced toward his own reflection in the mirror, and in that moment, Zack relaxed. He was lying. Lying and looking to see if his face reflected any changes spurred by his guilt. The glance was a reflex Zack knew well.

"I was Punished for lying," the accountant lied.

"Interesting." Zack in fact had no more interest in this conversation. He knew that his number-crunching friend had been protected from Punishments somehow, just as Zack had.

As he was preparing his exit, however, the accountant remembered: "I saw that social worker get Punished, too."

"When?"

"She got food poisoning, she was sick and throwing up for a couple days, and the next time I saw her, her face looked all messed up." Zack vaguely remembered her skipping a couple workouts.

"You don't know what she did?"

"Nope."

And then Zack had an idea. "Where did they take her? When she got sick?"

"There's a medic on the grounds. We passed his office on our runs, that building behind the big tree."

Outside. The medic was outside.

Zack left and found Jenna in her room, alone. "I know how to get you out."

Zack had faked being sick plenty of times, pre-Revelation. But Jenna had the advantage of never having been Punished for lying, so she was an expert. Within minutes, she'd worked herself into a sweat. She gagged herself to induce vomiting, leaving residue on her clothing.

"Authentic," Zack admired.

She grinned, the "sick" facade dropping immediately. "Thanks." She seemed to take pride in the ways she was able to deceive people . . . a trait that left Zack unsettled.

He helped Jenna draw a map based on their memories of the grounds, and she listened intently as he laid out the plan. "They'll take you to this room here. When the nurse goes into the storage closet to get you some medication, you'll have a window to escape." As he spoke, he wondered if he was doing the right thing. He could get kicked out of the program for this. He had a feeling jail time could be involved. Suddenly, he wasn't sure he trusted this woman—someone he knew all too well he *shouldn't* trust.

But she was out the door, with barely an expression of gratitude for the risk he might be taking. Whatever help he'd given her, it was up to her to escape.

That evening, he picked at his dinner, trying not to listen as others speculated on her absence. "I wonder if she figured out who it is," the NYPD officer pondered. "Maybe she moved on to the next phase or something." It hadn't occurred to Zack that he might be the only one who suspected her. He wondered if her attempt at escape might be the thing that led people to consider her.

But then, as dinner ended, there she was. All cleaned up. Grabbing food for the road. "How are you feeling?" Zack asked her.

She shrugged. "Medic told me whatever bug I had must have passed." She said no more. Zack suddenly considered the possibility that they were being watched, a worry that seemed to be confirmed moments later, as they were herded into a meeting room for a stern lecture.

"You've had a month to get to know your fellow recruits," Esther said. "Which leads me to believe someone's being held back by loyalty. Loyalty is not rewarded in this program."

There went Zack's theory about testing for piousness.

"In case you thought, 'perhaps this person isn't so bad,' I'm going to tell you a little more about them."

The story began simply . . . a person with two loving parents, who struggled to manage their difficult child. Then those loving parents went missing, presumed dead. The child, armed with their inherited life savings, began a life of conning. Growing close to people, earning their trust, seemingly innocent and helpless, and when his or her use for their mark was over, the mark would mysteriously disappear.

Jenna's face showed no emotion as Esther continued to list her crimes.

"You see, when one lives without Punishment from Great Spirit, there is no limit to the pain they can cause others. The peace that's swept around the world relies on human beings trusting one another. The moment they realize they can't, they shouldn't, that peace will descend into chaos. If any of you decide now that you don't want to be a part of this force, helping Great Spirit to preserve His utopia, you're welcome, as you always have been, to leave the program." Her words had a finality to them, and Zack realized then what he needed to do.

As everyone headed back to their rooms, still consumed by the mystery, Zack approached Esther, speaking in hushed tones. "It's Jenna."

Esther pulled him aside and pulled out a voice recorder. "Why? Why do you say that?" He was uneasy, speaking ill of his friend on the record, but he felt like he had no choice. After Zack listed his observations, Esther turned the tape off.

"Well done," she said.

Jenna was waiting in the hallway as Zack exited the room alone. Her voice was ragged, betrayed. "You gave me up, didn't you?"

Zack held firm. "You lied to me."

Her anger rose to the surface. "*They* lied to you. You believe any of that? You think this is anything more than propaganda?

We're in some kind of Nazi brainwashing center, don't you realize that? They're turning you into a monster, they're dehumanizing people like me. Even if my brain works differently, that doesn't make me evil . . ."

Zack was too exhausted to fight her. "Jenna, I don't want to have this conversation." He walked away, shaking.

The next day, he was the only one at breakfast.

7

No Jenna, no other recruits. No dining hall staff either, not even a speck of food. As he looked around in confusion, Esther entered. "Congratulations." Her voice was warm, welcoming.

Zack was still on edge. "Where is everyone?"

"They were all told they advanced to the next stage of the program, and that you and Jenna failed. But as I'm sure you've guessed, that's a lie. Each pool of recruits only nets us one agent. You're that agent."

It didn't seem fair to Zack. Jenna had pursued him. She was the reason they became close, not any special investigative skills on his part. Really it was luck, that the one person he got to know over the course of the program was the only one who mattered. He tried to express this to Esther, but his concerns were dismissed.

"Do you want to forfeit your spot? I'm sure one of the others would be glad to step in."

Zack almost said yes. The emotional toll the program had taken on him thus far was overwhelming. He still felt guilty for turning in Jenna—maybe she was some kind of devil-worshipping sadist, but he'd developed feelings for her. She'd thought she applied for the program just like everyone else—little did she know that in her psych profile, instead of vetting her to be CIA, they'd singled her out as an example, exploited her as a test case. He could chalk it up as karmic retribution for all the times she'd exploited others, but as a man who'd come of age in such a moral time, he didn't like the idea of retribution.

Then Esther started talking about duty, about honor, about serving one's country—ideals that had always struck a chord for Zack. And in that moment, he knew he had to do anything he could to protect the nation he loved so dearly. Though he believed in Great Spirit, he'd always worshipped a different master—patriotism—and when invoked, he had to glorify that god.

Zack followed Esther outside the compound, into the sunlight. He was released! Whatever training still lay ahead, just being out in the fresh air again was some relief. For a moment, he wondered where he should go, what he should do next. But then Esther answered the question for him; she walked into another building, and he followed her down another corridor, to a different set of doors. Dread built inside him—was he about to start this terrible process all over again?

"Step inside," Esther said, and he could tell that any questions he asked now would go unanswered.

So Zack did as he was told, and the doors closed behind him. He was alone in a large, strange, square room—every surface, walls, floor, and ceiling, were all composed of a hard, porous brown material. He ran his fingers across odd dents in the walls, wondering what might have caused them, before a door on the other side opened, and Jenna entered with a smirk. "So, you're the other sociopath."

"What?" Zack asked. They regarded each other, wary, from opposite sides of the room.

"There were two of us. You almost had me fooled, with that loverboy schtick. It was sweet."

Zack bristled. "I'm not a sociopath. I caught you, that was the game."

Jenna scoffed. "And I caught you. And first."

Zack was getting irritated now. He knew Jenna was trying to manipulate him, trying to gain the upper hand. She thought she could win something by messing with his mind, and he had no patience for that. "This isn't going to work, lying to me."

"Why would I lie to you? We're the same." She took a slinking step forward, never breaking eye contact with him.

"No, Jenna, we're not."

"Embrace it, Zack. It's a good thing. We're special. Great Spirit's favorites, right?"

It was then that he noticed a glass case in the center of the room. He couldn't see what was inside it, but he saw that Jenna had been edging toward it ever so subtly. As he worked his way closer, he asked her, "If we're favored, why did we spend all that time learning to identify people like us?"

"Because the government needs us. Needs people who can do things that others can't. It's our job to bring them in. Recruit them. Convince them to help us."

He finally saw what was in the glass case. An item he'd become so familiar with over the previous month. A gun.

8

He understood then why Jenna was distracting him. She was now much closer to the gun. He could make a gamble, run for it, but she might make it there first. He didn't know how hard the case would be to open, and even if he succeeded, Jenna might be skilled enough to disarm him.

So he didn't head for the glass, he headed around it, toward Jenna. He'd watched the way she manipulated people, the levers she pushed—and he had a feeling he could push hers right back. "I don't know what I am," he said as convincingly as he could. "I want to say you're wrong, but who's completely self-aware, right?" They'd taken enough of the same psych classes to share a chuckle at that. Zack continued, "I do know I have feelings though. Even sociopaths have feelings."

"They do," Jenna said evenly.

"And I have feelings for you. Maybe that proves I'm normal, maybe it doesn't." He was steps away from her—he just had to keep up this act a little longer.

She seemed wary, didn't like him this close. "You don't have feelings for me."

"Of course I do," he said, a little bit of the truth seeping in. "Why else would I have spent all that time with you? Why would I have waited so long to turn you in? I'm not saying I'm in love with you. I'm just saying—what you and I had was real."

Her voice was quiet now. Moved. "I know it was real." For a moment, they were both taken aback by each other.

Maybe Jenna was lying. Sociopaths don't have the same capacity for love, Zack reminded himself. But maybe, Zack thought, whatever had transpired between them did mean something to her.

And then he saw Jenna glance at the glass case. Instinctively, he lunged ahead of her, reached it first. In a race of strength and speed, he was always going to win. The case opened easily, with a latch at the bottom, and as her fingers reached ahead of him to grab the gun, he was able to wrestle her away, grab it himself, and back away to a distance of a few feet.

Whatever sweet moment they'd shared was gone. The facade of affection was over, and Jenna seemed genuinely fearful. But she gave him a sad smile. "I told you on the first day, didn't I? That it'd come down to just the two of us?"

"Prescient," he said, amused.

Jenna started to tear up. "Don't do that," Zack said, anxiety rising.

"I'm smarter than you!" she cried. It wasn't a manipulation this time, Zack realized, it was a meltdown. "This isn't fair. You aren't special, I'm special."

Zack watched, not sure what he was supposed to do with the gun in his hands. He didn't see a reason to kill her. She was locked up, what would be the purpose of that? But no one was coming out and declaring him the victor, saying he was ready to serve his country. And he knew Jenna well enough to know that his position of power wouldn't last. When her meltdown ended, she'd realize he was too weak-willed to kill her, which meant she'd have a chance to get the gun out of his hands. And unlike him, she wouldn't hesitate to use that chance. She'd see it as proving her mettle, proving her ability to thrive under pressure, to outwit a stronger opponent.

Maybe that's all this program was, he thought. Maybe she was right. Maybe it was a training ground for sociopaths themselves. Instead of a group of potential agents, rising to the top by sorting out who the sociopath was, what if the goal was to see if she could outsmart them all? Pick out her greatest competition, and pull his heartstrings as a defense. The more he considered it, the closer he came to pulling the trigger.

But still he didn't. Her lips curled into a sneer. "You aren't going to do it, are you?"

"I'd like to avoid it," he admitted.

She yelled up at the ceiling, "Okay, he got me!"

Silence.

"Well, I tried," she said. She sat down in the corner. "If you're not going to kill me, I'm going to rest my legs."

Zack's instinct was to sit as well, but he knew better. He kept the gun trained on her. "Face the wall, lie on your stomach, put your hands on your head."

"Jeez, chill out." But after a moment, she did as she was told.

He looked around the room. There must be some trick here. He looked at the glass case—flipped it open and closed, but nothing happened.

He looked back to Jenna, lying in the corner. And closed his eyes as he squeezed the trigger. BANG. Jenna screamed as the bullet hit the wall above her.

"What the hell!" She instinctively sat up and glared at him.

Zack had hoped his intentionally wide shot might evoke some response from the outside world, but there was still nothing. He walked over and took a look at the bullet in the wall—it was real all right. He opened the chamber—five bullets left.

"Hey, do I really have to kill her?" he called out to the ceiling. There must be a speaker of some kind in here, a camera, some way of monitoring them. No answer.

"What are you going to do?" Jenna asked, boredom seeping into her voice.

Zack felt defeated. "I'm not a sociopath. Great Spirit will Punish me if I kill you, so what's the difference?"

"Unless you're killing me in self-defense," she suggested slyly.

He glared at her. "That's not allowed either. Not that you'd know."

"So if you're not killing me, I guess, given enough time, I'll have to kill you." Her smile was vicious.

Zack looked at the imposing metal doors on both sides of the room. He raised the gun and fired all five remaining shots into them, one after another. Jenna covered her ears as the rattling metal echoed around them. "What the hell?" Zack kept shooting, click click click, even after the bullets were long gone from the chamber.

When he was finally satisfied the gun was empty, Zack heaved all his weight on the bullet-ridden metal—it still wouldn't budge. He stepped back to catch his breath, when one of the doors on the opposite side of the room cracked open, nudged from the outside. Zack ran toward the open door, only to watch another glass case slide through the small opening. Just as he reached the door, it slammed shut again. Zack didn't even have to look—he knew that inside that second glass case was a second gun.

This time, Jenna didn't hesitate. She was across the room in a second, lunging for the case. She had her hands around it, and Zack had to pry her fingers from the glass. Despite how poorly she'd performed in those physical trials, with her adrenaline rushing she was a force to be reckoned with.

"Let go of me!" she cried out. She clawed at his bare arms, drawing blood. He shoved her roughly, with a physicality he'd never used on anyone before, much less a woman. Her head slammed into the wall behind her, and she screamed expletives he hadn't heard since pre-Revelationary times. He scrambled away, glass case in hand, and pulled out the gun.

Jenna crawled to grab the first, now empty gun he'd left lying on the floor, then lunged at Zack's ankles. She slammed his Achilles' heel with the butt of the gun, bringing him to his knees. She grabbed for the loaded weapon, and Zack instinctively pulled the trigger. The bullet went over her shoulder, but it scared her, and she backed away, up against the wall.

"I'm sorry," Zack said, genuinely stunned himself.

Her eyes narrowed. "I bet you are." She was poised to pounce, pissed and ready to claw at him until she'd gotten that gun. As she moved toward him, he steeled himself, focused the sight, and closed his eyes as he pulled the trigger.

When he opened them, she was still there, advancing on him, angrier than ever. He found himself shooting again. And again. The last bullet finally made impact, hitting her in the side. The sound it made, she made, when the bullet hit, would stay with him for years to come, a kind of slick thump. She cried out and dropped to the floor, clutching her side.

He stayed poised over her, gun lasered in on her heart— but she didn't bleed, like he expected her to. She'd passed out when she hit the ground, and now she lay there, totally still. Still breathing.

They must not have been real bullets, he thought with immense relief. They were something else, like tranq darts, or maybe some other technology he wasn't familiar with. There was still a chance she'd survive.

He retreated to the other side of the room, gun still trained on her in case she woke up, and weighed down by the enormity of what he'd just tried to do. The sin he would have committed, if the bullets had been real.

The doors opened, a tease—just enough to dispense a tray with a grilled cheese sandwich and tomato soup. Zack went for the opening in the door, but it closed before he could reach it.

Though he felt ill with guilt, he also hadn't eaten yet today. The silence around him suggested that this was his next mandatory task, so in an exhausted, mechanical haze, he chowed down on the sandwich, never letting go of his gun, or losing sight of Jenna. As he ate, he felt his strength returning, his guilt melting away.

And just as he was draining the tomato soup, the door opened. All the way this time, revealing Esther, voice gentle and proud. "You're done now."

9

Zack didn't think about the mirrored hallway he walked through as he exited, nor did he think about his reflection, which showed he was his normal, attractive self. All Zack thought about through his post-"killing" delirium was the fact that he still didn't know what was going on. Moments later he'd learn the most important thing: that he'd passed this final test. He was relieved to hear that the gun had in fact been filled with a tranquilizer of sorts.

"Why didn't you tell me what to do?" he asked, all his frustrations and confusion tumbling out. "And why didn't you tell me I wouldn't have to kill her?"

"Not all decisions you'll have to make in the field will be so easy," was all Esther said.

Zack never learned what happened to Jenna. He knew there was some sort of holding facility for sociopaths, but he wasn't told any details. I of course knew exactly what he was talking about—Jenna was at a prison like the one that housed Ciaran in

West Virginia. Maybe it was even the same prison; I wondered if I'd passed her cell during our jailbreak.

Zack wanted to reach out to Jenna, apologize for his willingness to take her life, even if he'd ultimately been spared the horror of it. But he was afraid to ask—afraid what it would mean to the agency if he showed some kind of sympathy toward the people they were dedicated to hunting down. So he buried those feelings, pushed Jenna from his memories as best he could.

For the next several weeks, he was consumed like never before with training, with proving himself to be worthy of the job. He'd given up so much to get to this point: his integrity, his girlfriend, his innocence. If he didn't succeed, what would this recruitment process amount to? What meaning would it have? And, he wondered, if he failed, would they even let him leave?

The pills weren't handed to him until the very end of the program. As soon as he took one, he recognized the feeling—they'd been in every meal he'd eaten at that recruitment center. Even in that final grilled cheese and the tomato soup. No wonder that building felt protected by Great Spirit. He and the others had been flooded with uppers their whole stay.

The explanation Esther gave him for the pills was simple. "Like all of modern medicine, fighting cancer, fighting disease—Great Spirit has always had to use the laws of the universe He created in order to act in it."

"Why doesn't everyone get to use the pills?" Zack asked. "Everyone gets a chance to use chemotherapy."

"Great Spirit wants to create a heaven on earth; He wants

to create a world where His justice is law. If we give everyone the pills, He'll just find a new way to enact that justice. And who knows how much worse that next plague might be. Besides, we're only using them to further His will, to perpetuate His utopia."

Zack had never been particularly religious. He accepted Great Spirit, like everyone did, because it seemed to be fact, because all those who questioned Great Spirit, publicly or privately, had been Punished so dramatically that questioning itself seemed dangerous. But learning about the pills certainly gave him pause. He was an intelligent guy, and he came up with a dozen logical possibilities for what the pills could mean, what the Revelations themselves could mean. He even worked up the courage to pose one or two of his theories to Esther—armed with a handful of pills that could protect him should Anyone be listening.

"You know, I've had those same thoughts myself," Esther said, her voice full of empathy. "But I still think about religion the same way I did before the Revelations—*I just don't know*. I don't think I'll ever know. And I don't know anyone who can give you any more answers than what you're holding in your hand."

He'd look back and wish he'd asked more questions. Wish he'd posed his theories to more people. But the words Esther said next were the ones that hit home: "You wanted to make a difference in the world. Well, I can tell you, knowing a little more about this world than you do—this is the only place you can do that. But it's not the place you'll find answers to your questions. If you worked your whole life as a cleric, or a doctor, or even a scientist, maybe you'd get a little closer. But that's not what you want to do with your life. You want to be a soldier. Protect this peace that we have here, assist our prophet with his important mission. That's what you want to be doing, Zack. So accept that you'll never know, and accept that you've found your purpose in life. That's the path I chose.

He followed her advice. Soon he forgot he'd ever had those questions, and he accepted the new life that seemed to be laying itself out for him. And it came with a great salary, great benefits, lots of travel. Everything he'd always thought he wanted.

After proving himself on a few smaller cases, he was given his choice of assignments, and he picked the one that would change his life. He was drawn to it because the teenager he was sent to investigate reminded him of himself: smart, charming, growing up in a small town in rural Virginia. Clinton Ciaran Ramsey Jr.

Zack called his parents, said he'd be in the area for work. They insisted he skip getting a hotel. Come and stay in his old room. They missed him so much. He missed them, too; he must have. The experience of recruitment had left him desperate for something comforting, familiar.

So he went home, annoyed Macy, followed Ciaran, and, in the process, saved me. At least, that was how it started.

Zack knew he hadn't killed Ciaran when he shot him. But he felt guilty, thinking of what had happened to Jenna, and knowing that this young boy's life was about to be cut short, even if it hadn't ended. Zack recognized that he was being Punished for his actions, the worst one he'd ever received. And even though he could logically justify that what he was doing was for the greater good, each Punishment he got on the job gave him pause. Made him wonder if what he was doing was really so righteous.

When he returned to the road with Ciaran's unconscious body, he inspected Ciaran's truck and found nothing there that implied Ciaran had been accompanied by anyone. He'd arrived at our location after Ciaran had already entered the woods, so he hadn't seen any sign of me.

He visited with Ciaran's parents, asked a few questions while posing as a cop that led them to believe Ciaran was dead. But they weren't fools—they knew he was no cop. Zack was the reason Mrs. Ramsey had been so paranoid, the reason they suspected a larger conspiracy behind Ciaran's disappearance.

Thinking his job was finished, Zack prepared to go back to D.C. to start his next assignment. His superiors praised him for his excellent work. And then he saw his pills were missing. "That's when I came to you," he said. "To save Mary." I already knew that part of the story.

"Now what?" I asked him. "What happens next?"

"That's up to you."

10

I nodded, taking in the enormity of what he'd just confided in me. If he'd been trying to humanize himself, it had certainly worked. He seemed so much smaller now, more vulnerable, and I felt for him in a way I hadn't expected to. My fear melted away the more he bared his heart. *But you have to stay afraid*, I reminded myself. No matter what tragic tale he spun, he still reported to Prophet Joshua.

"So now it's your turn," he said. "Set me up with your people. I want to help you."

I'd been dreading this part of the conversation. Knowing I couldn't confide anything about the resistance without Dawn's approval, I tried to stall. "I have more questions first."

His patience was fraying. "Seriously? What else could you possibly want to know?"

I held my ground. "You said I could ask anything. There's a lot more anything left."

Zack crossed his arms, frustrated. "You want to move

on to how I tripped and fell in my fifth-grade class play? Go ahead."

"Fine. So to clarify, you're working for the government?" I asked.

"I'm paid by them at least."

"But you report to the prophet."

He shrugged. "Prophet Joshua is the highest authority in the country. And we see ourselves as holy warriors, defending Great Spirit. But there are quite a few layers in between me and him."

"Do you have any idea why the world is the way it is? Who might be responsible?"

His voice held a challenge. "I don't. Do you?"

I wanted so badly to tell him all the things I did know, but . . . as much as I wanted to trust him after hearing all that, that voice in my head reminded me that I couldn't.

I remembered Jude, who would be waiting for me at the train station—soon, I realized, glancing at the sun's position on the horizon. And a streak of fear went through me. I knew Jude would cover our tracks, but I still worried what might happen if Zack discovered I was skipping town. "Let me talk to my people," I said. "Give me a little space for a day or so?"

He nodded, buying my excuse. "You know where to find me." And then he reached for my hand. Instinctively, I pulled it away. As if he was reading my mind, he said, "I understand why you still don't trust me. I've been there, too. I hope I can earn that trust back someday."

"I hope so, too," I said. And for a brief moment, I didn't care if I trusted him. I wanted to grab him and kiss him and let the rest of the world disappear again. Out here in the middle of nowhere, there was only the smell of his cologne, and the way the reddish light of sunset danced in his hair. But I tore my gaze away, forcing myself to remember—there *was* a real world out there. A world where I had responsibilities.

As Zack drove me home, he looked at me with newfound ease, and a genuine smile. "I'll see you soon, Grace." And I felt bad now, thinking that he might actually like me for real. I flinched when I imagined what his reaction would be when he realized I'd fled to a whole other country.

As I got out of the car and watched him drive away, I couldn't help but replay how his hand had felt on mine, and that kiss in the library. I hated myself for having this crush, for thinking about someone like him that way. *You can't help who you have feelings for*, I told myself. *Objectively, he's attractive; he takes drugs to make himself look that way. But soon you'll be safe, far away from Tutelo, and you'll never have to see him again.*

It wasn't until I was walking through my front door that I thought about all the other people I was never going to see again, including my father. He'd devoted his life to raising me, his only child, for the past decade, all on his own. I had to say goodbye. But I couldn't tell him that was what I was doing—I couldn't risk him telling Prophet Joshua that I was leaving before I made my escape.

I could hear my dad in the kitchen chopping vegetables for dinner, and I walked in to find him alone, no Samantha. I was seized with a sudden pang of grief. It was easy enough to tell my dad I was going back to NYU, to "Skype him from the city" for as long as I could possibly get away with. But I couldn't escape from the fact that I was about to leave forever, abandoning him with no explanation, no hint of what world we really lived in. I couldn't do that to him. He never would have done it to me, no matter the risk to himself. And if my cover was going to be blown any minute, this was as good a time to be honest as any.

"How's it going, sweetie?"

"Good," I said brightly, for the recording devices I knew were picking up my every word. "Want to go for a walk or something?"

Certainty rushed through me. I was finally going to tell my father the truth.

11

After making my father a smoothie laced with Dawn's pills—I knew our conversation was sure to plague him with doubt—I finally coerced him outside. When I was sure we were out of earshot of any passing neighbors, I whispered, "I have to tell you something."

My father, always concerned for my welfare, picked up on the gravity in my voice. "What's going on?"

I should have been more nervous, but for some reason in that moment, I felt like I could trust him. I was sure that this time, I could confide in him and succeed. Confidently, I began, "You can't tell Samantha, or the prophet, or anyone. Okay?"

My father's concern only intensified. "If you're in trouble, I can't make that promise."

"I need you to. I can't tell you unless you do." I saw my dad wavering, and I doubled down: "For me. Please. Whatever I tell you, promise me you'll keep it to yourself. For both of our safety."

At the word "safety," I think my father's parenting instincts kicked in. "Okay. I promise."

And so I told him what I knew—that the world we lived in wasn't as it seemed. That after I'd come to him six months ago, speaking of inconsistencies in Great Spirit's Punishments, I'd met someone (I didn't say whom) who'd explained everything. Who'd told me that Great Spirit didn't cause Punishments, that brain chemistry did. That everything was a conspiracy, and it seemed like Prophet Joshua was at the top of it.

At first, my father kept interrupting me: "I thought we resolved this thing with that boy Ciaran . . ." And then, "Who are these people telling you these stories?" "This seems like paranoia . . ." and "Be careful what you say, Great Spirit is listening."

I kept explaining more and more, starting to ramble, hoping something I said would convince him, but he kept finding ways to discredit my arguments, growing more and more frustrated in his conservative, authoritarian way. Finally, he broke down: "Grace, this is absurd."

My father's unwillingness to listen angered me. "Why? Why is it any more absurd than a god who rewards us with beauty?"

He sputtered, "Because Great Spirit's word is the truth, and what you're saying is . . ."

"Blasphemy. I know that's what you think, but it's not. Look at my face, it's not changing. Because I don't feel guilty for telling you the truth, I feel like I'm finally doing something right. I'm done lying to you." I held my voice steady, still confident I was going to find some way to turn him,

My father stared at me, trying to process all of it. For a

moment, I thought I'd gotten through, made some tiny crack in his wall of obfuscation. But then he shook his head, his voice full of a kind of disappointment I'd never heard from him. "I thought I raised you better than this."

It was like a knife to my heart. "And I thought I could trust you," I said, voice shaking.

My father's attempts at kindness reeked of condescension. "You can trust that I have your best interests at heart."

I began to get very worried. "If you tell anyone, even Samantha, you could get me killed. Tortured and killed."

"Grace . . ."

"And this isn't going to make me sound less crazy, but: our house is bugged. Because Zack Cannon is following me, on behalf of Prophet Joshua."

My father was more confused than ever. "Macy's brother?"

"Yes," I said, knowing how insane all this must sound to him, and deeply regretting that I'd started down this path.

My father was grasping at straws now. "What can I do, how can I help you? A group at the worship center, or some kind of therapy . . . ?"

I tried to stanch the bleeding, find a way out of this conversation. "You can keep this secret. Okay? I'm going to go back to college, we don't ever have to talk about it again . . . I just . . . I thought I'd give it a shot, I guess, telling you the truth. Because you're the person I'm closest to in the whole world, and I didn't want to just leave you in the dark."

My dad saw how upset I was and gave me a hug. "I'm sorry you didn't feel like you could come to me. But we're going to get you some help, okay?"

I nodded, trying to placate him. "I'll go to therapy in New York, I promise. But please, just humor me—don't tell Prophet Joshua, or Samuel, or Samantha, or the Cannons, or anyone what I just told you? Just on the off chance that I'm right?" I quickly added, "Or at least, because it'll help keep me sane, knowing I can trust you?"

My father nodded. "You can trust me." I wanted to believe him. But I wasn't sure why I'd ever thought I could.

I looked at my watch. Jude's cab would be coming in an hour, I didn't want this to be the way I left things with my father forever. "I have to go soon. Should we go make dinner? No more talking about this?"

"Because the house is bugged," my dad said with a smile.

"Right." I sighed with relief. He was going to humor me.

We had a perfectly pleasant dinner . . . a little strained, as could be expected. While he was out of the room, I mixed some uppers into his coffee grounds, just in case our conversation left any lingering doubts.

When the time came, I hugged him goodbye, under the guise of going back to NYU.

"I guess this means I won't see you in South Africa then," my dad said, and I could see the sadness on his face.

I shook my head, wishing so badly that things could be different. "I'm sorry. I love you, Dad."

"I love you, too." But the way he looked at me—something was different. Something was broken and would never be the same. He would never see me as his perfectly pious little girl. He judged me now. I'd stepped over his imaginary line between "us" and "them," and while I knew he would always love me, it would never be in the same way. We would never be on the same team again, Great Spirit's team.

I held back tears as I prepared for a lifelong trip to an unnamed international destination. I emptied my pockets, like Jude had asked, except for a few twenties for transportation and emergencies. Instinctively, I also grabbed a bottle of pills and the green card from Samuel. My gut told me those things might still come in handy.

Finally, I stepped into my driveway as a cab pulled up outside, right on time. I got in it—I didn't want to, but I got inside. And then it drove away to the beginning of the rest of my life.

12

When I arrived at the station, I dutifully followed Jude's instructions: taking the train into D.C., then weaving through the subway, changing line after line in case Zack was still following me.

Once I finally emerged onto the platform in a distant suburb, muscles aching, I saw Jude sitting on the curb outside, a hoodie over his eyes. He pushed it back as I approached, and that first glimpse of his face made my heart quiver. As those romantic feelings rekindled, so, too, did a tiny bit of guilt; some small piece of me felt like I'd betrayed him by kissing Zack. But, I reminded myself, that was silly. Jude had already moved on. And if all went according to plan, I was never going to see Zack again anyway.

"Where's your tail?" was the first thing he asked, as though reading my mind.

"Zack?" I asked, as casually as I could. "I told him to stay away for a day or so."

"You *what?*" Jude was panicked. I quickly explained every-thing that had happened (minus the kiss), and he calmed down, mostly. "He really wants to help?"

"That's what he says."

Jude was still wary. "You didn't tell him anything about us, did you?"

"Of course not!" I said, a little offended that he thought I would give up Dawn's organization so easily to someone who worked for the prophet.

"Good," he said, relieved. "I'll let Dawn know, maybe she can reach out." Jude and I walked in step, and I caught him glancing at me—he seemed to note my lingering anxiety. "Is everything else okay?" he asked.

"Yeah," I lied, looking away. I might not have betrayed Dawn's trust to Zack, but I had definitely betrayed it to my father. I couldn't bear to tell Jude how badly I'd failed to con-nect with him. I knew he'd judge me for not keeping my prom-ises of secrecy, and I knew he would be afraid for our safety.

Truthfully, I was a little worried, too. I felt confident my father would keep my secret at least as long as my cover was intact, but could *his* life be in danger now?

I grabbed a pill from my pocket and quickly downed it, hoping to squelch the remorse I felt. Jude noticed, of course. "Doesn't seem like everything's okay . . ."

"I'm sorry that I can't just up and leave everyone behind without feeling a little guilty." I now felt additionally guilty for manipulating Jude.

"I get it," he said softly, and I knew he did—leaving his old life behind had been the hardest thing he'd ever done.

I realized that maybe I'd been a little harsh. "I know how hard it was for you to leave your family, too." I touched his shoulder sympathetically, but he instinctively tensed—thinking of his girlfriend, perhaps. "Sorry," I said, hurriedly pulling my hand away. I wished I knew what he was thinking behind those brooding eyes.

"We're running late, let's get a move on," was all he said.

We got into a car and drove for hours through rural town after rural town. Jude instinctively kept one eye on the rearview mirror, checking to see if anyone was following us. Anxiety and confusion churned together into a soup in my stomach. I'd spent all this time wondering what Jude was thinking, feeling, dying to know if he was angry at me. Finally here he was in front of me . . . and I still didn't know. Obviously he didn't hate me—he'd come to save my life, after all—but . . . had I damaged our relationship for good?

"About what happened six months ago—" I began.

He interrupted quickly, "We don't need to talk about that." I could tell how badly he wanted to change the subject.

"We do," I insisted. "I need to say I'm sorry. I never wanted to hurt you."

"I know. I'm not angry." But I wasn't sure I believed him. He didn't sound *angry*, exactly, just . . . hurt.

Nervous, I asked, "Dawn found you, right? She told you what was happening?"

"Yeah," he said, avoiding eye contact. "Eventually." He tried to keep up his impervious facade, but I could see the pain that memory caused him. I imagined him sitting all alone, for what . . . hours? All night? Until Dawn finally found him and told him I wasn't coming. I hoped she'd at least made me sound noble. Had he tried to contact me? I was afraid to ask any more questions, afraid of what the answers might be. And I was afraid that I was too late. This whole line of inquiry might not be appropriate anyway . . . he had a new girlfriend, after all.

"I'm really glad to see you again," was what I finally went with.

"Me, too. Thanks for getting in the cab. I thought we might need to stage a kidnapping to get you out of there." He smiled, a little joke, and I knew that our friendship, at least, was safe.

"Wouldn't be the first time," I joked back.

We finally parked somewhere in central Pennsylvania that felt like the edge of the earth—closed-up shops and a gravel parking lot. Jude strode confidently down a dirt path into the woods that seemed to lead nowhere.

"Where are we going?" I asked as I followed, but my question was answered the moment after I finished the sentence—we emerged into an open field with a dirt runway, where a small plane was waiting for us.

Jude handed me a passport with my picture in it. Apparently now I was Sevda Yazici, a citizen of Turkey. "You're going home," he said.

BOOK
FOUR

Why Turkey?" I asked, as the plane took off.

"It's the home base of the rebellion," Jude explained. I'd never given much thought to the resistance outside of the East Coast of the U.S.—of course Dawn wasn't the head of the entire worldwide operation; someone like that wouldn't talk so frequently to low-level people like Jude and me.

"What am I going to do there?"

"Hopefully, you'll keep your head down and avoid getting caught," he said pointedly.

"Yes, *sir*," I grumbled, and Jude noted my annoyance.

"Sorry," he said hurriedly. "I didn't mean it like that."

"I know," I relented.

He added gently, "It just seems like every time I turn my head, you're changing the plan, you know?" I did. Bailing on our trip to Nova Scotia. Forcing myself onto his rescue mission at the West Virginia prison camp. Putting myself in danger looking for my mother. He had plenty of reasons to worry about me bucking orders. "And I trust you, I do," he continued, voice shaking. "I just don't want to lose you. You know, again."

For a brief moment, I saw a hint of the Jude I remembered—the sensitive, supportive young man I'd fallen in love with. And a hint of what he'd once felt for me. His concern sobered me, and I changed my tone, promising, "Whatever you guys tell me, I'll do it."

He nodded, appeased. "Thanks."

"Where are we going in Turkey exactly?" I asked.

He seemed relieved to return to discussing logistics. "The headquarters of the resistance. I should warn you, people there are a little different from the rebels you're used to dealing with at home." His careful tone made me nervous.

"How so?"

"The group's made up of people from all over the world, all different cultures, including lots of new subcultures that have sprung up since the Revelations," he said delicately, trying to find the words. "And . . . they don't always get along."

I knew Jude and Dawn and I were members of a diverse crew of atheists and religious people, practicing as they had before the Revelations. But in my sheltered worldview, I'd never stopped to imagine what that might look like, on a larger scale. I guessed I was about to find out.

"You're coming at a rough time," he continued. "We're about to have an election, and tensions are high."

"What are people so tense about? Aren't we all fighting for the same cause?" I asked, curious. While I'd had plenty of my own issues with Dawn's decisions, I'd never stopped to think that there might be larger rifts within our group.

"Our cause is the one thing holding everyone together. But everyone has a different way they want to do things, different priorities. And honestly, underneath it . . . there are still all these old grudges. People tend to trust their own."

"So it's what . . . tribal or something?" I asked, dumbfounded, trying to translate his careful language.

Jude nodded, still treading delicately. "If you can call religion a tribe, yeah. People our age, we don't remember what it used to be like, but the adults . . . they haven't shaken that old way of thinking. They're all afraid of each other."

I knew that people used to fight over petty things like race and religion all the time, but in my naïve way, I'd assumed the Revelations had cured all that. At least—I knew they'd cured it for anyone who still believed in the word of Great Spirit. Apparently without that common deity, everything had fallen apart again.

The Universal Theology had taught me to trust people who looked like me, the non-Outcasts, the "normal" people. I knew we were all on the same side, the "good" side. Honestly, once I learned the truth, that had been the hardest thing to get used to—not knowing whom to trust, once I knew that beauty and goodness didn't have anything to do with each other.

For everyone in the resistance, then, things were more complicated. Perhaps without the Universal Theology's visual cues to tell us who was good and bad, we were reverting to our worst, most archaic selves . . . the kind that used a different kind of visual cue to guess who was good or bad. *If you look like me—if you're dressed like me, if your skin color is the same as mine—you must be good.* It was the kind of primitive thinking I remembered my mother warning me about before the Revelations . . . and it made me sick to think that racism and xenophobia might be making a comeback among the very people I'd allied myself with.

"If they're all afraid of one another, how does anything get done? How do decisions get made?"

Jude was clearly trying his best to stay neutral, apolitical— to avoid scaring me by passing on his own concerns, I assumed. "The resistance's leadership has always been secular. We thought it had to be, you know? To get elected, you need to get votes from people who don't agree with you. That's easier to do if you're more moderate, if you accept everybody."

"So why the tension?" I asked, trying to figure out what he wasn't telling me.

On Jude's face, I could see I'd hit a nerve. "Lately, a couple politicians have been riling up old divisions. Appealing to the hardliners."

"The superreligious people?"

"Yeah, they call themselves the Originalists. They're the ones who're angriest about the Revelations, and they're obsessed with going back to the way things used to be . . . though they can't agree on what that means, necessarily. They're making a lot of noise, but I don't think they'll be able to make much headway in the election. They're too fringe, there aren't enough of them to really matter, especially since they can't agree on anything, even among themselves."

"But you're still worried." His forehead had scrunched up with worry lines going in a thousand different directions.

"Well, getting extremists angry is never good . . . I'm sure you remember religious extremists?"

I remembered the stories about them. The violence people used to perpetrate in the name of the old religions . . . terrorism, wars, genocide. My father often referred to those events in his sermons: how hypocritical the people who committed those crimes had been, how wrong we knew them to be now.

I'd thought of his sermons often since I'd begun working with the resistance. Had I become one of those hypocritical people, doing questionable things in the name of my god? I'd convinced myself I wasn't, that my actions were different, justified, in service of the greater good. But I doubted that Great Spirit would have wanted me to ally with people who killed simply to promote their own beliefs. "There are extremists working with the resistance?" I asked, not trying to hide my horror.

Jude nodded, clearly desensitized to this kind of conflict. "Depends on your definition, I guess. The Revelations made a lot of people very angry. And when you channel that anger through religion . . ."

"You get a bunch of extremists," I finished for him.

He saw how worried I was and tried to reassure me. "But maybe it's not all a bad thing. These guys, their goals might be different from ours in the long run, but right now, all we want to do is take out the prophets. Which means we need people who are willing to do violent things . . . sabotage government installations, assassinations, maybe worse. And honestly, they're gonna be better at that than you or me." I could hear the skepticism clinging to his words, even as he tried to give them a positive spin for my sake.

"Yeah, I guess they would be." As outraged as I wanted to be that the resistance had made such questionable allies, I remembered I'd set off a bomb and killed an innocent man just days ago. Every time I thought of that guard, a new wave of regret came over me, a sickening, dizzying pulse echoing in my chest that felt like it would never stop. A guilt I knew I deserved to feel forever.

I wondered, would that bombing have been more easily accomplished by someone who was eager to kill in the name of their god? Someone who wasn't constantly plagued by remorse, like I was? The logic of it made sense, but the idea still sickened me—and from Jude's expression I could tell how much it bothered him, too.

"Who are you voting for?" I asked him, happy to change the subject. My real question of course was, *Who should* I *vote for?*

Jude shook his head and replied darkly. "Whoever has the best chance of defeating the extremists."

"And who's that?" I pressed.

He thought a moment. "There's a secular woman I like, Ariana something, but she's a little fringe. So I'll probably vote for the guy who's our leader now, Mohammed Bashar. He's the moderate with the best chance of winning."

"Why?"

"He's Muslim, and that's a big voting bloc, but he appeals to the moderates from other religions. The more liberal Hindus and Christians . . . their candidates are more conservative, so Mohammed's their best option, if they want someone religious at all. The religious folks tend to be skeptical of totally secular candidates. They think secularism is to blame for the Revelations in the first place. Mohammed's the one person most people can agree on." He hesitated, then added carefully, "He also happens to be my girlfriend's dad, so . . ."

I nodded, trying to let the statement pass, even though it had tied my stomach into knots. Jude's matter-of-fact way of describing this world suddenly made sense to me—he had to play the politics and support his girlfriend's family. I said airily, "So she's voting for him, too, I guess."

"Yeah." He paused, gauging my reaction. "Her name's Layla. You'll meet her soon. I hope you like her, since we're all going to be sharing the same space."

I hadn't thought there was anyone I would want to room with less than a bunch of religious extremists, but in that moment I'd gladly have taken them as bunkmates over Jude's new girlfriend. I managed a smile, repeating the ex-girlfriend mantra, "I'm just glad you're happy."

"Thanks." For a moment, the way he smiled back, it was like old times . . . but I forced that idea from my mind. I might be sitting here with Jude again, but I was still on my own.

All through the flight I was nervous. Would our plane be diverted, shot down? Would we be accosted when we landed? But we made it to an airport in Ottawa without incident, where we changed planes to board a commercial flight to Istanbul. My new passport worked just fine, and Jude said that even if Prophet Joshua was looking for me in the U.S., Dawn's intel indicated that he hadn't alerted the Canadian or Turkish government just yet.

On our long transatlantic flight, I wanted to interrogate Jude, wanted to find out what he'd been doing since we'd last spoken, but as usual he was not forthcoming with details about his past. In fact, the moment the plane took off, he fell sound asleep—exhausted from his journey out to get me, no doubt.

I wondered what Zack was doing back at home. Had Dawn contacted him? I couldn't help hoping he was thinking about me, missing me, having his own fantasies of seeing me again. That the kiss had meant something to him, something real.

Then I immediately felt stupid for thinking that way. *You can't trust Zack*, my brain reminded me. And I didn't. But I hated that I wanted to. I hated how I couldn't get him out of my mind. What had seemed like a harmless flirtation had, in his absence, blossomed into a full-on, incapacitating crush. I kept thinking of things I wanted to say to him, imagined what he'd say back. Found myself imagining a whole relationship: days, weeks, months that we'd never actually get to spend together.

Maybe it was just sitting next to my first love that made me wish for a second, for someone who could replace Jude, someone who could assuage that nagging loneliness inside me. Even inches away from my best friend, I felt so far from him. But, I reminded myself, there were more important things right now than whether or not some boy liked me.

Things like that guard, the one I'd killed. Left alone, my thoughts ran wild, kept returning to him, to the last time I'd seen him alive, frantically searching through those boxes. Was there something else I could have said to save his life? I imagined his family hearing the news, grappling with their loss. Did he have a girlfriend? Wife? Kids even? Who had I stolen him from?

I tried to push all my anxieties aside, get some sleep, but I couldn't—I was well aware that these moments on the plane might be my last. Had Prophet Joshua mobilized an army to meet me in Turkey? What horrors awaited us when this plane landed?

The answer turned out to be . . . once again, pretty much nothing. Once we passed through customs in Istanbul, we picked up Jude's car that he'd left at the airport. Jude had his own car on another continent—it felt so surreal. We drove deep into central Turkey, speeding through the wild, rocky countryside. Before today, I'd never been outside the United States, and barely outside of Virginia. Heck, even New York City had seemed exotic just a few weeks earlier.

This continent was completely foreign to me, in every sense of the word. As we stopped to grab gas and food, I curiously tried to eavesdrop on the chatter around us . . . before remembering I did not speak Turkish. Though I'd felt so isolated at home, keeping all those secrets, I already felt more isolated here. At least my father and Macy and Zack could speak my language. Here, I discovered, I couldn't talk to most people even if I wanted to.

Adrenaline and excitement to be with Jude had gotten me this far into our journey, but exhaustion was setting in, and before I knew it, the car was parked and Jude was shaking me—I'd fallen asleep in the passenger seat. "We're here," he said.

I looked out the window and thought we'd somehow ended up on another planet. Rocks growing tall like giant mushrooms with windows carved into them. The hillside dotted with abandoned cave formations. This was Cappadocia, Jude said, and it was the strangest, most beautiful place I'd ever seen. A tourist town, but we walked far beyond where I could see any people. For a moment, all my fears subsided, and I allowed myself to feel the awe of the majestic expanse all around me. It was an odd gift—that despite everything I'd been through recently, Great Spirit had brought me somewhere so amazing, somewhere I never would have gotten to see otherwise.

"Where are we going?" I asked, as our steps sent birds flying out of the tall grass tickling my ankles.

"Base camp," Jude said, and moments later, he moved some brush aside to reveal a hole in the ground. Stairs made of stone leading beneath the earth. When Dawn had said she wanted to send me underground, she wasn't kidding. Jude stepped in ahead of me and held out a hand to help me inside.

We descended deeper and deeper into a cave with ceilings so low Jude had to duck. The space was lit only by ornate, colorful lamps lining the walls, and I had to tamp down the claustrophobic panic I felt as we descended. All my instincts said to find fresh air aboveground, to find a way to leave. I tried to distract myself, examining the walls, which were etched with the alphabet of an ancient language. "Written by the people who built this place, centuries ago," Jude explained.

Soon the rock walls began to widen, and I gasped as we stepped out of the passage to discover we were in a massive meeting hall—just the entryway into an expansive underground city. Tall ventilation shafts carved up to the surface, from which small beams of light trickled down. Shelves were scored into the rock, littered with altars to gods I'd heard of but had never seen worshipped. The hall stretched on for ages, filled with people of more colors and creeds than I'd ever seen before, dressed in bright, varied garb I'd be able to recognize someday, but not quite yet. New York had plenty of racial diversity, but everyone was still essentially the same—they all worshipped Great Spirit, they all belonged to one worldwide culture. But down here was another world, a hundred other worlds. Young boys in yarmulkes, a cluster of men with long beards who averted their eyes as we passed. It was wholly foreign—a refuge at once belonging to everywhere and nowhere, and the stone created an echo chamber that reflected the voices around me in a strange, constant kind of cacophony.

"How did the rebels find this place?" I asked Jude, ducking out of the way of a large stalactite hanging over my head.

"This part of the country is full of these caves. This one had gone undiscovered since it was abandoned by the people who built it, centuries ago. At least, until a member of the Turkish resistance stumbled into it, literally. And we expanded it out from there."

I heard wings flapping, birds cooing, and I looked up, assuming the sounds came from wild birds, like the ones I'd seen near the cave entrance. But as we rounded a corner, I smelled them before I saw them: live chickens, squeezed four or five into large cages, squawking wildly. "Dinner?" I guessed.

Jude shook his head. "Animal sacrifices. Like I said, 'Originalism' is kind of the trend down here. A lot of people are afraid of anything new, thinking it's a perversion of the truth, like the Universal Theology. So they're going back to the ancient texts, taking them as literally as they can, practicing in what they feel is the purest way possible."

I nodded, trying to take it all in. "Animal sacrifices are pretty classic, I guess."

Farther ahead, I saw a group of white women wearing ornate saris, chattering in English. "Converts to Hinduism?" I guessed with a chuckle.

He nodded. "The Rig Veda's about the oldest religious text out there. People are learning Hebrew and Aramaic, too, trying to read the Bible in its original form."

I had to admit, that sounded much more fun than most of the

Universal Theology propaganda courses at NYU. "So it's like a contest, who can go back the furthest?" I asked, joking a little.

"A not very friendly contest," Jude joked back, with a hint of derision.

As we neared the center of the compound, a bright-faced young woman wearing a yellow headscarf spotted us. With a cry of joy, she ran over and hugged Jude, holding him like she was never going to let him go. "You are back! Thank goodness!" she cried, her accent thick and melodic. This was Layla, I assumed, as my heart twisted with jealousy, watching the two of them embrace, nose to nose, forehead to forehead. Jude lit up looking at her in a way that felt familiar—it was the way he used to light up when he was with me. I realized, that was what had felt so strange, so stoic about him—away from Layla, he didn't have that spark I remembered. Now, it was back. And as much as it hurt, it made me happy, too, to see him coming back to life like that.

Jude pulled away from her embrace and gestured to me, a little awkward. "Layla, this is Grace. Grace, Layla."

I put on a warm smile, and I saw her attempting to do the same. She knew who I was, that much was obvious. But for Jude's sake, she tried to hide any distaste and greeted me with a staid friendliness. "It is good to finally meet you."

"You, too," I said, mostly honest.

She immediately turned back to Jude, all sweetness and concern. "Are you okay? Did you have any troubles?"

"Everything's fine," he reassured her, in that comforting tone he used to use with me. It killed me to know I wasn't the only one it belonged to. "We should find a place for Grace to stay."

"We have a few empty rooms," she began, but abruptly she stopped speaking and stepped back a few inches from Jude.

A man had entered, tall and imposing. Everyone in the hall had an eye on him, too; clearly, he was an important figure here. My first and only guess: this must be Layla's father, Mohammed Bashar. The current leader of the resistance.

Father and daughter exchanged a few words in Arabic that I didn't understand—his gruff, hers timid. I watched Jude, who was looking back and forth as though he comprehended the conversation, hoping I could tell from his expression if Layla was begging for my imminent expulsion. But as Layla's voice raised in annoyance, I quickly realized this conflict was a more familiar father/daughter spat. Apparently teenage rebellion translated across cultures just fine.

Finally, the man turned to Jude, speaking in English. "Your trip was successful?" His accent had a strangely European flavor to it.

"Yes, sir." Jude gestured to me.

Mohammed gave me the kind of gracious smile that only an experienced politician could muster on command. "Ah, Grace. Welcome to your new home. We are all glad you are safe. Please, let us know if there is anything you need." He then said something else to Layla in Arabic, and she stiffened and turned to me.

"I will take you to your room." She didn't look happy to be tasked with showing me around, and I certainly wasn't thrilled by the prospect either. But Jude nodded at me to go, so I followed Layla through the winding stone hallways.

"Was that your dad?" I asked her, trying to make conversation.

"Yes." Her clipped intonation made it clear she wasn't eager to chat.

I carefully ventured, "Was he mad about something?"

"He doesn't like Jude," she said impassively. "He is from the old generation; they are all like that."

"Why not?" I genuinely couldn't imagine a parent not approving of kind, reliable Jude.

Layla looked at me like I was crazy. "Because he's Jewish. My father is angry I embarrass him, dating at all, but he thinks at least I should choose another Muslim."

Jude isn't Jewish, I almost said. As long as I'd known him, he'd been an adherent to the Universal Theology, like me. But now, I realized, he probably wasn't. He never talked about Great Spirit, at least not the way I did. If his parents had been Jewish before the Revelations, did that make him Jewish now? Apparently Jewish enough to garner the disapproval of Layla's father—a strange concept. "Can't we all just get along?" I joked. "Common enemy, all that?"

"We work together," she said, ignoring my joke and dodging the rest of the question. "Ten years, we have worked together."

A thought struck me. "So you've always known? The truth, I mean? That Great Spirit wasn't behind the Revelations?"

"Since I was very young, yes. My father learned not long after the Revelation in Palestine, and he keeps no secrets from our family. My mother and my brothers and I learned the truth when he did." I felt a deep pang of jealousy. I'd tried to bring my father into our movement, and it had gone so horribly. Here was someone who could speak freely with her family about everything, who'd never had to keep secrets from them. I was reminded again of my deep and unshakable loneliness.

As we passed a huddle of women in burqas, Layla asked, "Tell me, what are you?"

I was confused by the question. "American?"

She managed not to roll her eyes. "No, what do you believe? What religion are you?"

It was a question I hadn't been asked since I was a small child. "I believe in Great Spirit," I said confidently.

She stifled a laugh. "The Universal Theology? That is not a real religion."

I stiffened, defensive. "Just because Great Spirit didn't cause the Revelations, that doesn't mean He doesn't exist."

"Yes, it does," she said, a little condescending. "It is a religion that someone invented." Her demeanor lightened a bit. Perhaps because she thought I was so ridiculous, I couldn't be any kind of a threat to Jude's attention.

"Allah didn't cause anything either, and you believe that He's real," I pointed out.

Her voice grew sharper. "Allah speaks to us through the Quran, through the words and actions of the last prophet, Mohammed . . ."

"But Great Spirit *is* Allah, and Yahweh, and the incarnations of Vishnu . . . Great Spirit is the next step, the final step, in the evolution of our understanding of our creator . . ."

"I do not wish to argue religion," she interrupted, annoyed. "I just need to know where to put you. Muslim, Christian, atheist, Buddhist, Zoroastrian, you can choose."

As I looked down the halls she pointed to, I knew I didn't have a place in any of them. Once again, I'd landed somewhere where the beliefs of those around me didn't match mine, where I'd always be an outsider. And if I didn't have a place here in this rebel fortress, maybe I didn't have one anywhere.

Layla eventually gave up on trying to talk sense into me and deposited me in an empty room in the corner of the complex. "Our brand-new American wing," she said, covering a smirk. Though I knew she meant the comment in jest, I still hated her for it. Really I hated her for who she was, the person with a father who fought by her side, the person who'd taken Jude away from me. As she left, my anger swirled into exhaustion, and I collapsed into bed, falling deeply asleep.

My dreams were wild, vivid, full of strange places, strange people. Turkish travelers. Zack, in his CIA training. And finally—my mother, on the day of the American Revelation, slipping away from our worship center. Turning around to look at me one last time. *Her final moments.* The buzz of the crowd quieted to a hush as she began to speak.

"Follow me," she whispered.

"I can't," I told my dream mother.

"Great Spirit will show you the way. Listen," she said. I nodded, and she walked out, leaving me alone in the crowd. But her voice still echoed around me, repeating, over and over, "Follow me. Find me. Follow me."

I woke up in a cold sweat, her voice still clanging around my ears. *Follow me.*

3

I t took me a few days to adjust to life in this confusing, renegade underground city. For one, I was hopelessly jet-lagged, and being cut off from the sun didn't speed my recovery. For another, the only person I knew down here was Jude, and he spent all his time with Layla, whose aloof demeanor made it clear she did *not* want me around. At meals, I tried to make conversation with strangers, but more often than not, they didn't speak my language . . . or maybe they just pretended not to, suspicious of anyone they didn't already know, anyone who hadn't already been vetted as a member of their in-group. It was very clear that people stuck to their own down here, and I was no one's own.

The longer I stayed, the more I took on everyone's wariness. If all these people were afraid of one another, maybe I should be, too. Sometimes a random stranger's face would give me a spike of fear, a twist of apprehension. A feeling in my gut that, despite Jude's words, it still wasn't safe down here. I desperately wanted to flee this claustrophobic cave, fantasized about making my escape and starting a new life somewhere in Southern Europe, but I didn't know how to do it. So for now, this was home.

During the day, I roamed the halls, exploring all the nooks and crannies of those shadowy tunnels, hollowed out of rough, beige stone. The space was generally sparse, function over form, but it was big enough that my expedition took ages; each day held a new surprise. Everywhere I went had different smells— food cooking somewhere—but I was too timid to ask to try any. I was also too timid to ask why they called these mini neighborhoods quarters, when there were clearly more than four of them. The children were the only ones who, like me, ventured beyond the invisible boundaries here. I enjoyed watching them hurtling through the halls, as frustrated parents called after them.

After about a week, I stumbled upon a library with tons of books, many in English. Since I'd brought nothing of my own, it was a relief to decompress, just to read a few chapters of an old spy novel—books that had been banned and burned after the Revelations, full of violence and blasphemy. They'd preserved some of them down here, and though they weren't great art, they were still fascinating, a kind of literature I'd never been exposed to. Once I discovered that library, I spent most of my time there, devouring gruesome mysteries, subversive political thrillers, erotic romances.

Each time I visited, I saw the same familiar faces—including a young blond man about my age, head buried in a Greek textbook, who kept glancing my way. He was handsome enough, so I usually offered a smile when he caught my eye. But he never smiled back, like most of the people I met down here—and I remembered that constantly smiling at strangers is something of a small-town American quirk. Because he never spoke to me, and I was too proud to try and speak to him, we went days in silence—feet away but never interacting—until one day, he sat down next to me.

"You are new, yeah?" His accent was unmistakably German.

"Yeah," I said. "Grace."

He shook my outstretched hand. "Max. I heard about you."

The idea that strangers in this bunker knew who I was unnerved me. "What have you heard?"

To my surprise, he gushed, "You were fighting in America. You are the girl who has tricked Prophet Joshua. The one who destroyed his most dangerous weapon." I blushed—I guess my reputation could be worse. Max certainly seemed impressed by it, and it gave me a little rush of excitement, to think of myself that way.

"Yeah, I guess that's me."

He scrunched his face in contemplation. "You do not look like I expected you to look."

"Oh." I was suddenly conscious of my appearance. But the way he'd said it, I could tell he wasn't disappointed.

"You are Christian, yes?" he asked next. I was surprised by the question, but I shouldn't have been. Many Americans had been Christian before the Revelations. Heck, I'd even been, as a little kid . . . but after ten years of listening to my father preach that the old religions were crude, inferior ways of accessing the divine . . . I just couldn't go back to believing in any of them.

I couldn't define myself as something I'd spent most of my life trying to be "better" than. Even on the other side of the world, my father's sermons still stuck with me, convinced me to keep believing in a deity everyone else in the resistance had abandoned.

But I was also tired of being alone down here. And after my conversation with Layla, I knew better than to try to explain what I really believed, to make some futile case for Great Spirit. So I gave an answer that was technically true, though misleading to its very core: "My father was a Christian minister before the Revelations."

That seemed to please my new friend Max to no end. "I am part of a Christian group, people of all countries. We are going tomorrow to watch the debates together." Before I could ask if that was an invitation, he confirmed it. "You can join, if you want."

My first friend down here, and my first chance to make more friends. All of it was based on a lie, a lie of omission at least, but I didn't care. "That sounds great."

"See you soon," he said, leaving the library with a grin on his face, and I felt excited for the first time in a long time.

4

The next night, the Christian quarter was filled to the brim with young people in their teens and twenties. It was more of a party atmosphere than I expected; I saw cups filled with wine—my first exposure to alcohol, ever. "There is a black market not far from this underground city," Max explained when he saw my shock. "Down here, there are no Punishments, no Prohibitions." Everyone was taking the same drugs I was, he meant, the ones that prevented guilt from turning into Punishment. I marveled at the idea of a whole society, governed only by laws and conscience.

"Cool," I said, as a smiling Korean girl handed me a wineglass. My first sip had a strangely metallic taste—I heard one of the older partygoers grumbling that wine was supposed to taste better, but apparently this was the best you could get at a Turkish black market.

"These are the people to know here," Max told me. "There are many other groups of Christians, you know. This whole wing, they are all Christians. But they are not spending as much time with the Bible as we are, they are not reading it the way it was meant to be read." Apparently, Max and his friends were some of those Originalists Jude had been telling me about—Max's Greek textbook should have been a tip-off, in retrospect.

I nodded as though what he was saying was very important to me. "Thanks for bringing me here."

"You will like the debate. Matthew Graham, he is American, like you; he is fighting for the Christians here. I have met him, he is a good man." Graham must have been the conservative Christian candidate Jude had mentioned. I nervously sipped the wine, which filled me with a dizzy, happy feeling.

As we moved through the party, Max introduced me to everyone—lots of Americans, I was surprised to discover. Some were familiar—people I'd tried to start conversations with, who'd shied away from me. Now that I was vetted as "one of them," they were over-the-top friendly and welcoming. One girl was from a small town in Tennessee I'd driven through as a kid, though now she only wanted to speak in Hebrew. Names and handshakes swirled by in a blur—people from Brazil, Nigeria, the Philippines, Russia—and all were thrilled to meet me.

Or rather, the person I was pretending to be. Somehow I'd come all the way to Turkey, but I still couldn't shed my fake, pious persona. Except now, I was playing Grace, the "Christian" . . . a much harder part, because I had so much less experience with it. I tried to remember being seven, eight . . . what had I been like then? I doubted my memories of Sunday school art projects would be useful now.

Occasionally, people would wander through, coming and going from rooms in the Christian quarter. But they exchanged wary looks at my new friends, and passing as quickly as possible—clearly not in the "good" group of Christians that Max liked. I tried to guess what sect they might be . . . Catholics? Mormons? Jehovah's Witnesses? It was impossible to tell exactly what made you "good" or "bad" to Max and his friends, what lines they were drawing between themselves and others. And I was too afraid to ask . . . for fear of ending up on the wrong side of that line.

As the party wound down, Max put a hand on my back as we followed the group toward a cavernous meeting room. Several hundred chairs were already filled with people, and more filed in to stand behind them. Once again, the room was fractured into different groups along religious and racial fault lines, and in certain circles, people were further divided by gender. Another reminder that while we were all fighting for the same cause, this was far from the idyllic "everyone is the same" world I'd grown up in.

I spotted Jude sitting with Layla and her family near the front, and I hid in the back of Max's group, hoping he wouldn't notice me. I didn't know what Jude would think of my new friends . . . honestly, I wasn't sure what I thought of them yet.

Thankfully, the event began soon after we arrived. Volunteers passed out headsets, through which the multilingual debate would be translated. As the candidates stepped up to the stage, an English translation sprang into my ears, explaining

who all the candidates were, and which religions they repre-
sented. Even with all that, I still felt lost.

But I knew I needed to keep up. As the room descended
into a whirl of grave whispers, I could tell that whatever I was
about to witness would decide our future—the future of the
resistance, and the future of the world.

What are they all running for, exactly?" I asked Max, feeling dumb for not asking that basic question earlier.

He quickly explained that the political system of our organization was similar to your average parliamentary democracy, where everyone votes for their representatives. Except, instead of voting in a district based on geography, voting blocs were determined by religion. Taoists, Buddhists, atheists, everyone had their own representatives, fighting for their group's needs. Some groups, like the Christian coalition, chose to band together behind one leader, while other religions fractured into sects, each with its own goals, and representatives.

And right now, all those representatives were onstage, arguing about which one of them should be chosen as the leader of the whole organization—to be a kind of president, or prime minister. It all felt overwhelmingly complicated.

"Every year, that Mohammed guy wins." Max pointed to

Layla's father, Mohammed Bashar, who was currently speaking onstage about his ten-year plan for undermining the prophets. "All the Muslims are voting for him. The secular people, too, they like him. He listens to them. They know he is the best they can get, so they vote for him."

Onstage, an older French woman, the secular candidate Ariana Dupont whom Jude had said he'd liked, was trying to win back some of her demographic. "Have you heard Mohammed Bashar explain how he makes decisions?" Dr. Dupont was saying to the crowd with outrage. "It's always, Allah says this, Allah says that. If you aren't Muslim, why are you voting for this guy? I know, I know, he's a 'moderate.' But as long as he's basing his decisions on one religious doctrine, he's excluding everyone else. A *truly* secular leader is the only one who can listen to everyone."

"That's simply not true," Mohammed fought back, undeterred. "I lead by my faith principles, yes, as you live by your principles, Dr. Dupont. But I have no wish to impose my religion on anyone else . . ."

"'Leading by faith principles' . . . that's just code for making laws based on your religious beliefs. Haven't we all had enough of that?"

As Mohammed defended himself with a politician's grace, Max leaned closer to me, and I could feel the heat of his breath against my ear as he pointed to a handsome middle-aged Caucasian man. "That man there, that is Matthew Graham. He is an American reverend, like your father. He is the only candidate who represents real Christian interests. This is why he makes the fake Christians angry." The longer Max and I hung out, the more convinced I became that I had more in common with the people he called "fake" than with him.

Finally, Graham stepped forward to the cheers of Max's friends and began a fiery speech, one it was clear he'd been practicing for days. "Humanity has always squabbled over our divisions. But the one thing the Revelations proved is that faith can unite us. And while we can all agree, a false religion does no good, faith itself is the only thing that can save us from ourselves."

Max was nodding along, as though he'd heard this speech before, as though it were a favorite movie he'd seen many times but was excited to watch again. In fact, I noticed that all my new "friends" were rapt, applauding Graham's every point.

The reverend continued, "If we listen to the secularists, or the so-called moderates, Universal Theology wins. They're going to take away the thing that makes us strong, the only thing that can bind us together. Once we succeed in tearing down the false prophets—and under my leadership, have no doubt, we will—we can finally remake the world the way it ought to be. As a utopia governed by *real* religions."

Though I wasn't quite sure what he meant, that line got a huge reaction from the crowd. Cheers from my friends, of course, but I also noticed a few tentative claps from around the room, from members of other religious groups.

When Mohammed noticed Muslims clapping for Graham, he stepped in. "I strongly disagree. Religion is best practiced privately, and I believe it has no place in government. As a Palestinian who has seen firsthand the perils of letting religion and politics mix, both before and after the Revelations, I can say for certain that you have no idea what you're talking about, Reverend Graham. And after fighting against a worldwide theocracy for years, I cannot believe that you are actually arguing for establishing *another* one."

"Not at all," Graham corrected him. "America would be a Christian country, as it always has been. Israel would be a Jewish country. The surrounding areas, like Iran, Iraq, and Pakistan, would be Muslim countries. India would be a Hindu country." With each nation, he gestured to a rabbi, an imam, and a Hindu priest onstage, who all nodded approvingly. Meanwhile, my stomach turned, as I realized this kind of rhetoric was exactly what Jude had been nervous about.

The roar of the crowd grew fiercer; the cheers for Graham grew louder, as his opposition in the secular wing sharpened, booing and hurling insults Graham's way. Mohammed ignored the overlapping voices, firing back, "You're dreaming about splitting the spoils of war when our forces are backed into a corner, when we're losing that war badly. We need to focus on the present, the here and now."

I hoped Graham would back down, listen to reason, but he was on a roll. "I *am* focused on the present. Even now, we shouldn't be afraid to live our faith. The laws of our makeshift society should be the laws of the world we aspire to live in when this war is over. Even down below the ground, we must remake our society into a city on a hill. We need rules about the way we speak to each other. About the way we treat each other. We've lived so long without Punishments, we've forgotten what God's will is. Our laws must reflect God's laws, must reflect an

Originalist interpretation of religious texts. And I'm calling for an army to enforce those laws."

"We will be that army," Max whispered to me with a kind of sick delight, and I was overcome with dread. Watching him staring at Reverend Graham with such devotion, I realized that the violent extremists down here might not look or act the way I expected them to. And my ignorance had led me into the middle of a pack of them.

6

As cool as my new friends had seemed only an hour earlier, as the debate wore on, their cheers turned vicious. They screamed over all the other candidates, shouting nasty slurs—"Heathen!" "Judas!" "Jezebel!"

I thought back on those other groups of Christians who had passed through our party. They hadn't given us strange looks because they were from some other sect of Christianity, as I'd assumed—it was because the group I was with was trying to impose some kind of creepy religious law on them.

Before I could contemplate my escape plan, a Shia imam, Mohammed's Muslim rival, stepped forward onstage to declare, "As a man of faith, I also lend my support to Reverend Graham." There was a moment of stunned silence from the crowd as the imam continued, "And I urge all my followers to vote to support him. This is a vote for the values of Islam."

Next to me, Max was in awe. "You see the power of Matthew Graham? Never before has Muslim endorsed Christian. Never."

Mohammed was clearly just as surprised. "You couldn't have given me a heads-up?" he quipped, an edge to his voice.

The imam shook his head in apology. "I know I have supported my fellow Muslim brother in every previous election, but these past few months, I have been disappointed by his policies. He and his family do not live by the true, Originalist interpretation of the Quran. He has made too many compromises for his secular friends."

Graham continued, "We will base our laws on the Ten Commandments, on the five pillars of Islam, on God's laws. Members of the current secular party may choose a religion of their liking."

A rabbi onstage nodded his approval. "If we don't live according to our beliefs, we are no freer than we were under the prophets."

Graham reveled in both the cheers and jeers of the crowd. "Religion is dying. The Universal Theology has committed genocide against it. If we do not fight for our beliefs, the truth will die out."

Max saw the concern on my face and perhaps interpreted it as a reflection of his own concerns. He leaned in, both conspiratorial and reassuring. "Don't worry. Graham will not stop there. When we finish with the prophets, the next step is a Christian world."

"Hmm?" I asked, assuming I'd misheard him.

"It is not enough to kill off Universal Theologist scum. Next step is fighting for a Christian world. This is what we all know Graham really wants. Just as that imam wants a Muslim world, and on and on. They make an alliance now to get power. Then later, they will fight each other. But we are strongest, the Christian Originalists. We will win."

I couldn't hide my disgust any longer. "We've spent the past ten years living in a society that imposed religion on us. Why would you want that again, why would you want to do that to more people, to people who just got their freedom back?"

Max stared at me like I was crazy. "Religion *is* freedom. Only through God can you be free. But all people will not practice unless the laws make them. Real biblical laws. We need *real* prophets, who talk to the *real* god."

His intensity made me ill. I'd been impressed by Mohammed, that he had somehow united the moderates of every religion, even down here in such a divided world. But as I watched groups of cheering Buddhists and Sikhs and Catholics, I realized it was Reverend Graham who had done the truly impossible— he'd somehow united the *extremists* of every religion. For now, at least.

By the end of the debates, my German friend was in a frenzy of excitement, and I was in a state of dread. Eventually, Dr. Dupont, the secular candidate, threw her support to Mohammed in a last desperate plea, fearing what would happen if the ultrareligious coalition prevailed, but every word she said was drowned out by the echoing pandemonium in the room.

I wondered how Max would react once he learned I didn't believe what I'd pretended to believe. Whether, if Graham won, he'd try to impose some kind of Christian code on me, too. As Graham listed off the biblical laws I'd be expected to follow, I was overcome with despair. After everything I'd fought for, this is the rule the world might come under next? Back in New York, I'd thought that being under Prophet Joshua's thumb was the worst thing I could imagine. Apparently, I'd simply lacked imagination.

As ballots were distributed, I noticed Max glancing over as I began to mark mine. I shielded it with my hand, putting down a vote for Mohammed.

While Max was distracted, talking to one of his other friends, I slunk away without saying goodbye, dropping off my ballot and cornering Jude and Layla as they exited the hall. As I approached, I could see Layla's brows were furrowed, clearly disturbed by everything that had just transpired. In that moment, all our petty little squabbles evaporated, leaving only the concerns of the moment.

"What was that?" I asked Jude, unable to disguise my fear.

His voice was soft and calming. "Like I told you, the extremists are getting riled up. There aren't enough of them though; they can't win." It sounded like Jude was trying to convince himself more than anyone.

"I don't know, they were pretty loud," I said, worried.

"Well, you were standing in a mob of them," he said pointedly. My heart sank, realizing he'd seen me with Max.

Layla was shifting her weight back and forth, trying to reassure herself, too. "I do not think any of the Sunni vote will go to Graham. I do not think they will trust a Shia cleric."

"It's always the Hindu vote," Jude reassured her. "They're the swing bloc, and they're a huge group."

All these sects, and divisions within sects, seemed so meaningless to me. "Can't people cast a vote without it being based on religion?" I asked, feeling stupid.

As I said it, I remembered how often I'd made decisions based on what I felt like Great Spirit wanted me to do. But that seemed different—Great Spirit was speaking to me *directly*, I wasn't mindlessly repeating what some larger organization told me to think. But the more I tried to find a distinction between those two things, the more they seemed to blur together.

And like Layla, I was worried.

7

Days passed as we waited for votes to come in from around the world. I mostly hid in my room, afraid to go to the library or the mess hall for fear of running into Max and his friends. I didn't know if I could fake my way through even a casual conversation with any of them without giving away just how much I loathed the man they idolized.

One night though, I heard a knock at my door. *Did Max know where I lived?* I wasn't sure if I should answer, but I worried things might get worse if I made it clear I was avoiding him.

But when I opened the door, instead I found Layla, a nervous expression on her face.

"Hello," she said.

"Hey," I replied, trying to figure out why she was here.

"Jude said you have been in here alone. He said . . ." She stopped and corrected herself, "I want to invite you to meet my family."

"Oh." I was touched. "Thanks."

"Tomorrow, my father is hosting some friends to hear the results of the election. You should come."

"I'd love that," I told her. This time, totally honestly. As she walked off, I wondered how much of that invitation came from her, and how much from Jude, and ultimately decided I didn't care. Even if Layla still resented me, as I suspected she did, she and Jude were the closest thing I had to friends down here, and I wasn't in a position to turn away friends.

So the following night, I followed Jude and Layla to the Muslim quarter, where her family and some friends were gathered in a large suite, nervously awaiting the tabulation of votes. Her older brothers debated intensely with some friends in Arabic, as her father held court with his multireligious group of associates in a corner—I recognized one of them as Ariana Dupont, the French secularist who'd run against him. Though I got some strange looks as I entered, I was grateful to Layla's family for letting me be a part of this important, private moment.

As soon as we walked in, Layla's mother pulled her away from the crowd to sit with a group of women, and Jude and I were left to watch the excitement from a distance.

"Thanks for keeping me company," he said.

"Is this what it's always like?" I asked. "Layla brings you here, and you hang out in the corner?"

Jude shrugged. "Traditionally, men and women aren't really supposed to intermingle in Layla's culture, unless they're family. It's hard to do that, down here, because there isn't really space for people to keep to themselves. But Layla's mother still tries to enforce the boundaries as much as she can."

I nodded—another strange set of rules I didn't understand.

In this room full of Mohammed's friends, Jude looked as out of place as I felt. I saw him stealing glances at Layla across the room whenever he could. "Seems weird for them to invite you here and then ignore you," I observed.

He nodded—I'd clearly hit a nerve. "Mohammed's Muslim allies disapprove of his rebellious daughter, but I think I actually help him with the secular vote, make him look more progressive. Now that the election's over, I wouldn't be surprised if he tells me to get lost."

Instinctively, my heart soared. If Mohammed forbade Layla from dating Jude, then maybe he and I could pick up where we'd left off, without all this weird distance between us. But when I saw the sadness on Jude's face, my heart came crashing back down. I would never want my happiness to come at the expense of his. "I hope that doesn't happen," I managed to make myself say.

Jude seemed grateful to hear that. "Thanks."

Before I could say anything else, a man ran in shouting in Arabic, and the room went wild. Hugging, crying. "I assume he won?" I asked Jude, who looked just as unsure as I did.

But it was Layla who answered me in the affirmative, running up to us, beaming. "He won!"

Relief washed over me: nightmare averted.

Dr. Dupont popped a bottle of champagne—a nice gesture considering she was celebrating her own loss. Secular leaders passed around cups; a man in a Sikh turban handed me a glass, and I clinked it with dozens of strangers who suddenly felt like friends. As the room cheered around me, I finally felt a little bit like a part of something, for real this time.

Over the whoops of victory around me, I could hear other sounds outside. Shouting, clomping feet. Of course, I remembered, there were plenty of people out there who were less thrilled about this election outcome. People I definitely wanted to continue avoiding.

But something about those pounding footsteps felt familiar, felt dangerous. No, this wasn't a few unhappy voters, this was something else. *Something violent.* As their voices grew louder, dread built inside of me, even as everyone else seemed oblivious, wrapped up in the glow of victory. In all my anxiety over the election and my silly little love life, I'd forgotten about the larger threats facing us—Joshua, and all the other prophets, gunning for us. It was like watching a tsunami in slow motion—dozens of people with no idea they were about to be engulfed.

I tried to find someone to tell, to warn . . . and then a gunshot rang out in the hall, and the room fell silent. Another, and then another, echoing as the bullets ricocheted off the stone walls. We could hear screams now, and pounding footsteps. It all seemed so clear now. It was happening—*Joshua had found us.*

Everyone else was already taking shelter behind furniture, in corners, but I was frozen where I stood.

Layla grabbed my arm, jerking me out of my haze and to the ground. "Get down," she hissed. "Put your head between your legs and don't say a word."

8

*W*hat was happening? I couldn't ask, I knew better than to speak—the whole room had gone silent. How had they found us? Despite Jude's reassurances that we were safe, had Joshua tracked us down, tracked me all the way around the globe?

As the gunshots came closer, I heard voices accompanying them, though I couldn't make out yet what they were saying. I heard crashing sounds—doors being kicked open, terrified screams. I scrunched myself into an even smaller ball, covering my head, hoping they would move past us.

Finally, the voices, deep and gruff, were right outside our door. I stole a glance at the others in the room—they were all just as terrified as I was. Shouts I couldn't translate vibrated the stone walls. I heard high-pitched shrieks, footsteps running away.

The voices didn't say anything for a moment. And then—BAM—our door crashed open, and two dozen heavily armed men burst in. "Put your hands up!" several people shouted at once, in multiple languages. Everyone complied.

As I threw my hands in the air, I peeked between my knees to try to see who these people were, and my heart sank to recognize a familiar face, half hidden behind tactical gear—*Max*. I recognized a few of his friends flanking him, fanning out, guns trained on our heads. This wasn't Joshua's army, it was Matthew Graham's. I kept my face buried, hoping to conceal my identity as long as possible, as a man I didn't recognize reached down next to me and grabbed Layla, pulled her to her feet. Her shrieks echoed in my ear, and I could smell, almost taste, her captor's sweat.

"Let go of her," Mohammed shouted, but the gun barrels pointed at his chest forced him to stay put. He changed his tone, imploring the man restraining Layla. "Don't do this, brother." As Layla's captor snarled back in Arabic, I realized, this crowd wasn't made up of just my Christian extremist friends. In fact, as I looked closer, I recognized other familiar faces from the debate crowd—two Hindu men, a Jewish one, a Buddhist one . . . these were all the Originalists of different faiths who had cheered on Reverend Graham. His army was even more formidable than I could have imagined.

Max stepped forward, his gun trained on Mohammed. "Reverend Graham is the rightful leader of this movement."

But Mohammed kept his focus on the man holding his daughter—the one he believed he might be able to turn. "This is not Islam," Mohammed implored him, voice steady. "Islam is peace."

But the man didn't release her, firing back a stream of angry Arabic.

After a moment, one of the Hindu men stepped forward,

shouting over everyone. "Step down. Or we will start killing hostages." Terror spiked through me. The man's gun was pointed at Jude.

Mohammed looked at his daughter, at the tears streaming down her face, then back to the rest of his family. His older son shook his head, saying something in Arabic I could tell meant something like *Don't you dare step down.*

Mohammed turned his gaze back to our attackers, keeping his voice level. "Your government will not be legitimate if you take this place by force."

"The people are on our side," the Jewish man said.

I stole a glance at Max and saw he was already looking back at me, his eyes cold. As Mohammed and the others continued their standoff, Max moved closer to me. "Grace?" he asked, his voice full of shock and distaste. "You are one of them?"

"Please don't hurt me," was all I could think to say.

As the other gunmen moved to tie up Mohammed and his family, Max stooped next to me, binding my hands. I could feel his anger as he dug the wire into my wrists. "You did not tell me you were friends with this man."

"I just met him," I said, an idea forming. "I just got here." If I could convince him not to tie me up, maybe I could find a way to help the others.

Max didn't buy it. "Only his inner circle is celebrating with him."

"Wrong place, wrong time," I said.

"She's not with us," Jude piped up from a few feet away, and I realized he'd been listening in; I shot him a thankful look.

Max moved over to Jude, who'd already been restrained by one of our other attackers. "Who are you?"

Jude took a deep breath. "I'm the one who brought her here. She's only here because she doesn't have any other friends in Turkey; I told her to tag along. She didn't have anywhere else to go."

Max looked to one of his comrades, who shrugged his shoulders. "Please," I said. "You want a Christian world. Why start by killing another Christian?" I forced myself not to look at Jude, knowing the reaction he'd have to hearing me describe myself that way.

Max pondered the question as he sized me up. I tried to look as timid, as useless as possible. Making a decision, Max pulled me to my feet. "This way," he hissed, walking me out into the hallway.

As we emerged from the room, I saw a crowd of onlookers scatter—people who'd heard what was happening but were too afraid to intervene. Now that we were alone, Max pulled out a pair of wire cutters and removed my restraints. "Now, leave this place." He turned to go back into the room.

"Wait! What's going to happen next?" I called after him, hands shaking.

"That is being decided by the others. The fate of Mohammed's family is not up to Christians."

"Why?"

"Muslims police their own. I am responsible for Christians only. That is the deal we have made."

I wondered if I could convince Max to turn against his

compatriots. I'd already convinced him to let me go—maybe I could exploit his own prejudices. "Why are you working with them?" I asked.

"What do you mean?" Max seemed genuinely confused.

"You think Mohammed has made too many compromises, but what do you think you're doing?" I tried to think of the words most likely to sway someone who thought the way he did. "What's the difference, him working with the secularists, versus you working with all those extremists, all those people killing for a god that isn't your god?"

He seemed unconcerned. "Once we defeat the false prophets, we cannot risk having a new government with secular laws. Secularism is what caused the Revelations in the first place." His matter-of-fact way of speaking about things that weren't facts drove me crazy.

"Jesus never asked anyone to take up arms," I pointed out, trying to keep my frustration in check. "In fact, I think he was pretty against it."

Max shook his head, undeterred. "He asked us to spread his word. This is the best way. It will be worth it, when the whole world follows Christ. You worry now, but you will see."

His stubbornness infuriated me. "All your talk about Originalism, it's just an excuse, isn't it?" I shot back.

"What do you mean?"

"All that time you spent studying ancient scripture, it wasn't about finding the true meaning, it was about cherry-picking examples to help you find cover for oppressing everyone else." As I finished, I was breathless, and terrified . . . I knew I'd just made a risky accusation.

But he took my words in stride, unmoved. "You have not studied like I have. If you do, you will see."

I nodded, numb, realizing there was no way I could convince this guy of anything approaching sanity. I changed my tack. "Please, the other American in there. Jude, the one who spoke up for me. Please don't let him get hurt."

"He is also Christian?" Max asked.

I worried getting caught in a lie might make things worse for Jude, so I just said, "He's a good person."

My omission told Max all he needed to know. But he nodded. "I will keep watch on him."

"Thanks," I said, and I believed that he would try. And I hoped, desperately, that Max's small-mindedness, his tribal outlook, would help keep Jude safe.

Max disappeared inside the room, closing the door behind him. Moments later, a gunshot rang out from inside, followed by screams and wails.

I ran to the door, pressed my ear against it—but I couldn't tell what had happened. My nails dug into the wood; I wanted to weep, scream, collapse, but I couldn't. If there was any chance my friend was still alive in there, I had to try and save him, and everyone else in that room.

I tore myself away from the door. I needed to find help.

9

I scrambled through the halls, stopping everyone I passed, breathlessly stringing together syllables. "They've taken hostages. They have guns. We have to do something." But everyone turned away from me, walked away quickly with their heads down. Some of them might not have understood my jumble of words, but I think most were too afraid. Afraid to take sides, afraid to put themselves in the middle of yet another conflict. And some, I'm sure, must have been Originalists who supported the insurrection, even if they weren't willing to take up arms themselves.

In a flailing haze, I started yelling down the dark halls. "Anyone! Can anyone help me?"

But no one answered.

My feet fell heavy on the stone pathways, my breath pressing against the silence of the fearful corridors. Doors slammed as I approached—everyone lying low until the coup had resolved one way or the other.

This place had never felt so huge, so barren, so empty.

I tried to think of where I might find allies. The atheist quarter maybe? I found myself walking in circles; in my panic, I couldn't remember the layout of this place, and I didn't know whom I could trust to ask directions.

As I pressed on, legs aching from exertion, I finally heard voices arguing ahead of me. Friends, foes, I had no idea, but I was just relieved to find anyone who wasn't in hiding.

As the voices grew louder, I realized I'd arrived: this was the atheist quarter, buzzing with angry and terrified people. A woman holding a baby was near tears: "This is our home, our future. We can't just let them take it."

Another man bellowed, seemingly to no one, "They want to outlaw secularism. Outlaw it!"

The woman shook her head. "We don't know who's in there. We can't mount a counteroffensive without some idea of what's going on, on the ground."

"I can help," I blurted out. Everyone turned their skeptical eyes toward me. "You're talking about the coup, right? I was in there, I escaped."

A bald, burly man, who seemed to be the ringleader, pulled me into a nearby room, some family's living quarters, and a few others followed, forming a hushed circle. "Tell us everything," he said.

Invigorated, I quickly related what I'd seen: "They've got about thirty hostages, held by maybe a couple dozen gunmen. They want Mohammed to step down, so Graham can be the leader."

"So it's the Christians, figures . . ." the ringleader muttered.

"No, it's everybody. It's all the religious extremists working together."

That floored the atheist wing. "Working together?"

"They're saying it's temporary . . ." I tried to cut in, but I was drowned out by all the other voices:

"There's no way . . ."

"Graham rose to power by demonizing the other Originalists, they'd never team up with him."

"You saw that debate, they already have."

"To form an army . . . ?" asked a skeptical voice.

"That's what Graham said he wanted, didn't he?"

"Let those Originalist assholes kill each other," one woman snorted. "When the dust settles, we'll take over again."

Another man concurred. "I'm not putting my ass on the line for some Muslim guy. Do you think he'd do the same for me?"

The woman with the baby shouted back, "You're not fighting for 'some Muslim guy,' you're fighting for us. They want to outlaw the secular party!"

The ringleader whistled sharply, and the room fell silent. "Save the politics. You said there's two dozen? We can take on two dozen." He looked around the rest of the crowd, fixing them with a hawklike stare. "Anyone willing to put their ass on the line, we're going in."

"Wait," I interjected. "They've got really big guns. Scary-looking ones."

He opened a closet, revealing dozens of assault rifles, just as big as the ones the extremists had been holding, and he couldn't help but grin. "Scary enough for ya?"

I nodded, scared indeed.

He continued, "We heard the Originalists had a line in to a black market, and we knew they'd be secretly stockpiling weapons. We figured we oughta do the same."

The guns made their way around the circle, followed by a bottle of pills—to guard against any sins we were about to commit. A tough-looking young woman extended a loaded rifle to me, but I shook my head. "I don't know how to use it."

She pointed. "Safety. Trigger. Now you do." I reluctantly took it from her. It was heavier than I expected, the metal colder. Would I really be willing to shoot it? Would I kill one of those masked men to save Jude's life? I'd been torturing myself over that guard's accidental death . . . could I really take another life, on purpose this time? As I looked around the circle at this mustering army, an icy wave of terror washed over me. *You should leave now*, that nagging feeling in my gut said. But I shook it off. I had to save Jude.

"We don't have long," our leader said. "If they're threatening hostages, we have to move now." And despite that nagging feeling in my gut, we did.

10

None of this felt real. As I followed these strangers down the dimly lit halls of this underground city, I couldn't believe I was really holding a gun in my hands, really going into battle with strangers I'd just met, against a group of quasi friends I'd just learned I should oppose. Was this what the pre-Revelation era had been like? All this hatred and violence and chaos? Constant fear, a constant struggle for power?

As we approached the Muslim quarter, I felt dread billowing up inside me. I'd been gone nearly an hour . . . who knew what might have transpired in that time? Who knew if Jude was even still alive in there? Maybe the gunmen had been joined by reinforcements. Maybe I was leading this secular army to their deaths. Maybe I was about to die myself. My finger shakily rested near the trigger, and I was terrified I would pull it too soon . . . but more terrified I wouldn't be able to pull it at all.

When we got close to Mohammed's suite, our leader nodded to me. *Is this the place?* I nodded back.

We took a collective inhale of anticipation. I could see in my compatriots' eyes that this wasn't a new experience for just me. None of these people looked battle tested. Unlike Max's army, we hadn't trained together, hadn't prepared for this. Our odds seemed slimmer and slimmer with every step we took.

But it was too late to back out now. Our leader threw his weight against the door, and as it fell down, a hail of gunfire rang out. From my spot at the back of the pack, I could see bright muzzle flashes, I could smell the smoke wafting out of that room.

The screams were loud, but the gunshots were louder, rattling my eardrums with an endless fury. On my tiptoes, peering over the heads of the people in front of me, I could see hostages fleeing for cover, Originalist gunmen falling.

But Jude. Where was Jude? I didn't see him, didn't hear him, or Layla either. My finger tightened around the trigger as I imagined the worst. Tried to stay focused. If I wanted to see Jude again, I needed to stay alive, too.

As the group in front of me moved into the room, I took cover at the doorframe and peered in, gun up, prepared to shoot. Eyes peeled for Originalist gunmen in their tactical gear, for anyone who might be targeting me.

But the battle was already over, before I'd even crossed the threshold. My breath caught in my throat as I took in the slaughter splayed out around me. Our leader, that bald, burly guy, lay dead on the ground—but so did all the masked men. We'd won.

I picked my way into the room, surveying the scene. Jude. Where was Jude? In all the chaos, the crying, I didn't see him. I still couldn't find him.

My eyes roved across each of the dead and wounded bodies, feeling a sick kind of relief with each face that wasn't Jude's. The atheist army moved from hostage to hostage, freeing them from their bonds . . . the ones who were alive, anyway. The Sikh man who'd handed me a glass of champagne earlier was unmoving at my feet. The secularist leader, Ariana Dupont, lay still against the wall, a bullet drilled through her forehead, execution style. I wondered if that was the shot I'd heard right before I ran for help. I saw Layla's brothers—one applying pressure to the other's wounded stomach. Mohammed, hugging a sobbing Layla, whose face was beaten and bruised.

But no Jude. I could feel my chin begin to quiver as tears fell. Where was he? Was he dead, caught in the cross fire? Had we just killed my best friend?

"Grace?" I turned to find the voice . . . but it was Max, on the ground a few feet from me, his eyes boring into me with the deepest hatred. A pool of blood spilled out of his stomach. Someone had confiscated his gun, but I was certain his glare was enough to kill me outright.

"I'm sorry," was all I could say to the man who'd freed me. Who'd saved my life, even while trying to harm so many others. I was afraid of whatever he might say next . . . but nothing came next. He was dead.

11

I stared in horror at Max's lifeless eyes. Wishing desperately that they'd fill up with that hatred again, be full of anything again. But Max was gone.

I tore myself away. Jude. I still hadn't found Jude. He could still be alive, somewhere in this carnage.

I picked my way through the bodies, glancing at each face with apprehension. Would this one be Jude? That one? But the faces I saw went with hands that held guns—soldiers, not hostages.

As medics streamed in, doctors who'd been called for help, I was close to giving up the search, when I heard a voice.

"Over here!" Jude's voice. I turned to see him, covered in blood, calling to a medic . . . As I followed the medic over, I saw Jude stooped behind an overturned table where he'd been caring for a fallen hostage, one of Mohammed's political allies. "She's unconscious, but she's breathing," Jude told the medic. "I used a piece of my shirt to tie a tourniquet, but she's lost a lot of blood . . ."

As the medic went to work, Jude finally looked up and saw me. I ran to him, as he turned to meet me. The slow, stilted way he was moving worried me. "Are you okay?" I asked him.

He nodded. "A couple bruises, nothing too bad." I saw relief in his eyes now, too, and gratitude. "Your friend wouldn't let them shoot me." He nodded to Max's body, and I felt a new wave of conflicted guilt.

"I asked him not to," I admitted. Jude hugged me, as the shock and horror of it hit me all at once. I whispered, rambling, "I know he was awful, but I didn't want him to die. I didn't want any of these people to die . . ."

Jude shook his head, not willing to let me wallow in my misery. "If your rescuers hadn't come when they did, Layla would have been next."

I nodded as I looked to Layla's shaking form, now huddled with her mother, watching one of the doctors carry away her brother. "Is he going to be okay?" I asked Jude.

"I think so. There are others wounded much worse."

Across the room, I saw Mohammed conferring with one of his advisers. He looked up, and they both briefly made eye contact with me—then quickly looked away.

Jude tugged on my sleeve. "We should go. Let the medics do their job." I nodded—I didn't want to be in this room one second longer.

But as we moved for the exit, the room went silent, as we saw Mohammed, standing solemnly, as though preparing to give a speech. But he didn't . . . he just uttered a few, quiet words. "Call everyone to the meeting room." He paused, his eyes full of fury. "Everyone."

12

As Jude and I followed the hushed crowd back to the meeting hall, my anxiety brewed. I'd seen death, I'd been trapped in a carton full of dead scientists, I'd taken the life of that guard. But I'd never held a gun in my hands, prepared to kill another human being, and that unnerved me like nothing else. I felt like I was tumbling off a cliff, falling deeper and deeper into a kind of evil and sinfulness I'd never thought I was capable of.

I'd always known I lived in a utopia, a world stripped of the violence and misery people once assumed was inevitable. When I'd promised to help Dawn restore things to the way they used to be, I knew I was dooming all of us to return to that same violence and misery. But now that I was actually faced with it, I wasn't at all sure our goal was worth fighting for.

When we arrived in the meeting hall, Jude warily eyed the crowd. "Will there be more violence?" I asked. "Will Mohammed retaliate?"

"I don't know," he said, and I could tell he had no clearer idea than I did what might come next.

The room buzzed as Mohammed walked in, his family following somberly behind him. His voice was steady, containing his anger. "Tonight, an army tried to overthrow me, by taking my family hostage. Those men are now dead. The man who incited them, Reverend Graham, is under arrest, as are his accomplices. We do not have time to fight among ourselves. The people who live above us are not free. It is our responsibility to help them. And we must work together.

"I know some of you are waiting to see what I will do, how I will take my revenge. But I'm not going to do that. I will not ask for penance. We must move forward, to survive. We must defeat the prophets, because I can see as well as you can that this alliance we have, it's not going to last forever.

"This is why winning this war as soon as possible, before we tear ourselves apart, must be our highest priority. And I have a plan."

He was all politician now as he walked toward Jude and me. "The answer has been standing among us all along, someone with the tools to help us take down the prophets for good." Mohammed stopped a few feet from me and looked me in the eye. "Grace Luther, will you step forward?"

I froze, as everyone in the room looked around, confused. Most people had no idea who Grace Luther was. I turned to Jude, desperate for help, but he reluctantly nodded his head from me toward Mohammed, a gesture that meant, *Go on.*

I nervously took a step or two forward. "Where are you from, Grace?" Mohammed asked.

"Tutelo," I said by rote. Then remembered to say, "In Virginia, America."

"And which god do you believe in, Grace?"

I hesitated before admitting, "Great Spirit." I could tell Layla had told him to expect that answer, because his face showed no surprise, unlike the rest of the crowd.

"You worked for the American prophet, Joshua, no?"

The crowd's interest in me grew even more intense. "I was undercover," I explained, "but my cover is blown." Many seemed not to know that particular English idiom, so I explained, "Joshua knows I'm working with you guys. Or he will soon."

"We can help with that," he reassured me.

I looked back at Jude, a little desperate. "I thought I was supposed to lie low." Looking back to Mohammed, I translated, "I'm supposed to hide, so I don't implicate anyone else. If they catch me, it could be bad for everybody."

Mohammed seemed confused. "You would turn in your friends?"

"No, that's not what I'm saying," I stammered.

Mohammed seemed tired of my wavering. "Are you willing to help us, to follow the orders you're given, or not?" he asked.

"I . . . Okay," I said timidly, not sure how I felt about wading into the mess of politics down here. "What do you want me to do?"

But Mohammed returned his focus to his assembled followers. "You will help Grace with her mission. All of you. We have one enemy. Anyone who forgets that is no longer welcome in this refuge."

And with that, he exited the room, leaving a crowd of people staring at me warily. I looked to Jude, terrified. "What am I going to have to do?"

Jude's trembling voice did nothing to ease my fears. "I have no idea."

13

I could tell Jude was keeping something from me, some piece of knowledge about what Mohammed's strange declaration might mean. I tried to find a moment to corner him privately, but as soon as the meeting ended, Layla arrived by his side. "Are you sure you're okay?" Jude asked, stroking her cheek. They were in their own little world, completely focused on each other, and suddenly I felt invisible.

I excused myself, trying to be polite—Layla had just gone through something traumatic, and I didn't want to keep Jude from her. As I walked back to my room, I was inclined to listen to that voice constantly tugging at me to bolt from this place . . . but I didn't know where I'd even go, what I'd do, so far from everyone I knew.

I thought Jude would come and find me later, but he didn't. I tried not to be angry—going to comfort his ex couldn't be high on his to-do list after everything that had happened. I tried to sleep, but failed miserably. How could I stop my brain from agonizing after everything that had just happened?

I couldn't get Max's lifeless eyes out of my head. Not because I'd felt some great bond with that violent man, but because I felt like whatever kindness had existed between us, I'd betrayed it. He was dead because of me, because I'd lied and exploited his feelings of connection toward me and used what I knew to arm his killers.

I tried to shake off the guilt. Max was dead for one reason: because he'd threatened my best friend. He'd made the decision to be part of a violent uprising, and the consequences fell on him, and him alone.

But as I tried to force out Max's visage, it morphed—Max's lifeless eyes became the lifeless eyes of the guard in the bunker. Had his face held that same empty stare? Or, I shuddered to think, maybe there hadn't been any face left intact after the explosion. I wondered what his final moments must have been like . . . the frantic searching through boxes, interrupted by the sudden heat, the noise, and then . . . whatever it is that comes next. The Universal Theology had taught me of so many possibilities that might come after death, but it gave me no comfort to imagine the guard living in any of them.

And ironically, his death might have been the thing that saved my life. He couldn't identify me, couldn't speak my name to Joshua, and that had given me time to leave the country, even with the delay I'd taken to search for my mom. The relief I felt, thinking of how lucky I'd gotten, made the guilt sting even worse.

As I lay awake, tossing and turning with my own inner torment, the halls around me began to quiet, until eventually, everything was silent. Restless, I tiptoed out of my room and moved through the compound, wandering until my heart stopped at the sight of a familiar door—I'd ended up back in the Muslim quarter, at the scene of the crime. But now, its wailing terror had faded into an eerie silence. Everyone seemed to be sleeping, or hiding.

Except, apparently, one person, a voice behind me. "Grace?"

I jumped, startled, then turned, relieved to see it was Jude, padding toward me in his pajamas. "I didn't think you'd be awake."

"The time change is still killing me, too," he said. "Hard to adjust when there's so little natural light coming in."

"The time change, the constant state of panic. Yeah, I'm with you," I said. Had he come looking for me? What other reason could there be for him to be roaming around the women's side of the Muslim quarter . . . no, I knew the explanation. He was coming from Layla's room—no wonder he was eager to blame his presence on jet lag. I tried to push that thought from my mind, not imagine what they might have been doing in there.

He eyed me with concern. "You ran off, right after the meeting. I was worried about you. Are you okay?"

Not wanting to vent my feelings about his new relationship, I dove into the larger problem that was consuming me. "What was that back there? Why would Mohammed pick me out of all the people here?"

"You did work for Prophet Joshua . . . maybe it's just strategic." But I could tell Jude didn't really believe what he was saying—he was holding something back for my sake.

"Or . . . what?" I asked, nervous about what the answer might be.

He tried to speak as delicately as he could, but I could hear his worry building. "Well, you've seen the kind of conflict we have here. It's tough to balance all these different points of view. Make people think they're being treated fairly. Sometimes people from opposing parties think Mohammed's protecting his base, the people who vote for him, at their expense. And right now, after everything that happened . . . maybe Mohammed wants to make sure everyone knows he's not going to do that. You know, to protect his family, he has to make a show of being fair, of not retaliating against his enemies."

I said what Jude was afraid to say. "So if someone has to die, better that it's someone neutral."

"Basically."

My voice quaked. "Whatever my mission is—you think it's a suicide mission?" Panic surged through me—maybe I should have run when I had the chance.

Jude saw how freaked out I was and walked his statement back. "Maybe. There's no way to know. I already sent a message to Dawn. If you're in danger, she can help you. I don't have much power here, especially since . . ."

"Layla," I filled in for him.

"Yeah, like I said, I'm not Mohammed's favorite. But Dawn has some sway. If you need to be protected, she'll do everything she can to help."

"Thanks." But though he spoke in smooth, calming tones, his words did nothing to calm the new fear brewing inside me.

I could tell he felt bad about upsetting me. "And *I'll* do everything I can to help. You know that, right?"

"You've saved me enough times, I've gotten the hint," I said, jabbing him in the arm playfully.

"Good," he said, suddenly serious. He took my hand, and my heart fluttered in spite of myself. "I don't want you to think I stopped caring about you or something," he said quietly.

"I know you didn't," I said, breathless.

His voice stayed quiet, measured. "I didn't want to lead you on, I didn't want to be unfair to Layla, but I don't want to do the opposite either. I don't want to shut you out. I don't want you to think that what we had meant nothing to me."

I could feel the tears gathering behind my eyes, eager to spill out. "It meant something to me, too," I whispered.

"That night . . ." He paused, composed himself, and then continued, "The night you didn't show up . . . Look, I've had a lot of bad nights. Tonight was one of them. But that night back in Tutelo . . . it was hard."

"I'm sorry," I said again, my heart breaking.

"Dawn told me why you stayed, and I got it. I get it. I'm glad you did that. But I'd spent so much time alone, away from everyone I loved, and I just had this moment where I thought, maybe things could be different. Anyway, I've been trying not to think about it, I've been trying not to lay that on you, but . . . if I've seemed rude, or cold . . . I don't want you to think I'm mad, or that I forgot, you know . . . everything great about you."

"Thank you," I said, moved. Then, I wondered aloud, "This isn't just because I'm gonna die, is it?"

"Grace . . ." Jude warned.

"You know what I mean."

"No, it's not." He squeezed my hand tighter. "You'll be okay. You'll survive this. And then I'll see you back in Tutelo, or New York, or D.C., or I don't know . . . Tokyo, who knows."

I smiled. "And everything will be better."

"Yeah," he said, enjoying our little fantasy.

"Back to normal. Simple again." Back to the way things were before the crash.

He nodded. "Don't lose hope, okay?"

I fixed him in the eye. "How could I stop hoping for that?"

He held my gaze, not breaking away, and my heart ached, as I imagined three years ago, his truck rounding the corner . . . but instead of crashing into that sedan, *missing* it. The two of us continuing on to that prayer rally. Jude finishing whatever it was he was going to say—telling me how he felt, maybe. Me telling him what I'd been feeling. Prom. Spending the summer in love. And then . . .

"Do you ever think about how things would have turned out, if you hadn't been in that crash?" I asked him, breath catching in my throat.

He nodded, solemn. "I used to, all the time. But now it makes me sad. To think how easy it would have been to live my whole life and never learn the truth."

He was right. I couldn't imagine the rest of that other future, the one where we were just ordinary college students, the future that didn't end in this underground city. I couldn't imagine graduating from high school and still not knowing the truth. I couldn't imagine Jude still being dorky and awkward, me still being judgmental and self-righteous. I couldn't imagine those two people connecting the way Jude and I had. Our relationship had been forged in struggle, in loss, in absence.

"To never become the person you are now," I said softly. He nodded, and I continued, "I like this you. And this me."

"Me, too." He still hadn't broken eye contact, and the longer he held it, the more it felt like six months ago, like the night we decided to run away to Nova Scotia. But just for a moment . . . and then he shook himself out of it. Remembered where we were, when we were. "I'm going to try to get back to sleep," Jude said, as he let go of my hand. Or get to sleep for the first time, I guessed.

"Good idea," I said, back to politely platonic.

"I'll walk you back."

He seemed wary as we navigated the quiet halls, as though our moment of connection had scared him. When he dropped me off at my room, my instinct was still to kiss him good night. I wanted to say more, I wanted to tell him I still loved him, that I'd always love him . . . But every time I tried to get the words out, my conscience caught up with me. Jude seemed happy, genuinely happy, and if I got in the way of that, I would always hate myself.

"Good night, Jude," was all I said.

"Good night, Grace." He walked away, and I shut my door softly.

drifted off, maybe even slept a few hours, but it felt like just the blink of an eye before someone was banging on my door.

I bolted upright, on guard. My first thought: *What now?* I didn't have the energy for another coup, an invasion by Prophet Joshua. I considered staying in bed, pretending not to hear it . . . but as the banging continued, I groggily pulled myself out of bed and cracked open the door.

Professor Irene Hernandez, Dawn's wife, was standing in front of me. I stared at her, shocked.

"Sorry, did I wake you?" she said, as though it wasn't early in the morning, and she wasn't the last person in the world I'd expected to see right now.

I shook my head groggily. "It's okay. I'm glad to see you're safe."

"You, too. Dawn sent me to check on you."

So Irene had heard about Mohammed's request. The concern in her voice made me think Jude was probably right about what that request meant. "Well, maybe I was safer back at home," I grumbled.

Irene nodded solemnly. "When do you have to go?"

"I have no idea. Jude said maybe Dawn could help?"

Irene hesitated, then said, "I hate to say it, but Dawn doesn't have much help to offer."

"Why not? Is she still angry at me?" Had I burned all my bridges by jumping out of that taxi?

"It's not you." She looked me square in the eye and said bluntly, "Dawn doesn't care about anyone."

"What do you mean?" I asked, thrown.

Her tone was markedly different from the last time she'd mentioned her wife. Clearly something had happened between then and now to change her outlook. "Dawn only cares about what's strategic for the resistance," Irene said, and I could hear the resentment in her voice. "You don't know her like I do. She'll hang you out to dry, if it helps her cause. It's never personal, just business." I thought of the cruel way she'd let those scientists die, and I wondered what other horrors Irene might have witnessed.

"What do I do, then?" I asked desperately. "Jude thinks Mohammed might be sending me on a suicide mission." I looked around, getting frantic. My instincts to run had been right all along—Great Spirit had been telling me I wasn't safe down here. "I need to find a way out."

"Don't. If you run, and you get found somewhere in Cappadocia, the prophets of the world will know we have a safe house here." Though her words seemed logical, they didn't quell my desire to get the heck out as quickly as possible.

"Is there anyone here who can help me?" I asked. "Do we have any allies?"

Irene shrugged. "None that will go out on a limb for someone they don't know. You saw what just happened. Jude's right, Mohammed can't afford to alienate anyone politically important, and I'm sorry to say, hon, you aren't important. The extremists might be down right now, but they're not out. The secular wing of this group held power for a while, longer than I thought they would. But sooner or later, the religious radicals are going to take over. It's inevitable."

"But they just lost," I argued. "First in the election, and then when they tried to stage a coup."

Irene clearly missed being a professor and reveled in the opportunity to give her own little lecture. "That's just it. We think we have them beat, but trust me, being in the middle's a losing proposition. Moderates aren't passionate, they're not recruiting, they're not proselytizing like the Originalists. Do you know how fast that movement is growing? And after years of being ignored, being ridiculed, now all the radicals are teaming up against us . . . in the long run we can't defeat a coalition like that. Eventually they'll all turn on one another, but until they do . . . the centrists might as well leave."

I shook my head, determined it couldn't be so inevitable. "There has to be a way to find common ground . . ."

Irene laughed a little, in that way that made me remember how naïve I was. "You mean, convince everyone to believe in Great Spirit? That's your religion, right? I think we tried that one already."

"Yeah, it's my religion," I said, not wanting to defend my ideology to yet another mocking nonbeliever. "So what?"

The woman shrugged. "So, nothing. None of my business. It's *all* bullshit as far as I'm concerned."

"All religion?" I asked her. Though it was the kind of statement that instinctively made me cringe, at this point I could at least discuss ideas that felt blasphemous.

"Sure," she continued, still in lecture mode. "The Revelations were just a natural outgrowth of religion in general. I try to stay impartial, as a professor studying religion, but the larger trends are obvious. Every society has some kind of worldview you have to buy into in order to join."

"Not secular ones," I pointed out, but she shook her head.

"Even if it's 'democracy,' or 'communism,' or a flag—we have plenty of secular 'gods.' And every society's gods serve a purpose. Religion, a common worldview, that's the glue that holds us all together, keeps us moral, keeps us acting in ways that help the greater good."

"Those sound like good things."

"Of course they are. Doesn't make God real."

"It doesn't mean He isn't," I fought back.

"True. But ultimately, that isn't what matters." She seemed to enjoy getting on her soapbox. "The question is, can we survive without one? Are human beings mature enough to make our own decisions? Or do we need a god to control us? Because, historically, if you invent a fictional deity that's watching over you, telling you what to do, then your society functions better than one that's godless. Gods give us rules, laws. That's why we have them in the first place, because the societies who invented them were the ones that survived to give birth to us. God's always been the fictional thing keeping us in line." She eyed me with a smirk. "Where do you think the inventors of that nano-tech got their inspiration?"

"You say 'fictional,'" I said, getting more and more frustrated, "but you haven't explained why all that can't be true and Great Spirit can't be real."

"Because it's just too easy. That there's some all-powerful being ready to help us out? Isn't that exactly the fiction we'd make up, to reassure ourselves?"

Her words gave me a moment of pause. But then I thought of all the times I'd felt guided by Great Spirit. The times I'd despaired, when things seemed hopeless, and I prayed and felt a little less alone. And I felt sad for this woman, who'd never felt that kind of comfort. "I guess we'll never know for sure," is all I said. Looking for a subject change, I added, "If Dawn can't help me, why are you here?"

Irene's expression grew grave as she pulled something from her pocket. "I do have one gift from Dawn, in case you're captured. Cyanide. Better than torture." She handed me a small vial, and my insides convulsed with dread.

I pocketed the vial. "Safer for everyone," I reassured her, throat dry. Though I knew Dawn had given it to me as a protection, it still felt ominous. And I wasn't sure, if the time came, that I'd be brave enough to use it.

As Irene left, I realized just how much I needed Great Spirit's guidance right now. Irene had warned me, Jude had warned me, about the dangers of leaving this place, but I kept coming back to one thought: *You aren't safe here.* I knew the threats that lurked in the world aboveground, but staring at that vial of cyanide, deep down I felt it—*the risks of staying outweigh the risks of leaving.* And the more I meditated on it, the more I felt Great Spirit wanted me to get out of here.

But just as I was planning my path out, Layla appeared at my door. She was back to her old, standoffish self—or at least, she was faking it well enough to avoid talking about her recent trauma with her least favorite person in the world. Her voice was even, robbed of any emotion. "My father would like to speak to you."

15

Don't we need more time to prepare?" I asked, hoping to delay the inevitable.

"As you said, your prophet could notify the others at any moment. My father says you must go now." My own words, coming back to bite me.

"What will I be doing?"

She remained impassive. "My father will explain."

I had no desire to die just yet, but I couldn't see any way out of this. The halls were starting to fill with early risers as we walked to Mohammed's office; no one we passed said a word, but I could feel their eyes inspecting me, judging me, pitying me.

As we entered, Mohammed was already waiting. "Grace!" he called out, as Layla left us alone. "I am grateful to Allah for bringing you to us."

"No problem," I said sardonically.

"Do you have any proof that you are a member of Prophet Joshua's organization?"

I remembered the little square card—and then kicked myself for bringing it along. Without it, I might be off the hook. I could always lie and pretend I'd left it behind . . . but I remembered how my gut had told me to grab it—clearly Great Spirit knew I might need it for a moment just like this. Feeling like it must be important, part of Great Spirit's master plan, I reluctantly pulled it out, and Mohammed examined it, curious. "This should work."

"For what?" I asked hesitantly.

"We need to learn the identity of one person. We think someone with your credentials can help."

"Why? What's so special about this person?" I asked.

"This person can lead us to a device, which will remove the machines that live inside your brain."

"The nanotech, you mean?" I asked, hope rising.

"Yes. There is one person who can give us the key to turn them off."

Turn them off. It sounded too good to be true.

Mohammed continued, "This key is something you breathe in, a gas, which acts as a kind of fail-safe. It will signal the computers to destroy themselves."

My breath caught in my throat. If the nanotech in our brains died, everyone would be saved, and no one else would have to die. "Are you sure this gas exists?"

"Yes. But the last time we tried to steal the key, we failed, and the prophets destroyed all paper and electronic record of it. Meaning the only copies of the key are held within the minds of a few trusted individuals. Memorized."

"And we're looking for one of those people," I put together.

"We have a spy working in the prophets' office in Israel-Palestine. He witnessed this man being called once before, and he even knows the name for the event: Protocol 44. But because our spy was not anticipating it, he was not quick enough to trace the call. If we re-create the conditions that led to the last Protocol 44, we are certain we can trigger another one."

"So my job is to convince the prophets' office to call this one guy?" I asked. I knew from experience it would probably be ten thousand times more difficult than it sounded.

"That's correct. Once we have this man's identity, we can capture him and find out what he knows." I didn't ask how they planned to find out—I didn't want to think about any more terrible things I might be responsible for.

"But I told you, my cover is blown," I said. "Joshua knows I'm working with you. No office will trust me until they check with him, and when they do, they'll arrest me and kill me. Whatever your plan is, it's not going to work."

"A couple months ago—with your help, I have heard—we were able to hack into Prophet Joshua's computer system. We will change your status in the system. If we succeed, no one will know you have betrayed the American prophet unless they talk to Joshua directly."

I hesitated, thinking of what Jude had told me. "And if they do?"

Mohammed paused, looking at me with compassion. "Then you will likely not return." There it was, as Jude had predicted. Mohammed was okay with the risk that I could be captured, or even killed.

"What if I *want* to make it back?" I asked. "What if I want to survive?"

He nodded, sympathetic. "Then it is your choice not to help us. And you are young, I understand why you would not want to take that risk. But your sacrifice would mean humanity's freedom."

Why on earth would I agree to this? I didn't know this man, had no reason to trust him. And in fact, every cell in my body was telling me not to trust him, not to trust any of these people I'd just seen engaging in a kind of civil war. But I had to admit, I'd never trusted Dawn either, and I'd been fighting on her behalf for six months. Was helping Mohammed now really any different?

I thought of Jude, of how grateful I was to be fighting along-side him. Of my father, still trapped in a prison of his own certainty. Of how much bigger all this was than my one little life. And when I thought of the prophets in Israel-Palestine, a sense of calm came over me. It felt like a message from Great Spirit, that I was supposed to go there. That I was supposed to perform this mission, get to those prophets, get out of this claustrophobic cave.

So I was able to push aside my fears and my prejudices and nod. "I'll do it," I said, my voice shaking only slightly. I was desperately afraid, but I also had hope that I was finally back on the path that Great Spirit was laying out for me.

Mohammed smiled. "Thank you. If the worst should happen, your sacrifice will not be forgotten down here."

"You'll keep Jude safe?" I asked him. "If I die."

Mohammed nodded with a chuckle. "Of course. My daughter

would never forgive me if I didn't." Apparently he approved of Jude and Layla's relationship more than they thought. "Layla will accompany you on your journey," he continued. "There are very few people that I know I can trust, and she is familiar with your destination."

Great. The last person I'd probably ever speak to would be Jude's new girlfriend.

I had the rest of the day to say my goodbyes—to Irene, and then to Jude. I hugged him for a long time, not caring what Layla thought. "I'm going to miss you," I said. I'd lost him so many times—I couldn't bear to imagine that this might be goodbye for good.

Jude wouldn't even humor the thought. "I'll see you soon," he insisted. His words gave me a boost of confidence. When Jude believed in me, I always felt like I could do anything.

I hoped that he was right.

That evening, I emerged into the humid country air—it was fresher than I remembered air could smell, after weeks in that cave, and I inhaled deeply, grateful for a moment of peace.

Layla appeared next to me, clucking like a protective older sister. "Do you have your passport?" I showed her my fake Turkish passport, and she nodded. "Good. Our bus for Israel-Palestine leaves in an hour." Amid all the fear, a bit of excitement surged through me. Whatever awaited us on the road ahead, I was ready.

BOOK
FIVE

1

M ost of you know the history of Israel-Palestine, but
for those who might not, a quick primer.

For thousands of years before the Revelations, various religious and ethnic groups had been fighting over the land southeast
of the Mediterranean Sea, a fight particularly bitter because of
the area's importance to three of the old religions—Islam, Juda-
ism, and Christianity. But since the Revelations, those feuds had
become irrelevant. Sure, some of the old prejudices remained,
as they did everywhere, but discourse became more civil, and
populations that had once been entirely separate began to work
together as they never had before. The nation was heralded as
the greatest success of the post-Revelation age. Great Spirit had
finally ended a conflict that most people thought would last a
few more millennia.

I had always dreamed of going there. In such a religious era,
the holy sites that littered the land were a massive tourist attrac-

tion. And, in fact, the bus we took from Ankara into Syria was packed with ardent worshippers of Great Spirit, eager to make their pilgrimage to the Holy Land.

"We'll blend in," Layla told me, and indeed, the swarms of people did feel like a welcome disguise, a cloak to wear over my anxieties until we reached our destination.

The two of us rode in silence for a few hours, before our silence began to feel uncomfortable. I'd already asked if Layla was okay enough times that it was clear I needed to drop that particular topic. Though I had little else I wanted to say to her, I started to feel rude staring at the back of the seat in front of me, avoiding eye contact. So I tried to be civil, while also being a little nosy. "How did you and Jude meet?"

She seemed pleasantly surprised by my question. "He never told you?" I shook my head. "About six months ago, he asked for help leaving the United States, from the woman who leads the Washington, D.C., group . . ."

"Dawn."

"Yes, Dawn. He wanted to go to Nova Scotia." He wanted to go *with me*. I wondered if she knew that part of the story. The way she watched me out of the corner of her eye suggested she might. "When he could not go there, Dawn suggested he come here. She had heard rumors of unrest . . . the unrest you have now seen. So he came to Turkey, and we met here."

Essentially, they had only met because of me.

Perhaps she saw the sadness on my face, because her voice softened, almost like an apology. "He was very unhappy when I first met him, to be away from you. I know he cares about you very much."

I thought back on my late-night chat with Jude, the moment we'd shared, and I suddenly felt guilty. Here she was being so sympathetic toward me, and I wasn't sure I'd shown her the same consideration. "I'm sure he does," I said carefully.

She admitted, "That is why I tried to convince my father to choose someone else for this mission. I did not want you to be in danger."

I was surprised. "For Jude."

"I do not know you very much, this is true, but Jude still loves you. If something happens to you, he will be so sad. I worried that if he believed you were in danger, he might do something stupid, to try to help."

"Well, he's got a few hours still till we get to Jerusalem," I said flippantly.

"You want him to put himself in danger trying to save you?" she asked scornfully.

"No . . ." I said, realizing my mistake.

"He has already risked his life for you many times."

"I know . . ." I wish I knew how to convey to her how stupid I felt.

Her voice was breathlessly irate as she listed off my sins. "You should have stayed in that taxi in New York, but you did not. You did not listen to any of the people who wanted to help you. You should be dead right now, but Jude flew all the way to Washington to find you, putting himself in great danger."

Her indignation made me defensive. "So you *are* jealous," I shot back. "That he'd do all that for me." I hated the way she judged me, the way she acted superior to me. Or . . . maybe just the way she reminded me of my own faults.

"I am not jealous," she said. "Why would I be jealous? I have Jude." She didn't say it to hurt me, but it hurt anyway.

"Well, I'll be out of your way soon enough," I said, hoping to end the conversation.

And indeed, we slipped into a tentative silence again for a few more miles. Until she finally said, "I will try to help you. Even if you do not deserve it."

I resisted the urge to say something nasty back—I knew my anger wasn't at her, really. "I appreciate that," I managed to squeak out.

As she turned to look out the window, I watched her a moment longer. Though her mere existence drove me nuts, right now she was all I had. I hoped I could trust her when I needed to.

In Damascus, we made a pit stop for food, and the clocks on the wall implied that this was supposed to be breakfast. A friendly Syrian family at the table next to us wanted to know where we were going, and I glanced at Layla, hoping she'd know what our cover story was supposed to be. But she stared resolutely at her plate, so I answered with a big smile: "Israel-Palestine."

The kids, probably eight and ten, who'd known nothing but the Revelation age, squealed with excitement. Their mother explained, "They think Israel-Palestine is the best country in the world."

"Do you?" I asked, then felt stupid, remembering the history of this region, the violent conflicts that this woman would have remembered from her youth.

But she smiled, undisturbed. "Syria is the best country in the world."

I also remembered the stories of war in Syria, waged by religious extremists and a callous government. Indeed, on our bus ride from Turkey I'd seen plenty of bombed-out buildings that still hadn't been rebuilt—remnants of that war, over for more than a decade now. But looking around this bustling square in Damascus, you never would have known the pain this city had once suffered. The peace brought by the Revelations was swift and all encompassing.

I talked to this family awhile longer, bonding over our mutual love of Great Spirit, how we believed that Great Spirit had a plan for all of us (though I didn't mention that His plan for me at the moment seemed to involve a suicide mission). Layla watched with a cynical smile at first, and then that smile transformed into something more genuine. Perhaps she was moved by my ease at talking to these strangers? I'd never know.

When we got back on the bus, she turned a kind eye toward me, suddenly inquisitive. "Why *did* you stay behind in New York?" she asked. "Jude said it was something about your mother?"

I reluctantly explained what had happened during my mission in the hospital. "I thought maybe there was a chance my mother was still alive."

Layla considered this. "I understand why you would search for her."

I shook my head, embarrassed. "I think maybe I was wrong. I found out why she was Punished, and it seemed real, it seemed true."

"But you saw her," Layla argued, and a small bit of hope resurged.

I tried my best to quell it. "Even if she is alive, I'll never find her. I tried, but all my leads went nowhere."

"I think if she is out there, you will find her someday," Layla said, the confidence in her voice reassuring, though I was pretty sure she was just trying to be nice.

Our bus rolled into Jerusalem in the afternoon, depositing us a few blocks from the gates of the Old City. I paused to take in the view: the magnificent stone structures, built thousands of years ago. Coming here had been a bucket list dream of mine for years. It seemed I'd get to see it just in time to kick the bucket.

I looked around—this was my last chance. Did I dare make a run for it? But thinking about the plan calmed me. *Go to the prophets*, my inner voice told me. Stay on the path Great Spirit was laying out for me, that's what I knew I needed to do.

"Are you ready?" Layla asked, handing me a small, shriveled fungus: what the hippies of my grandparents' generation would have called a "magic mushroom." I took it from her, put it in my mouth, and started chewing. The mission had begun.

During the Revelations, prophets around the world had forbidden the production and sale of many drugs, for reasons that—I knew now—were quite logical. By changing brain chemistry, drugs interfered with the way the nanotechnology in our brains worked. Because of the Prohibitions against them, I'd never seen a human being on hallucinogens, and I'd certainly never gotten to try any myself—or wanted to, for that matter.

But here I was, nervously swallowing and waiting to see the effects as Layla took my arm to guide me. "This way." It took us about thirty minutes winding through the labyrinth of souvenir stalls, finally emerging at the Western Wall, with the beautiful golden Dome of the Rock right next to it. One of the most holy sites in all the world, according to the old religions. This was one of the places mankind had fought over in the dark ages before the Revelations, and now, it was the site of Israel-Palestine's joint prophetship—one former rabbi and one former imam, ruling together, passing commandments over their joint territory. Their office was small because it had to be squeezed in between this assortment of holy relics, but it was beautiful, built of light-colored Jerusalem stone and adorned with marble eight-pointed stars.

"What do I do now?" I asked, fear bubbling up inside me. I was pretty sure the drugs hadn't kicked in yet, but I wasn't sure what I should be waiting for exactly.

"Go inside. I will be here in case you need anything." And to make sure I didn't bolt, I suspected.

Determined to get through this alive, I pushed through the crowds of the devoted to step up to the doors of Prophet Itai and Prophet Hamza, showing the guard my ID card. Luckily, I'd been to Walden Manor enough times to feel comfortable navigating this part of the plan. "I'm here on behalf of the American prophet, Joshua." The guard squinted at the green square, and after consulting with a second guard, he waved me by.

The entryway was beautifully adorned with a combination of Jewish and Muslim iconography: paintings and architecture that evoked the history of both religions. Mosaic tiles lined the walls, forming scenes that stretched back centuries: images from the Torah and the Quran, and more recent depictions of the Revelations.

I looked carefully at everyone I passed, a staff evenly split among the country's ethnicities. I knew that someone in here was an agent working for Mohammed, but I had no idea who it might be. Someone with the ability to monitor the phones in this place, that was all I could say for sure. But Mohammed had specifically chosen not to tell me who our man on the inside was, for fear that I might give away his cover under torture, if I was caught.

Before I could get very far inside, I was intercepted by a harried woman, who spoke to me in very clear English: "You are American? Can I help you?"

"I'm here on behalf of Prophet Joshua. I have a message from him for your prophets. It's urgent."

She glanced at the green card, and the grave expression I was putting on, and walked away at a fast clip. "Follow me."

She took me immediately into an empty office. "Wait here, I'll be right back."

And that's when the shrooms kicked in.

3

should tell you, while I've done my best to correctly re-
count everything that follows, my memories while on drugs
are obviously a little compromised.

What I do remember is feeling like I was melting into my
chair. There was no barrier between me and the room around
me. It was peaceful—it reminded me of the Moment. Which
made sense—Dr. Marko had explained that during the Moment
we all experienced temporal lobe epilepsy, which created the
spiritual experience of being connected with everything. But
this trip on shrooms was so much more intense, and because of
the high-stakes circumstances, the drug also served to amplify
my fear. I could feel myself vacillating between panic and bliss
from moment to moment.

I tried to hold myself together as my escort returned with a
glass of water. "Our prophets apologize for the wait. They both
want to be here to hear this urgent news, so they're finishing
their current appointments as quickly as possible . . ."

"Thank you," I said, trying to keep my cool. I took the glass of water, took a sip. If it had any uppers or downers, I couldn't feel them over the craziness that was happening in my head.

Finally, two men entered: Prophets Itai and Hamza. Before the Revelations, I might have been able to tell them apart by their dress, but as they stood before me in suits and ties, I struggled to tell one jovial salt-and-pepper prophet from the other. There was a lot of "we apologize" and "praise Great Spirit," before they finally broached the question: "What message does Joshua have for us?"

Mohammed had given me a fake message to tell them, in case I needed it, but in my drugged-up haze, I couldn't remember it. I couldn't remember much of anything. Looking into their faces, I could almost see halos above their heads; I felt like these two people were the best creations in the whole world, and I wanted to tell them everything—everything about the resistance, every secret I held dear. As I sat in silence, trying to pick which words to say to express what I was feeling, the prophet duo stared at me, trying to figure out what was happening. "Are you okay?" Prophet Itai finally asked.

And then they exchanged looks—something was happening. I pulled a mirror from my pocket and saw the insane way my face was morphing, melting like a Dali painting. Though maybe the intensity of what I saw was just a hallucination, I knew some piece of it must be real—in fact, that was the whole plan. The only way to stop my face from spinning out of control was by removing the nanotech in my brain altogether. And everything relied on the hope that these prophets were loyal enough to Joshua that they would call the one person who knew how to remove my nanotech, in order to avoid starting some kind of international incident. We knew that these prophets had made that call once before, when an agent from Russia had suffered similar symptoms. In fact, they might even assume that my symptoms were caused by the same, still unexplained source.

And once our spy in this office traced their call, and figured out which person the prophets were contacting, the resistance would know whom to target.

"What's happening to me?" I asked, feigning panic and ignorance.

"Have you experienced anything like this before?" Prophet Hamza ventured. His suspicious voice made me think that, on drugs, I might not be the greatest actress in the world.

I snapped back, defensive, "Of course not!" I looked down at the glass of water in my hand. "Did someone in your office poison me?"

They knew exactly what I meant, and they talked over each other, saying no, of course not, they would never do that.

"I don't believe you!" I cried.

They looked at each other, both a little accusatory. I saw them silently asking—*Did you? Did* you? Both denying it.

Mohammed had hammered this next part home, so in my delirium I repeated it over and over. "Help me!" I kept saying. "Something's wrong, help me!"

But instead of picking up the phone and calling for help, they eyed me suspiciously. "What did you say your name was?" Prophet Hamza asked.

"You're suspicious of me?" I spat back, trying to turn

around the accusation. "You poisoned me, and now you're accusing me?"

They didn't back down. "If you're really working with Prophet Joshua, tell us your name."

I was backed into a corner. "Grace. Grace Luther." I showed them the green ID card to prove my identity.

Prophet Itai quickly typed something into his computer, and a file came up. He turned the screen toward Hamza, and Hamza nodded—indeed, my face matched the image on the screen. The resistance's hack had been well timed—my record on the computer was spotless.

Hamza pushed a button to call someone, speaking in his most measured voice. I didn't understand the Arabic, but I did catch one English phrase: *Protocol 44.*

With any luck, I'd just accomplished my mission. A spy somewhere in the prophets' office was tracing the call now. I wondered where in the world that call might be headed to . . . How long it would take the resistance to kidnap the secret knower, and interrogate them.

And I wondered how the heck I was going to get out of here. Considering I had no idea how to do that, I was less afraid than I should have been, and significantly more interested in the thick, grainy texture of the carpet on the floor.

Prophet Hamza was less focused on carpet fibers. "Come with us, we will help you," he said reluctantly. I was thrilled as I stood to follow these two prophets. They must be taking me to remove the nanotech. The plan was working perfectly.

But as we exited our meeting room, I saw a familiar face

standing at the other end of the hallway. I stared, trying to figure out how I knew her, but by the time I'd placed her, she'd placed me. It was Aviva, that sorority girl from NYU whose files I'd stolen. I finally recognized her unplaceable accent—she was Israeli-Palestinian, reporting to these exact prophets. Her eyes narrowed as she strode toward us. "What is *she* doing here?"

looked around—was there any way I could escape? I knew how many guards were in this building, and with a face going crazy like mine, there was no way I looked trustworthy enough to make it past that gauntlet.

Aviva ranted, ratting me out. "This is the girl who stole my research on that professor!"

The prophets turned on me. On a less powerful hallucinogen, I might have found a snappier comeback, an explanation that made sense. But at that moment, I was flummoxed. "Nuh-uh," was all I could think to say.

"We should notify the Americans," Hamza began, but Itai interrupted him.

"Not yet. We need more information."

"I'm not telling you anything until you fix whatever you've done to me!" I cried, thinking maybe I could sway them with anger, trying to return to my real goal. Heads were turning—maybe if I created a scene, people nearby would help me. At least, I was convinced they would all be on my side—right now a lot of them had halos, too.

"I do not believe we have done anything to you," Itai said sternly.

"Then he did!" I pointed at Prophet Hamza, hoping to turn them against each other. I knew the divisions that existed within the rebels. Perhaps they still existed between these two prophets, too.

But Hamza bore down on me, indifferent to my attempts to sway him. "Whatever has been done, you did to yourself. We both know this."

I held my ground. "You want to bother Prophet Joshua, go ahead. But the way I see it, I came here on a diplomatic mission, and I was poisoned the moment I stepped through those doors. Now, you find some way to solve this, or I walk right back out there and I tell Joshua everything that's going on here." While this is what I remember saying, I'm pretty sure Grace on drugs was far less eloquent. And she definitely didn't convince anyone.

For a moment I was convinced I was hallucinating this whole event. Maybe the drugs had invented these two prophets, or Aviva, or both. Maybe I was still back in the cave in Turkey, or New York, or Tutelo, or the womb even. But the more I looked at everyone, trying to gauge their realness, the more suspicious and angry they became. My pleasant high was turning paranoid.

I was running out of options, and thinking through any kind of plan required all my focus—but my thoughts were so jumbled. I could keep talking or make a run for it. But then maybe they'd restrain me, and I wouldn't be able to get to the cyanide capsule that remained in my pocket.

Irene's cyanide—that was pretty much all I had left. Could I do it? Could I really end my life, right here right now? In the abstract, sure, it had been simple enough. I wanted to protect Jude, Dawn, Irene, Mohammed, Dr. Marko, Father Dennehy, and all the other people who were working toward a goal I thought was noble—whether I approved of their methods or not. I'd gladly give up Layla in self-preservation, if you asked my very worst self. But everyone else, including Jude, would fall if I was weak.

I reached inside my pocket. I could feel the cyanide pill there; I could take it at any moment. I *should* take it, this was the time to take it. But I was going to have to do it quickly, or these two prophets would stop me.

As I grasped the pill, I silently prayed—something I used to do all the time, but had fallen out of the habit. If there was ever a moment I needed guidance, this was it. *Great Spirit*, I thought, *please help me. Please get me out of this. Please help me save Jude, please help me save everyone.*

And then, as clear as day, I heard a response. *Tell them the truth.* The voice was at once deep and melodic, and light and ethereal, as though spoken by a chorus of all shapes and sizes. The voice was so loud, instinctively I turned my head—but no one had entered the room. It spoke again, *Tell them the truth. You can trust them.*

Was this just the drugs talking? I had a feeling it was the drugs. But it felt familiar—it felt like the voice I'd been hearing in the back of my mind forever, the voice that had been growing louder and stronger as I grew more confident in it. The voice that had told me to save Dr. Marko, the voice that had told me to look for my mother, the voice that had told me to leave the rebel compound and come here. If I could indeed talk to Great Spirit, maybe all it took was a little hallucinogenic push to give me the ability to listen.

Or . . . maybe I was just being foolish. I reminded myself, I was supposed to take the cyanide. If I didn't now, there would be no second chance. Should I listen to the voice?

Take the risk, it said. The risk of being tortured.

I found myself letting go of the pill as the prophets moved toward me. "Well, I guess she's not talking," Prophet Itai muttered, and I realized he'd been asking me questions for nearly a minute and I hadn't noticed.

"Wait," I said loudly, drawing their attention. "You're right."

All three of them were shocked at my bald admission. "About what?" Hamza finally asked.

I forged ahead; the more I spoke, the more I got a gut feeling that I was doing exactly what Great Spirit wanted me to do, whether I understood His reasoning or not, and the words poured out of me. "I'm a double agent. I'm working with the resistance." As I said it, I realized I needed to buy myself more time and quickly improvised: "But I want to be on your side."

The prophets and Aviva went silent for a moment. Had my ploy worked?

But then Prophet Hamza gestured to two armed guards, who moved to handcuff me. "Call Washington," he said to Hamza. "Let's see what Prophet Joshua has to say about this."

I was being arrested.

As the guards led me down the hall, everyone stared at me, horrified. Decorations on the walls that had once seemed beautiful now seemed menacing. My darkest thoughts were amplified—every terrible thing I'd ever done played on a loop behind my eyelids, and every fear seemed real, tangible, possible. Because, at this moment, they all were. I prepared myself for whatever torture I was about to face as they deposited me in a white, windowless room and handcuffed my wrists to the table. "Stay put."

I didn't let up with my protests: "I want to help you, I'm trying to help you." "Great Spirit is going to Punish you for this." "Ooh, that mosaic is pretty." The guards were not swayed.

And then I was left completely alone. Time passed, though in my shroom haze it was hard to be sure how long time was, exactly. I could hear voices outside, speaking in a language I didn't understand.

The bliss of interconnectedness couldn't mask my terror.

That voice in my head, Great Spirit or whatever it was, had reassured me that everything would be okay, but this didn't feel okay. Any moment, someone would speak with Prophet Joshua, and they'd find out the depths of my treachery, including the guard I'd killed, and these foreign prophets would return, ready to torture me. It felt like torture already, the way this high had turned sour. I needed to find a way out of here.

But I couldn't. My thoughts were dark, the darkest thoughts I'd ever had, screaming, wailing, stabbing at me. This was what I'd imagined hell must be like. I felt like I belonged in this cell. That I'd been drawn here because Great Spirit thought I deserved to be imprisoned, to suffer for my sins. Nothing would ever be okay again, that was the only thing I was sure of.

It'll be okay, that ethereal voice chimed in again. *You're in a safe place.* I tried to trust it, tried to believe that salvation was on its way. In this state, at least, it was easy to believe I was talking to something real, even if what it was saying seemed so obviously impossible.

"What do I do?" I asked the voice. I think I actually said that out loud.

You can trust these people, the voice whispered.

That seemed objectively false. These prophets were working with Joshua, weren't they? Weren't all the prophets working together, declaring one another as the true word of Great Spirit? That was what Dawn had told me, at least.

Trust them.

"I don't trust anyone," I told the voice. "You're in my head, you should know that by now. After everything that's happened, the only person I trust is myself. And maybe you, I guess, if you're Great Spirit. Are you Great Spirit?"

Listen to me, it said. *I'll show you. I'll make you feel better. I'll protect the people you love. I'll help you find your mother.*

"My mother?"

And then, it whispered an echo of a dream, two words that shook me to my core. *Follow me . . .*

"Where?" I asked breathlessly. "Where should I follow you?"

But before it could answer, I heard footsteps coming down the hall. Someone was coming for me.

I braced myself as the door swung open—it took me a moment to realize I was looking at Layla. Dressed like the guards and holding a tray of food. Was she working with these prophets? Was she an agent for their side? Her smirk seemed to confirm my theory.

I tensed as she approached. "What are you doing here?"

She glared, placing the food in front of me as she whispered, "Aren't you hungry?"

"You're working for them?" I whispered back, incredulous.

She put her finger to her lips, annoyed. "Be quiet."

And then she pulled a key from her pocket to unlock my cuffs. My mistrust had been misplaced. She'd come here to rescue me, almost certainly risking capture herself.

"We don't have much time."

Indeed we didn't. Before she could unlock my cuffs, one of the guards entered the room. "Who are you?" he asked her.

She hid her fear, calmly gesturing to the tray. "I was asked to bring food."

The guard inspected the tray. "You're new?"

Layla nodded. "First day." She was a good actress, I was impressed.

"Come with me," he said, gruffly. With a nervous smile, she left the room, surreptitiously pocketing the key.

The only rescue party that was coming for me had just failed, and now Layla was in trouble, too. Would she be able to talk her way out of this? She seemed plenty smart and capable, but this was the belly of the beast—escaping from the hands of the prophets wouldn't be easy. I wondered how long it would be until she was inside this cell with me. As my mind swirled with fears and worst-case scenarios, I began to despair. There was no way out of this.

I thought about what that voice in my head had just said. *Trust them.* What did that mean? A thought occurred to me . . . what if it'd meant I was supposed to trust *Layla*? Had the voice predicted what was about to happen? I'd questioned her, because I was suspicious of her, and that had alerted the guard that someone was in my cell. If I'd listened to the voice and trusted her, might our silence have given us the time to escape? It seemed like a stretch, but hey, everything's a stretch once you start hearing voices.

I listened again. Did it have any new wisdom to impart? *You're safe here.*

I tried to trust it. *Safe.* My mind still spun, trying to figure out what was real and what was imagined. But the more the voice spoke, the more I began to feel *safe* again, the more it brought me out of the dark place the drugs had taken me to. And given how little I could do here in this cell, I was happy to take a little hope, wherever it came from.

After what felt like an interminable number of hours, I heard the door open again: it was Prophets Itai and Hamza this time, circling me with skeptical eyes. A guard joined them, unlocking my cuffs.

"You're free to go," Itai said gruffly.

"I am?" I tried not to appear too confused—this could be a trick, an interrogation tactic. They'd asked me no questions. It didn't make any sense.

"Someone likes you in America, after all," Hamza grumbled.

I looked down at my free hands. *You are safe.* Apparently I was. But for some reason, I felt *less* safe as they walked me outside. My gut wanted to walk back in, stay in that cell until I knew better what was happening.

But here I was on the outside, left all alone near the Western Wall.

"Now what?" I asked the voice.

For once, it seemed not to know either.

As I took a few steps through the bustling Jerusalem crowd, I looked around desperately for a familiar face. Aside from Layla, there was no one I knew in this whole country. On this twisted drug trip, the crush of tourists now felt oppressive: they were freaking me out, their eyes wide and buggy, their expressions contorted and biting. In retrospect, these folks must have been even more weirded out by my frightening, morphing face. I saw more than one family take a look at my strange features and quickly divert their course.

Layla had set a meet point in case I got out, a train station where I could find my way back to the underground city in Turkey. But though I knew I should go there, I found my legs wouldn't move. The thought of being back in that cave sickened me. I didn't want to go back and work for Mohammed and Dawn anymore, I didn't want to sit and watch Layla and Jude falling deeper in love. My body physically rebelled against the idea. But where could I go?

As I tried to work out some kind of plan, I was startled as someone walked up behind me, hushed and intense. "I've got a car not far from here." I turned to see Layla—she was alive!

"You're okay," I whispered, relieved.

"Of course." She seemed offended that I'd even consider she might be incapable of protecting herself. "Now, come."

Though everything inside of me resisted the idea of returning to Turkey, I forced myself to follow her back through the winding alleys, where the shiny souvenirs on sale kept distracting me.

"Are you all right?" she asked, still keeping her voice low.

"Yeah, other than this drug trip." I paused, then added, genuine, "Thank you for trying to help me."

This time, she grinned. "We are on the same side, remember."

"Why did they let me go?" I wondered.

She gave me a puzzled look. "You don't know?"

"No, I don't."

My uncertainty seemed to make her nervous. "I thought you talked your way out."

"I didn't say anything," I insisted. "Itai and Hamza said 'someone likes me in America, after all.' What does that mean?"

She shrugged. "Perhaps you have a friend working for the American prophet?"

I thought of Zack—could he have somehow manipulated the Israeli-Palestinian prophets to help me? But I didn't think he'd have the access, or the power—like he'd said himself, he wasn't the kind of person who got told high-level secrets. Though all I had was his word—who knew if anything he'd told me was the truth.

"I have no idea," I said honestly, as my mind roiled with the question of who my savior might be.

Layla, however, wasn't one to find fault with a bit of good luck. "Well, we don't have time to find out. We need to move quickly."

Our car was waiting outside the walls of the Old City, and after we got in, Layla stepped on the gas, speeding us through the hilly streets. "Where are we going?" I asked, a little disoriented.

"To meet your friend Dawn," she said dispassionately.

"Dawn's in New York," I replied, confused. Also, I'd recently been told she was not my friend, by none other than her own wife.

"No, she's at the airport in Tel Aviv; she's here to meet you."

"We're going to pick her up?" I asked.

"No, I am dropping you there. They did not tell me where you are flying. But the plan worked."

It took me a moment to remember what plan she was talking about. "We found the person?"

"Yes. And soon we will have the information we need." The key, the code, that would unlock our brains from this collective cage.

As we drove, I realized that all my animosity toward Layla had disappeared—and it wasn't just some hippie-dippie drug thing. She'd been a true friend, risked her own life to try to save mine. "I'm glad you're with Jude," I told her impulsively.

"You are?" She seemed appropriately surprised.

I nodded. "He's happy. I just want him to be happy."

And then I stared out the window to watch the houses roll by. Layla watched me with amusement—to be fair, I was being pretty amusing. "Thank you," she said tentatively, and I felt a new kind of bond forming between us. Trust, maybe even friendship. After a moment, she glanced at her phone, and relief washed over her face. "They have the source in custody."

"The guy who knows the code? Already?" I asked, surprised.

"The resistance moves quickly," she said gravely. "There is not much time."

Imagining what horrors might be done to that man, because of my actions, filled me with disgust. But I pushed those thoughts out of my head with better ones, of a world where my friends would be safe, and people could be free.

As if reading my mind, Layla echoed those thoughts. "Thank you for doing what my father asked. You saved our lives. Jude's life."

"Of course," I said simply. "I love him." Later I would remember I said that and kick myself.

But Layla just smiled warmly, moved, and I was genuinely sad to be saying goodbye to her.

That said, while I'm sure I did say goodbye to her, I don't really remember it. The next thing I remember is standing in line to check my bags at Ben-Gurion-Abbas Airport. I must have been coming down off my high at this point, because I began to wonder what could possibly be in those bags. I chuckled as a cursory examination showed that Layla had packed up some drab, ugly clothes for me. One final jab at her romantic rival.

Suddenly, Dawn was next to me. "We need to talk, but not here," she murmured.

I nodded, glad for the excuse to stay silent while I waited

for my thoughts to sort themselves out again. As we moved through the line, Dawn made sure I had my passport, which I had not considered I would need until that moment but which thankfully Layla had put in my bag. When Dawn handed me my ticket, I audibly gasped. "Johannesburg?" I hissed to her.

She shot me a look—*not here.*

When we'd made it through security, Dawn pulled me to a private corner. "What's happening? Why are you here? Why are we going to South Africa?" I asked.

"Because that's where your father is," she said. I saw an anxiety on her face I never had before—something was clearly up.

"My father?" I asked, trying to make sense of why that would matter to her.

Her gaze was unflinching, startling me. "You have to convince him to help us. He's the only one who can."

"But I can't," I said, embarrassed to admit it. "I tried already. He's a true believer, like you said—there's nothing that will ever convince him that Prophet Joshua is anything other than Great Spirit come to Earth."

Dawn looked worried, but she shook herself out of it. "Your cover isn't the only one that's blown. In a few days, they'll know about all of us. This is our last chance. If you don't convince your father to help us—this is the end of the resistance."

8

I stared at Dawn, hoping this was just the intense way she talked sometimes, hypothesizing a worst-case scenario. But when I asked for more information, she wouldn't elaborate, not somewhere there was any chance of being overheard.

Her evasiveness, her cold way of relating such bad news, reminded me of what Irene had said—that we were all just pawns in her chess game. Still in my drugged-up haze, my feelings spilled right out. "Why should I trust you? I know you don't care about me."

She was dismissive. "Of course I care about you."

"I almost died, and you haven't even asked me if I'm okay."

"Grace, I asked you, like, six times if you were okay."

"You did?" I genuinely didn't remember.

"Yes. Well, maybe not six. But you kept saying that the bells would ring if you weren't okay, so I took that as a yes." Apparently I was still higher than I'd realized. And glancing at the clock on the wall, I discovered it had only been a few hours since

I'd taken those shrooms . . . my stay in that cell must've lasted mere minutes, even though it had felt like eons.

"Oh."

I saw real concern cross her face. ". . . *Is* everything okay?"

Should I tell her? I couldn't think of any reason not to. "Your wife told me some things," I said, staying vague enough to let Dawn speculate on what I might mean.

But Dawn just sighed. "She's still mad at me, I assume?"

"Mad?"

A look of real sadness crossed Dawn's face. "She wanted me to come with her to Turkey, and I said I couldn't. I had things I needed to do for the resistance that I couldn't do from there. Now she thinks all I care about is my work."

I had to admit, that explained a lot. "Was that it?" I asked, suspicious. "Nothing else happened?"

"Nothing else." Dawn hesitated, then added, offhand, "Except that I shouldn't have married her." So their relationship troubles went deeper than just squabbles over work.

"Why did you?" I asked, feeling like I'd stumbled into a sinkhole of awkwardness.

"Because she wanted to marry me, and I knew there was no one alive who would make me happier."

I furrowed my eyebrows. "That seems like a good enough reason."

"Alive, that was the key word there." Dawn took a moment to collect herself, then explained, "My first wife, Sonia, she died in the Revelations. Her family had always put a lot of guilt on her, for the way she lived her life. You know, being gay. I thought she'd moved past it, but . . . Anyway, that's why I never believed the Revelations were real. I knew Sonia was a good person, I knew she'd never done anything wrong. So I started asking questions, and I found someone who, like you, had gotten their hands on some pills. I took them to a chemist, had them analyzed and reproduced, and started my network. Eventually we linked up with a few other networks abroad, and . . . here we are."

"How do you know Sonia didn't do something bad?" I asked, thinking of my mother and Prophet Joshua. "Maybe there were things she hadn't told you."

Dawn shook her head. "I knew her. I've never known another human being like that. She was good through and through. And Irene . . . she knows, I think. That I can't . . . that no matter how much I love her, there'll always be Sonia. That everything I do, for the resistance, it's for her."

Irene's evaluation of Dawn was off then—it wasn't that Dawn was heartlessly slavish to a cause—she was hopelessly devoted to a person who wasn't Irene. For the first time, Dawn began to shade in as a person for me. She was intensely pragmatic about loss of life because the only human life she valued was already lost.

But as quickly as Dawn had opened up, she closed off again. "It doesn't matter what Irene thinks right now. If we don't act quickly, she'll be dead right along with us." I nodded, understanding her focused concern, as we moved toward our gate.

Once we got on the plane, we couldn't talk at all, so I was left to stew in my anxiety, infused with the remnants of my mushroom high. For hours, I tried to focus on the saccharinely sweet, Great Spirit–approved onboard entertainment, but I had trouble following it. I kept hallucinating other plotlines, creating imaginary sinister backstories for characters. The plane itself seemed to change shape as we flew, expanding and contracting, and I grew massively nauseated and claustrophobic.

By the time we landed in South Africa, the shrooms were finally wearing off for real. Dawn had to reexplain our entire plan to me, which she said she'd told me a few times already back in Tel Aviv, and it went something like this:

My father had already arrived at the spiritual conference in Johannesburg. The biggest draw of this conference was a worship service, held at FNB Stadium. It would be full of music and inspiration, with a sermon given by Prophet Joshua himself, as well as the prophets of other countries. Close to a hundred thousand people would be in attendance.

"That's when we have our chance," she whispered, her voice breathless. "Thanks to you, we succeeded in extracting the code from the source we captured. Now we need to enter it into a specific kind of machine—and one of those machines is hooked up to the ventilation system in FNB Stadium. It's the same system that was used during the Revelations, to install the nanotech in the first place."

I'd always wondered how all these little machines had gotten into our brains, and this made sense. On the day of the Revelations, we'd all been told to go to worship centers— clearly that made it more efficient to infect everyone, by dumping a whole boatload of bugs into the air all at once in one location. The original nanotech had been piped through those stadium vents ten years ago . . . and now, ten years later, we could use the prophets' own infrastructure against them.

"The nanotech is like a computer," Dawn explained. "The bugs you have in your brain are the hardware. But they can be updated with new software. And all those pieces of software are encoded in chemicals that you can inhale. The code you helped us get in Israel-Palestine will create a molecule you can breathe in, which will disable the nanotech in your brain completely. It's a tiny piece of malicious software that will cause it to turn off and self-destruct, just like it would when you die. A back door in case of malfunction."

I spoke slowly, trying to make sure I understood everything. "So you want to disperse this chemical, the software chemical, into a crowd of tens of thousands of random people, to disable the nanotech in their brains?"

She nodded, continuing at her usual breakneck speed. "Exactly. Once those people have the tech removed, we can tell them the truth—any guilt they feel at doubting their ingrained beliefs won't kill them. A group that large is dangerous—it doubles the potential size of our fighting force. The prophets of the world will have to deal with it somehow."

I was a little skeptical. "Won't they just kill everyone?"

Dawn was unmoved. "Assassinate a stadium full of people, at a rally where Prophet Joshua is speaking, and no one gets out alive except the prophets? How would that look?"

"Not good, I guess." Though I didn't think any of the alternatives looked great either.

Dawn, however, seemed plenty confident in her plan. "We'll cut off video feeds and cell service right beforehand, creating a ticking time bomb. Joshua can't let these people back out into the general population, or he risks a chain reaction of deaths—the freed people telling their family and friends the truth."

I thought of my father—even with the harshest of warnings, I'd only been able to resist telling him for a few months. No one can keep a secret like that very long from the ones they love. "But we don't want that either, right? Once they know the truth, we recruit them all into the resistance? Then what?"

"We ask for a truce."

Her words surprised me. "A truce? What about everyone else, the rest of the world that's still under their control? We just abandon them?" I asked.

"Not forever," Dawn promised. "But long enough to save our own skins. We ask the prophets to give us our own country. A piece of land somewhere where we can practice our own religions in peace, cut off from the rest of the world. They have their world, we have ours."

That was the grand plan? "You really think Prophet Joshua would give you that?"

"The resistance has been a thorn in his side for years. We've been able to do an enormous amount of damage relative to our size. Our back channels within his office have been whispering that he's at a breaking point; he's ready for a ceasefire. The prophets want to maintain their control, even if that means letting a few people live outside it." For a moment, I saw Dawn's concern breaking through as she admitted, "And right now, a safe haven is the only thing that can protect the resistance from total annihilation."

I thought of the country I'd just come from, Israel-Palestine—a nation created out of the ashes of World War II, intended as a haven for Jews after the Holocaust. I thought of what had happened there between then and the Revelations—the wars, the instability, the oppression. I thought of the armed coup in the bunker, a reminder of the past and a harbinger of the future. I thought of the peaceful family breakfasting in Syria, and the terror that had once enveloped their country. Voice shaking, I ventured, "Even if we do it, the plan works, we get a safe haven—how do we know it'll really stay peaceful? With all those people, all those different religions, won't we just go back to fighting each other again?"

"We've come too far for that," Dawn insisted. "After everything this world has gone through—we won't go back to fighting over petty things. How could we? We've learned how to coexist . . . for all the horror the Revelations brought, I believe they did give us that one gift."

Based on everything I'd seen in Turkey, I was pretty sure Dawn was wrong, and it was a gift we'd have to return.

But the future wasn't the problem right now. Right now, I had to focus on saving our lives. "The only person who can get to this ventilation system is my father?"

"Any of the clerics backstage could, but he's the only one we have a connection to. All he has to do is get into the right room and enter a code into a machine."

"What if I can't convince him?"

"You will," Dawn said. Insisting on optimism, I knew, because she couldn't bear to consider that everything she'd worked for might amount to nothing.

I, however, was consumed by all those negative possibilities. They seemed so much more likely than the remote possibility that this crazy plan would work. "There really isn't anyone else who can help us . . . ?" I searched through my mind, and then remembered—"What about Zack!"

I quickly related the story he'd told me, and his interest in helping our side. Dawn's face grew pitying as I talked, until she finally interrupted me to say, as gently as she could, "Jude told me all this. I looked into him already. Grace, Zack isn't on our side. He's the one who turned you in."

My heart sank so fast I could almost hear it thudding to the floor. "What?"

"He reported you to his bosses right after you left. I can show you all the correspondence if you don't believe me," she said, her voice still gentle.

I wasn't ready to simply accept that explanation. "But someone helped me. Someone got me out of prison in Israel-Palestine."

Dawn shook her head. "I don't know who helped you."

"Maybe it was Zack, then. Maybe there's something we don't know."

Dawn shrugged. "Maybe. Or maybe not. But we don't have time to find out. Right now, your *father*'s our best shot."

After a moment, I nodded. After my experience with the feuding factions in Turkey, Dawn's brusque focus was a welcome change.

Dawn handed me the code to give him, scribbled down on a slip of paper.

"My dad will help us," I said softly, trying to reassure her, and myself.

But I couldn't shake the question: What would happen if he didn't?

BOOK

SIX

Johannesburg was a bright, busy city—a beacon of post-Revelation modernity, safety, and industry. The once stark divide between the rich and the poor had narrowed since the Revelations, and people of all races mingled freely.

I was antsy as I stepped out in public, remembering stories of the old days during apartheid, when racism had been the law of the land—a time when I wouldn't have even been allowed to visit white neighborhoods. But as I walked up to my father's hotel, I felt no animosity from anyone I passed, of any race. In fact, I felt a deep sense of belonging, in this city where so many people looked like me, a belonging I hadn't even realized I was missing back at home. Though I remembered, Johannesburg's multiracial paradise had come at a cost—a new kind of legalized apartheid, against Outcasts this time. Indeed, I'd seen many Outcast encampments on my way here—even more ramshackle than the ones at home.

I waited in the lobby, unobtrusive in a corner, until I finally spotted my father strolling in. He was accompanied by a woman in her forties, a British cleric I recognized who'd begun her career as a New Age mystic. Both here for the conference, I assumed.

Since I couldn't find an easy way to signal my father without attracting attention, I followed behind them—as close as I could get without being seen. As they wove through hallways that led into bustling conference rooms, I kept my head down, terrified. Surely there would be someone here who would recognize me as Paul Luther's daughter—or worse, as Grace, the traitor.

As the elevator doors closed my father in, I watched the little light above it, blinking yellow as it passed each floor— eventually stopping on the fifteenth.

I hopped in the next elevator, hitting the button for 15. But just as the doors closed, I noticed a man in a black suit staring at me, speaking into a cell phone. My heart skipped a beat. Was that man working for Joshua, or one of the other prophets? Was I caught? I'd have to do this fast.

I arrived on the fifteenth floor just in time to see a door closing halfway down the hall. I ran to it and knocked, hoping it was the right one.

I got lucky. My father opened the door and froze, shocked to see me. "Grace?"

"I need to talk to you," I said, shutting the door behind me, knowing we didn't have time to waste with pleasantries. "Where's Samantha, is she here with you?"

"She's out sightseeing, giving me time to get ready for my speech. What are you doing here?"

"I came for the conference." For a moment, I saw his heart swell—he thought I'd finally given up on my crazy ideas and come here to support him, to cheer him on during his big sermon, to close the distance between us. And now I would have to break his heart all over again. "And no," I said carefully, "what I believe hasn't changed."

My father's face fell. "How did you get to South Africa?"

"I had some help," I evaded.

He lowered his voice. "You mean from your . . . 'friends'? Who *are* these people? Have you gone to see a psychiatrist yet?"

"No," I said, disappointed that my father still trusted me so little.

"Have you been spouting this nonsense around Prophet Joshua? His office called me with all these questions . . ."

"What kind of questions?" I asked, heart skipping a beat.

"When did I last see you, what have you been saying to me . . ."

My voice shook a little as I asked, "What did you tell them?"

A strange mix of emotions washed across my father's face. "Exactly what you told me to say. Nothing." I'd never loved my father more than in that moment. I hugged him, but he barely returned it; he was busy being full of fatherly concern, intent on questioning me about my whereabouts. "Where have you been?"

"It's a long story." I knew telling him about Turkey wouldn't win me any brownie points.

"I'm keeping this quiet for now, but after a certain point, humoring your condition won't be helpful." He was still so obstinate, so resolute.

I tried a new tack: "Are you sure that's why you lied? Are you sure there isn't some little part of you that thought I might be right? That I was in danger, and you didn't want me tortured or killed?"

He was getting frustrated. "No, Grace, I'm sorry." He certainly didn't seem conflicted.

I pushed harder. "Why not? Leave aside everything you believe about Great Spirit for a second. Everything I'm saying about the way the world works—it *could* be true, right? Hypothetically?"

He thought a moment. "I suppose, but you could say the world was . . . run by gremlins from Mars or something, and tell me a story that made sense."

"That's true," I agreed. "But if they both make sense, the only difference between my explanation and yours is that yours is the explanation you heard first. And just because you heard it first, just because you've decided it's right—that doesn't make it true."

I could see I'd touched a nerve. "Everyone else in the world believes what I believe, that must count for something."

"Plenty believe what I believe," I said. "You just don't know them. But there are lots, all over the world. And Prophet Joshua is going to kill them all—"

"Grace . . ."

"—If you don't help me."

My father was startled. "Help you?"

That wasn't the subtle way I'd intended to bring up the plan, but I forged ahead. "Let's say there was a way to prevent yourself from receiving Punishments and Forgiveness. And Great Spirit's fine with it, it's not like you're making a deal with the devil," I added in a rush. "If you did that thing, you could decide, without being afraid, if you believed me, or you believed Prophet Joshua. You wouldn't have to worry about feeling guilty and dying because you doubted Great Spirit. Right?"

My father was clearly only half following me, but he said, "Okay . . ."

"Would you be willing to do that? To yourself?"

"I don't know . . ."

I was getting riled up. "If I'm crazy, nothing will happen if you help me, right? You have nothing to lose."

But my father was barely listening to me. "I can't say what will happen, because I don't know what you're doing."

I interrupted him, determined to make him hear me. "There's a device that releases a gas. You type in a little code, and you breathe in the gas, and then all the little computers in your brain are gone. If I'm right, once that happens, you'll never be Punished or Forgiven again." I saw on his face what I thought might be a moment of consideration. A moment of understanding. I carefully suggested, "Would you be willing to do it? Just to humor me?"

"I guess," my father said warily, clearly only down for the humoring me part. "Where's this device?"

I sighed with relief. For the first time, it finally seemed like this plan was on track. "In the stadium."

My father looked at me suspiciously. "Why is it there?"

"Because it was used to infect a bunch of people with the nanotech in the first place. It's hooked up to the air ducts, to get to everyone in the stadium." The moment I'd said it, I realized I'd made a huge mistake.

"You want me to put this gas in the whole stadium?" My father was appalled.

Again, perhaps I hadn't phrased this delicately enough. After weeks in the rebels' underground city, maybe I'd forgotten how to talk to people like my father. "Maybe," I said, trying desperately to reel him back in. "I've never used the machine, I'm not totally sure how it works. But if I'm right and it's real, and you could do it to a bunch of people at once, wouldn't that be better anyway?"

"Who's giving you these ideas?" He was panicked now, pacing the room.

"The people I'm working with."

"Let me get this straight. A stranger told you to ask me to go into a room and push some buttons and unleash a gas over a stadium full of people?"

I was not making my case particularly well. "They're not strangers . . ." I tried to explain.

But my dad wasn't finished. "These same people are filling your head with blasphemous ideas, sabotaging your relationship with Prophet Joshua and the good work you can do with him . . ." I could see the fire and fear in his eyes.

"Dad . . ." I tried to interject, but it was too late. I'd lost him.

"Grace, I want you to think very carefully about what you do next." My father's voice was level, projecting authority, certainty. "I am in a position to help an enormous number of people through my influence, and I think I do a pretty good job. If you damage my reputation, I may lose that influence, and an untold number of people's lives might be hurt."

I saw it suddenly—my father's denial wasn't about spirituality; it was rooted in his own sense of self, his own importance. He would never believe me, even if every single sign pointed to the truth, because accepting the truth would mean that instead of a great man, he'd been a great fool. That all his hard work had amounted to nothing, that he'd wasted his life—no, that he'd been an agent of the very devil he'd spent his life trying to combat. That he'd devoted a decade to spreading ignorance instead of wisdom.

Realizing the futility of our conversation gutted me. My father was a lost cause. We'd never be able to connect the way we used to, we'd never get to live in the same world again. He was still my father, but he was separate from me now, maybe forever.

And my failure meant my friends were still in danger. My father had been our one shot, our one chance. I despaired, imagining what horrors Joshua might unleash on everyone I cared about. But I drew on my reserves of resilience. I had to find another way. I had to get into that stadium myself.

Which meant, I had to leave now. I hugged my father, not wanting to let him go. Worried this might be the last time I saw him. "I love you," I told him, eyes brimming with tears.

"Is this the end now?" he asked, a note of caution in his voice. "No more talking to those people, no more crazy talk about computers in my brain?"

I nodded, composing myself. "I'll keep quiet, I promise. I won't damage your reputation." It was a promise I never intended to keep—a promise I knew I probably couldn't keep.

"I have to get ready for my sermon, but please. Let me help you," he begged me.

"I will," I said, voice as bright as I could muster.

"I hope you'll come to the service. Get some inspiration." The eagerness in his voice broke my heart.

I nodded. "Wouldn't miss it."

I remembered the man in the black suit who'd seen me come up here. If he was still waiting for me, he'd be watching all the exits. I glanced out the window of my dad's room—fifteen stories down, no way I could survive that jump. I had to find a safe way out.

For now, I put on a smile. "I'll see you soon, Dad."

But as I exited my father's hotel room, the futility of making any kind of plan became even clearer. Zack was standing at the end of the hall.

"You never came to meet me," he said. He seemed hurt, almost as hurt as Jude had been about Nova Scotia.

"Yeah, I got tied up," I said warily, remembering Dawn's warnings about him.

He tensed in response to my standoffishness. "No. You never intended to see me again, did you?"

I felt bad—it was true. But it had been the right call. "Not like we would've hung out much once you got me locked up in some government prison."

Zack's face was somber. Apologetic. "There are agents stationed all through the hotel. I've been sent to bring you in."

2

He moved toward me, and I began to back away. "If you run, they'll catch you," he warned me.

I was afraid of him now, in a way I never had been before. As he closed the distance between us, I turned to bolt, but in a split second, he'd grabbed my arm, was holding me in place. "Let go of me!" I cried, but this time he didn't, and no one else was around to hear.

"I trusted you," he hissed. "I told you everything. You said you'd help me . . ."

"I didn't promise you anything," I countered. "And I was right not to, wasn't I? You turned me in."

Zack was spitting mad. "What choice did you leave me? For all I knew you were running to the prophet to tell on *me*. Maybe *you* were monitoring *me*; maybe my whole assignment was just a ruse. And then you vanished and I was screwed."

Zack's dizzying paranoia felt familiar, and after the story he'd told me about Jenna, I could see why he might not trust me.

"I'm not monitoring you," I promised, and a fear I hadn't even noticed was inside him seemed to ease. Then I remembered, "In Israel-Palestine. Did you help me?"

He seemed totally confused. "What are you talking about? I've never been to Israel-Palestine."

I couldn't help but be disappointed. "It wasn't you who called the prophets and told them to let me go?"

Zack shook his head. "No. How would I do that? I don't have any authority, especially not in some other country."

So it *hadn't* been Zack who'd arranged my release from prison. And it hadn't been Dawn, or anyone on the side of the resistance.

Could it have been Great Spirit? I *had* prayed in that cell—and my prayer, in that dire moment, had been answered. Could it have been a miracle after all?

"My offer still stands," Zack was saying. "I still think we can work together. But if you won't work with me, I don't have a choice. I have to protect myself; I have to be honest with my employers."

"Okay," I said carefully, knowing I was backed into a corner. "Let's work together. Can you get me into the conference tonight?"

He seemed suspicious, surprised by my sudden turnaround. "Why? What does the resistance want with this conference?"

I had no patience for his games. "You don't get to know why. If you really want to help me, help me." Off his hesitation, I added, "You turned me in. You don't get any more than that right now."

Zack seemed less than pleased as he eyed me warily, trying

to figure out if he could trust me. "Fine. You want me to prove myself to you *again*? I'll do it."

Don't trust him. It wasn't Zack who said it—it was that voice in my head, the one who had spoken to me in my moment of need. The one I'd assumed was a hallucination, now echoing louder than ever. I'd felt sober for some time now . . . was I wrong? Or was some mystical presence actually making itself known to me? I lived in a world where so many prophets claimed to speak to Great Spirit. Maybe I could actually communicate with a higher power, for real. Don't trust Zack, is that what Great Spirit was telling me?

My hesitation was clearly unnerving Zack. "Well? Are we going or not?"

I'd already told him half of Dawn's plan—it seemed irresponsible to cut and run now. But Great Spirit had guided me well so far. This voice had prevented me from taking a cyanide pill, it had saved my life once before. Was I walking into a trap if I followed Zack?

"We have to go now," Zack was saying. "If I don't bring you downstairs soon, they're going to come up after us."

What should I do? I thought frantically to myself. I got no additional advice from Great Spirit this time. And I couldn't think of any other good options. At the very least, if that man in the suit by the elevator had been one of Prophet Joshua's agents, I could probably use Zack's help getting out of this building.

I had to take this chance. "Okay, let's go."

I followed Zack down to the opposite end of the hall, where he swiped a room key, and we entered what looked to be an occupied but currently empty room.

"Whose room is this?" I asked.

"No idea," he said flippantly as he opened the window, which led to a fire escape. "You ready?"

I looked down the fire escape—it was a frighteningly steep descent. "Yep."

Zack hesitated before stepping out. "Don't screw me over again, okay?" He tried to sound casual, but there was a vulnerability in his eyes that seemed genuine.

I nodded. But as I slowly descended the ladder, nervously looking down at the honking cars so many stories below, I became more and more convinced that *I* was the one who was going to get screwed.

If the voice was right, I was walking right into a trap.

We moved through a massive, eagerly pious crowd, all heading into the stadium.

"Should I try to disguise myself?" I asked Zack.

"You mean with a pill? They'd never let an Outcast into this place." As little as I trusted Zack at this moment, I had to admit, he was probably right.

As we passed a cluster of security guards, I heard, "Zack? Grace?"

I turned to see Macy heading toward us, jaw hanging open. "Macy!" I angled my head away from the guards as best I could, giving her a bright, surprised smile.

As she approached, she wrinkled her eyebrows in confusion. "You guys didn't tell me you were coming! What are you doing in South Africa?"

"Work," Zack said quickly, looking at me.

"Helping out my dad," I said at the same time.

Macy narrowed her eyes at me. "Your dad said you weren't

coming. He asked *me* to help him with stuff." She glanced back and forth between us, clearly seeing how nervous we were. "Oh, heck, you're dating, aren't you? You've been secretly dating this whole time, I *knew* it!"

From the corner of my eye, I saw Zack's cheeks turn red. "I'm here for work, I can't stop and talk," Zack said, quickly walking off.

Macy now looked at me, expectant. "Uh, I've gotta go help him with his . . . work thing," I said, quickly moving off after him.

Macy called after us, "Best man *and* maid of honor at the wedding, I'm calling it now!"

I rejoined Zack, keeping my head down as we moved toward security. "Well, that wasn't awkward at all."

Zack seemed almost as embarrassed as I was. "Tell your dad to stop inviting my sister to things." He gently nudged me toward an unmanned door. "This way."

He scanned his badge, and the door opened immediately. "That was easy," I whispered.

But then we walked into a room full of guards. I tried not to panic, gave a polite smile. Zack nodded to them—he clearly knew at least one or two—and then pulled me toward a stairwell. Having him here for cover seemed to be working out well so far.

"You're going to have to direct us from here," he said.

Dawn had told me where the maintenance room was—I'd needed that information to pass it to my father. Just a few flights of stairs and a long corridor remained . . . our objective was within reach! But as I climbed the stairs, the voice in my head returned: *Run.*

Great Spirit had led me well so far. Did I really want to ignore His advice now that we were so close? Now when it mattered more than ever?

I turned and looked at Zack, and he gestured for me to move forward, harried. "We need to move," he whispered.

If he was, like I suspected, still playing me, I needed to ditch him now that I was inside. "I've got it from here," I told him.

Zack was flummoxed. "Grace, don't be stupid. There are a million other doors I may need to open."

"I've got it," I insisted, a little rudely.

Clearly not wanting to argue with me anymore, he threw up his hands. "Fine, I'll be down here when you realize you need my help."

That had gone better than I expected. But as I continued up the stairs, I heard that voice again. *Run.*

Something was still wrong. And the fact that I didn't know what filled me with unease. *Run!* The voice was getting more insistent. I tried to ignore it and looked down at Zack—he was almost out of sight now.

The voice wanted me to run, so I ran. Up one flight, and then another. But when I got to the sixth floor, I reached another locked door. Zack had been right; I needed his card to swipe myself through. I kicked myself. What was I supposed to do now? *Run away!* the voice screamed at me. Why, why was it so insistent? What did I need to be afraid of?

I peered through the glass window in the door. I couldn't see anyone at all on the floor, no one I could signal to let me in.

I was ready to give up, go back and ask Zack for help again . . . but then I heard the voices. Two women. Though

I couldn't figure out where they were, their voices must have been coming from somewhere on the other side of that door: they were so loud it sounded like they were right next to me, screaming in my ear.

"Is she here yet?" one asked.

"The prophet will be so happy," said the other. "He's been dying to torture Grace Luther." Their tinny laughter echoed, and I felt sick.

The voice in my head had been right all along. This was a trap. Zack had led me straight to the people who were going to arrest me, and I'd been stupid enough to follow.

I finally came to my senses and ran. Back down the stairs, past a startled Zack. "Where are you going?" he called after me, but I ignored him. *Backstabber.*

I was out the stairwell door, out of the building, but I kept running. The voice in my head kept urging me on. *Run!*

I was close to ten blocks away before I finally stopped to catch my breath. *Run!* it kept insisting.

But I didn't, because Dawn pulled up in a car next to me. "What the hell are you doing?" she asked me.

"I got into the stadium . . ." I panted, out of breath. "My dad wouldn't help, but Zack did . . . he scanned a key card."

Dawn looked relieved. "So he *is* on our side? Why did you leave?"

And then the voice in my head piped up again. *Don't trust her.*

4

Dawn? I couldn't trust *Dawn*? I'd always been suspicious of her, true, but she'd recently seemed like the best option I had, outside of Jude.

Don't trust her, the voice in my head repeated, louder. I didn't have time to argue with it, so I listened. I began to run, and Dawn's car followed me.

"Grace? What's going on?" Dawn called out the window at me.

But I kept running. Block after block, turning unexpected corners, pushing through the pain that was throbbing deep in my chest, my lungs aching to stop. I was getting away. Until—a figure cut in front of me, blocking my escape.

I cried out, stopping myself before I ran headlong into Zack—in my panic evading Dawn I'd ended up right next to FNB Stadium again.

He grabbed me by my shoulders. "Where are you going?"

"Away from you!" I cried, struggling to find a way past him.

Get away! the voice was screaming.

He was scared, angry. "Away from *me*? What are you talking about?"

Dawn ran up next to us. "What the hell is going on?"

Zack's attention was diverted for a moment, and I took that opportunity to bolt—only to have Dawn grab my arm this time. Her grip was surprisingly strong. "Grace, are you okay?"

"I know what you're up to," I said, trying to cover. "I know you're working against me. Both of you."

Zack and Dawn exchanged a look. Zack didn't know who Dawn was, but Dawn had clearly figured out who he was, and I saw her make a decision. "Get her in my car. Now."

Zack squinted at her. "I'm sorry, who are you?"

As he hesitated, I begged him, "You can't trust her."

Dawn moved closer to Zack and said, hushed, "I'm with the resistance. I'm the person you've been trying to get in touch with. If you want to help us, get her in the car. There's something wrong with her, and I think I know how to fix it."

Zack was convinced enough by that to take me by the shoulders again and push me toward the car.

"There's nothing wrong with me!" I cried, trying to attract a scene. "Zack! Let me go!" A few passersby gave us strange looks, but no one would do anything about it, I knew—we all looked pious, so no one would suspect any of us of criminal activity.

Run! Get away! But I couldn't obey the voice this time. There was nothing I could do except allow Zack to force me into Dawn's car and glare defiantly as the two of them interrogated me.

"Now, Grace," Dawn said, "why do you think I'm working against you?"

Don't tell her! Get away from her!

"I just know," I said, embarrassed to admit the reason, and nervous to show my ignorance about any details.

Don't trust either of them!

And then, ever so delicately, she said the words that chilled me to my core. "Grace, is there a voice talking to you?"

She knew.

Now could she know? Zack looked at me expectantly, perhaps waiting for me to contradict her. But, dumbfounded, I nodded.

"Oh, great, so she's a crazy person," Zack muttered, and I could see his mind working through the implications of that.

But Dawn shook her head. "Not crazy. Infected."

"Infected?" I asked.

"Remember those bugs you destroyed? At the hospital in New York?"

"Yes . . ." I said.

"Do you remember what they did? What the weapon was?"

Don't trust her! the voice was screaming. And kept screaming, all throughout our conversation.

My hand flew to my mouth. "Mind control," I whispered, putting it together. "You said it could put thoughts in people's heads."

I felt monumentally stupid. The voice had never been Great

Spirit, it wasn't even my own thoughts. *It was nanotech.* "But how did they get in my brain? I thought I destroyed them all."

"Since they're airborne, they likely infected you during the explosion itself. They've been multiplying in your brain ever since. Has the voice been getting louder as time's gone on?"

"Yes," I said tentatively. I didn't want to believe her, but I had trouble even hearing the words she was saying over all the yelling inside my brain.

I thought back on everything the voice had told me to do. To jump out of the cab when I should have been getting to safety. To escape that underground city and potentially expose myself to capture again. To meet with not one but three prophets, tell them everything, and remain in their prison. To bail on my mission at the stadium just when I was getting close. To . . . *find my mother.* To put off going into hiding and risk everything to find her.

I started to ask, "My mom . . ."

Dawn's gaze grew sympathetic. "When you were first infected with these mind control parasites, it's possible you could have had a brief hallucinatory experience. It would explain what you saw in the hospital, particularly combined with the oxygen deprivation caused by the fire. There was probably no woman there at all. And the bugs, the stronger they got, seized on something they knew would divert you from your goal. That's how they work."

"Parasites . . ." I said with horror, my mind consumed by the idea of something eating me from the inside.

Dawn explained, "Have you ever heard of toxoplasma gondii?"

"No . . ."

"It's a parasite, a microscopic creature, that replicates in the intestinal systems of cats. A cat's intestines are its home, and it'll do anything to get back there."

"Gross," Zack said.

"When the parasite infects a mouse, it gets into its brain, and it makes that mouse less afraid of the smell of cat urine, of cats themselves. Meaning those mice become easier for cats to find and eat, leading the toxoplasma parasites, and the mouse along with them, right back to their breeding ground—the intestinal tract of a cat."

I tried to wrap my parasite-filled mind around that. "You're saying the bugs in my brain are leading me to my death?"

"Something like that. They hijack your gut feelings, your instincts, and make you do things that will sabotage our cause. They make you more trusting of the prophets and their ilk, and less trusting of everyone else. They're even programmed to recognize the faces of known subversives and instill fear of those people. They're designed to lead you straight to the prophets for questioning."

That was why I'd jumped out of the taxi, why I hadn't trusted Dawn or Zack. Why I'd walked right up to Prophet Joshua, so fearlessly asking questions that might have blown my cover. Why I'd trusted Joshua when he said my mother was dead, accepted his words as truth when I'd doubted Dawn's and Zack's. Why I'd suddenly trusted my father, a noted cleric, why I'd felt so sure I could convince him of the truth. Why I'd felt safe with Samuel, and the prophets in Israel-Palestine. Why that voice had told me to confess to them, to stay in that cell. It was why the voice had told me to run just now when it knew I was close to accomplishing something the rebels wanted. Every action I'd taken since leaving that storage facility in New York had been driven by someone other than myself, had been compromised by Prophet Joshua himself.

"I'd guess that your mother was a weakness the bugs found," Dawn continued. "To keep you from getting yourself to safety.

She's lying to you! Your mother is alive!

My mother was dead. The truth of it hollowed me out, left me shaking and numb. As much as every part of me had wanted to believe she found some way to survive, I couldn't anymore. The proof was shouting in my brain. I'd spent all this time mistrusting everyone around me, but the only person I'd truly put my faith in—myself—that person turned out to be the least reliable of all.

But still, I tried to find excuses. "But this voice, this feeling . . . it did some good things for me. It kept me from taking cyanide. And there were people waiting to torture me, inside the stadium . . ."

"What people?" Zack asked, confused.

Then I remembered that when I'd looked through that window, I hadn't seen anyone at all. *I'd hallucinated those voices.* I'd hallucinated them saying exactly the thing that would compel me to turn away. I'd run away for no reason, just when our goal was within reach.

"Okay, maybe there weren't any people," I said, embarrassed and a little defensive. "But I stayed safe, didn't I? When you told me that Joshua would arrest me at any moment?"

"Because you had people helping you," Dawn said, frustrated.

"I destroyed the evidence linking you to the hospital bunker, but I still don't know how Zack hid everything else so well." Dawn nodded to Zack, and he gave an appreciative smile.

"I did what I could," he said humbly.

I looked at the two people I was sitting across from, two people whom this voice, this feeling in my gut, had warned me not to trust. I wondered if that proved their trustworthiness.

"What do we do now?" Zack asked Dawn.

Dawn regarded him warily. "Are you still willing to work with us?"

Zack nodded, clearly overwhelmed. "I want my freedom back."

"Help us, and that's the freest you can get."

Zack lit up with excitement—possibly the happiest I'd ever seen him. Thrilled to be fighting for a cause he believed in again. "Just let me know what I need to do."

Dawn looked at me. "Grace? How are you feeling?"

I was still reeling, but I steeled myself. "A little crazy. But ready to try this again."

6

"Are you sure you're prepared to go back in there?" Dawn asked me, as we approached the side door of the stadium. "The closer we get to the ventilation system, the more the bugs in your brain will try to convince you to sabotage the plan."

Even now, that voice in my head was booming, urgent— telling me to run, telling me I couldn't trust these people. But I recognized it for what it was. "I understand. I can do it."

"Are we sure we should bring her?" Zack asked. "You know, in this . . . state?"

"We need backup. If something happens to me, I need someone else to step in. They've already arrested all our allies in South Africa. The three of us, we're all that's left."

As we stepped through the door, I had a moment of hesitation. Was it still possible the voice in my head could be Great Spirit? I couldn't rule it out, could I? But then I remembered the conversation I'd just had with my father, and my own words rang in my ears, louder than the voice, for once: *Just because it's the first explanation you believed in, that doesn't make it the right one.*

I ignored the voice as much as I could as we moved up the stairwell, Dawn giving orders: "Zack, you know the players here. I need you to stand guard outside the room while I activate the device. Grace—stay here, out of sight. If we're not back in fifteen minutes, something's wrong. And then I'll need you to go and enter the code yourself."

Don't trust her!

"Got it," I said, almost shouting over the voice in my head.

They disappeared into the building, and I hid myself in a corner of the stairwell, out of sight of the door. *Stop her! Don't trust her!*

Ignore it, I told myself. You have to ignore it. *Stop her!* Ignore it. *You're an idiot! You can't trust either of them!* Ignore it.

Now that I knew what the voice was, I had to admit Dawn was right about how dangerous this tech was. And as horrifying as it had been to ride in that truck full of dead scientists, I understood why she was intent on preventing it from being unleashed on the public. From what she'd said, the bugs in my brain weren't even done replicating . . . who knew what this voice might be like once it reached full volume. Who knew what it might ask me to do, what Prophet Joshua could program any of us to do at any moment.

I tried to distract myself. I thought of Jude—but that only increased my anxiety, wondering if he would be safe, if my actions would keep him safe. *You're an idiot! Don't trust them!* Finally, I heard a sound—two sets of footsteps entering the stairwell.

But my relief was short-lived. It was too fast—Dawn and Zack couldn't be back already. And then I heard a familiar voice: "You don't have any more information than that?" It sounded like Guru Samuel Jenkins. And the legs I saw descending the stairs meant that I probably wasn't hallucinating this time.

A female voice I didn't recognize answered him. "They were trying to enter an unauthorized area. The woman is a suspected subversive. The young man is one of ours."

"One of ours?"

"I trained him myself. Zack Cannon." *Trained him myself . . .* the words struck a chord in my memory. This woman must be Esther, the one who'd recruited Zack. A hint of black fabric swishing at the woman's feet confirmed my suspicions. "He was one of our most promising new agents, although his record of late has been spotty."

"Find out how long he's been working with these subversives. I'll speak with Dawn."

The door slammed behind them.

Dawn and Zack had been captured. It was up to me now. *Don't go, you can't trust them!*

I had to activate the device myself. And to do it, I would have to fight my own thoughts every step of the way.

7

If Dawn and Zack had been apprehended while trying to get into the ventilation room, that meant Dawn's initial plan of just walking through the door wouldn't work—it must be too heavily guarded. And I didn't have any other ideas, because I didn't know these people, or this facility—but Zack did. That meant I needed to find Zack before Esther got to him, so I could find some way to free him.

But where would Zack be held? I was woefully underprepared for this. Luckily, I had one vital piece of information that might give me a lead—the name of the person interrogating him.

I slipped back into the building, hoping that since this was the last place Joshua would expect me to appear, he might not have the whole staff on high alert. I approached the first person I found, putting on my best innocent young girl voice. "Have you seen Esther? I'm supposed to give her a message, it's very important."

No response except a headshake and "Sorry."

I asked another person, then another. No one knew. I was starting to despair, when a young woman passing by overheard me. "She's heading for room 20A, I just saw her." She gave me directions, and I called out a thank-you as I ran off, clock ticking.

Moving deeper into the stadium, I heard the service on the loudspeaker, a South African cleric presiding: "I'm pleased to introduce one of my personal favorite clerics to the stage—all the way from the United States of America—Paul Luther!" The crowd cheered, and I couldn't help but peek at the jumbotron—there was my father, walking up confidently, ready to give his sermon. I teared up a little, watching his beaming face. This was the greatest accomplishment of his life so far, something I would have been beyond proud to witness just last year. But now, I tore myself away from the screen. I didn't have time to listen. I had to get to Zack.

When I found room 20A, there was a man standing guard outside. Even if the door was unlocked, which I doubted, I had no idea how to get past this guard, or how to bypass Esther. But since I'd been lucky the last time, I tried some social engineering again. "Prophet Joshua would like to move the prisoner downstairs," I said firmly.

Run! The guard seemed confused to be getting orders from a teenage girl. "Esther's inside with him now. Who are you?" *Get out of here!*

I quickly flashed him my little green business card—I couldn't believe how useful it still was, even now that I was burned. "I work for him."

You'll die if you don't leave right now. The guard straightened up. "Where downstairs?"

Shoot, I didn't know any more room numbers in this building. "He didn't tell me, he said Esther would know."

The guard nodded and headed into the room.

I didn't want Esther to see me when she emerged—I'd been lucky so far, but I didn't want to risk interacting with more people than necessary, and definitely not anyone high-ranking. I looked around for a place to hide; the best I could find was a large pillar, a few feet away. I slipped behind it, straining my ears to hear if someone was leaving the room.

"Well, I don't know, why would I know?" I heard Esther's voice saying, growing louder.

"She said you were supposed to know," I could hear the guard say.

"Who?"

"She was right here. Some kid who works for the prophet."

"Great Spirit, I'll go find him."

I heard heels clicking—away from me, thankfully. When it seemed like enough time had passed, I moved back toward the door, a plan in mind. *Turn around, run, turn around, turn around, turn around . . .*

I couldn't take it anymore. This voice was driving me crazy; I wanted to follow its orders, just to shut it up. I took a breath, steadying myself. *You can do this*, I told myself. *You can silence the screaming in your head.* And slowly, I worked to push the voice deep into the back of my mind. *Run.* Though I could still hear it faintly, it was easier to ignore. I moved forward, resolute. I had a job to do.

The guard glared at me as I approached. "Where did you go?"

"To find out the room number. The prophet wants them to move right below us."

"What room number?"

"I think it's 10A, it's the one exactly below us, should look the same," I said. "I can show you, if you want to grab the prisoner."

The guard looked confused, and for a moment, I panicked. I'd gotten too cocky. But the power of that business card compelled him to open the door.

As we entered, I saw Zack handcuffed to a table, looking miserable. But as soon as he saw me, he had to stifle a smile. "You want me to uncuff him?" the guard asked.

"Yes, please," I said, maintaining my aura of importance.

The guard leaned down to unlock Zack's handcuffs, and the moment Zack's hands were free—POW. Zack's elbow was in the guard's face, and the guard cried out with pain.

Another punch, and the guard was on the ground, unconscious. "Nice," I said, both impressed and appalled by Zack's ruthless efficiency, as he used the handcuffs to lock up the guard.

"Yeah, well, I joined up with you and kept my cover for all of five minutes. Not sure that deserves much praise."

"It's harder than it looks." I smiled, a little proud I'd kept mine as long as I did.

"What next?" Zack asked. "Dawn? Or the device?"

I looked at the clock on the wall. We were running out of time. The service would be over soon, and all these people would leave, taking with them our last chance at survival. "The device. If you know how to get to it without getting captured again."

"I have one idea. It's not a smart idea, but it's the only one I've got."

"What idea is that?"

A devilish smile crossed his face. "We get Esther to help us."

was not amused. "Are you kidding? Why would she help us?"

"We'd have to force her to. Gun to the head, that kind of thing." He gestured to the fallen guard, who had a gun at his hip.

"You're right, that sounds like a terrible idea!"

"Dawn and I got caught because my security badge doesn't have access to that room. Esther's will. All I have to do is hold her hostage for a few minutes, and that'll give you time to use her badge, get into the room, and enter the code."

"And then what happens to us?"

"Like Dawn said, if we can remove the nanotech from ninety thousand people, that's our bargaining chip. All sins will be forgiven, even this one. It's not like either of us is walking out of here alive otherwise."

"Right," I said, not pleased to be reminded of that. "So how do we do it?"

"We could find her in her office, but that would mean walking through a stadium full of guards who all know I tried to break into the maintenance room."

True. "But she's probably coming back here. She only left because of my message."

"Right. Hopefully she'll be alone."

My stomach flip-flopped. "Maybe not though."

"I guess we'll see." He picked up the guard's gun and turned to me, serious. "If this is it, I just want you to know, it's been fun." His wink threw me off guard again. The tangle of my thoughts these last few weeks had been so muddled—and now I knew I couldn't even trust them. I desperately wanted to know what was real and what wasn't.

And somehow at the top of that list was, "So that kiss . . ."

Zack blushed a little, to be reminded of it. "Well, yeah, I guess if we're dying, we can talk about it."

I tried to let him off the hook. "It was manipulation, wasn't it? You knew I had a little crush on you, and you wanted to convince me to help you?"

He looked at me, startled. "Is that really what you think?"

"I don't know. That's why I'm asking."

Zack smiled. "Well, I'll say I didn't know you had a crush on me."

Now it was me doing the blushing. "Little. I said little."

Zack's expression turned serious. "I promise I was not trying to manipulate you into doing anything other than kissing me. That said, I definitely wanted you to kiss me."

In that moment, with all my adrenaline rushing . . . I really wanted to kiss *him*. Zack wasn't Jude, and I wasn't in love with him, but . . . I might never kiss anyone again. And that last kiss had been a really, really good one.

I tore my gaze away from his and stared at the door, my cheeks burning. We had an objective. If we achieved it, I could kiss lots of boys, for the rest of my life. If not, I wouldn't have long to worry about it.

Zack was poised by the entrance, gun at the ready, as we heard the door begin to creak open. Lightning fast, he grabbed the burqa-clad woman who entered, pulling her inside. She screamed, but the door slammed shut, muffling the sound for anyone outside.

"Hey, Esther," Zack said, taking a bit of pleasure in turning the tables on his interrogator.

"Let me go!" she shrieked. Though I knew what part she played in this conspiracy, I still felt bad for her, this helpless woman fearing for her life. I wondered if that feeling came from the impostor in my brain.

"Not yet," Zack said, pushing her away from him and training the guard's gun on her. "Keep your hands up."

Esther walked into the light, hands raised, and a shiver of recognition went through me. All I could see beneath her veil was her eyes, and the dark skin around them. But the way those eyes looked at me . . .

Arms still raised in surrender, Esther lifted her veil, revealing a wild mane of curls. I stared and stared, until I finally believed it. And as I saw the apology on her face, I knew for sure I wasn't hallucinating. Esther was Valerie Luther. My mother.

My voice came out weak, childlike. "Mom?"

9

Esther stared at me, her expression a jumble of emotions. "Grace."

"Wait, what?" Zack said, taking a step closer to her, gun at the ready.

"Don't shoot her!" I cried instinctively. I wanted to run and hug her, but . . . I'd heard her with Samuel. She'd trained Zack. She was the enemy.

My mother moved closer to me. Her brown skin was coarser than I remembered, and her expression a jumble of emotions— but it was her, there was no question. "I'm sorry, Grace. I never wanted you to be involved in any of this."

"What do you mean? You were dead, you're supposed to be dead, where have you been? Why does he think your name is Esther, why are you here, working with Prophet Joshua . . ."

I had a thousand more questions, but I stopped talking as Zack hissed in my ear. "Grace, we don't have time. Do you still want to go forward with the plan?"

I looked at my mom. Did this change anything?

Don't do it! The voice in my head was resurging. *Don't do it!*

"Do it," I said.

Zack handed me the gun—it felt slick in my hands, and I had the same sickened feeling holding it that I'd had during the coup. I'd finally found my mother, and now here I was pointing a gun at her. "Watch her," he said, grabbing Esther's security badge from around her neck. As he headed to the door, she tried to follow.

"Don't move," I said, as forcefully as I could, voice shaking. I'd waited all this time to meet my mother—would I really shoot her a moment later? I couldn't, I knew I couldn't, but she didn't know that. And I had to make sure she didn't figure that out before Zack came back. As the door slammed shut behind Zack, she stayed put, watching me closely.

"I can explain everything."

All this time looking for her, I wanted that explanation. But . . . "You can't explain why you abandoned me for ten years."

"We make sacrifices, we give up the people we love, if we think it'll make the world a better place." Her excuse made my heart sink: it was the same reason I'd given for abandoning my Nova Scotia plans with Jude. She continued, "The world is at peace, for the first time in all of human history, and I helped create that. Don't you think that's worth whatever it costs?"

"Create that? *You* created it?" My voice stuck in my throat.

"Not just me. Dozens of us."

I shook my head, unwilling to believe it. "You worked in a battered women's shelter. I remember it, I visited you there."

"Every CIA agent has a cover. But that cover was informative. Every week I'd meet some husband, full of guilt for abusing his wife and children. And the women who loved them, returning time after time. Because their husbands were handsome or charming, because they believed they'd changed. I wanted so badly to show them the ugliness inside the men they loved . . . and then I finally had that chance."

I couldn't hide my horror. "People *died* because of you, millions and millions of innocent people. Guilt shouldn't be a death sentence."

"But love should? Loving the wrong people, loving your country enough to fight for it? You may think things are unfair, but I can tell you, this is more fair than the system we had before. You don't remember, you were too young."

"Don't *you* feel guilty?" I asked her. "For leaving me, for any of it?"

Her eyes looked pained. "Every day."

"Do you think you deserve to die for that guilt?"

She took a moment, before saying, "Probably. I imagine you'd agree?"

I noticed then that my eyes were filled with tears. I pressed my arms straight, keeping the gun trained on her, determined to stand my ground. "What about Dad? Didn't you love him?"

"Of course I did. I wanted to take care of him. I wanted to take care of both of you. How do you think your father became one of Joshua's most trusted local clerics?"

So my father wasn't magical with his words. The position that was so important to him, the sermon he was giving mere feet away from us, it was nothing more than nepotism, and he would never know. "He mourned you for so long," I whispered.

"I'm sorry, Grace."

"No, you're not!" My voice was hoarse.

"I am. Truly." Her eyes were wet now, too. She moved toward me, and I couldn't help taking a step toward her. I was sobbing, but I never broke eye contact, never lost my grip on the gun.

And then I remembered. "You were seeing Joshua, weren't you? That didn't have anything to do with why you left us?"

Her eyes narrowed. "Who told you that?"

"Joshua himself," I said defiantly.

She laughed miserably. "I wasn't *seeing* him. I was recruiting him. We were planning the American Revelation together."

Recruiting him. "I don't believe you."

"Does it really matter what the truth is?" my mother asked ruefully. "An affair is just a drop in the bucket, isn't it, of all the reasons you have to hate me?"

All those reasons piled on top of one another, and it felt like they were suffocating me. "A week ago I thought you were the best person in the world. I was fighting with the resistance because I thought the Revelations were a bad thing, because they'd taken you away from me. But the truth is, I was better off without you."

My words seemed to land, to burn her. "I'm sorry."

Her regret made me even angrier. "Stop saying that."

She reached out a hesitant hand to touch my shoulder, but I pulled back. "I'm not going to hurt you," she whispered.

"You're a mass murderer," I hissed.

"Over the past ten years, I've saved as many lives as I've taken. More, so many more. The number of people who would have died through violence, through money spent on armies instead of on prevention of accidents, or disease? You have this black-and-white idea of right and wrong, and I understand that—I created the culture that gave that to you. But things are so much more complicated than that." She took a step forward again. "Do you know why I wear this burqa? Because even though I knew I had to leave you behind, to help with this cause I'd spearheaded . . . I knew I couldn't really leave you. I still wanted to go to your recitals, your class plays. You won't remember, but I was there. In some small way, I wanted to be in your life as much as I could, even if you'd never know."

I tried to remember if I'd ever seen a woman in a burqa at my school events. I wanted to say yes, but I wondered if I was only imagining her there, because Esther had just planted the idea in my mind. And I'd had enough ideas planted in my mind.

"You didn't have to leave," I insisted. "If you had to be awful and evil, you still could have done it in Tutelo, with us."

My mother shook her head ruefully. "And put you in danger? I've made a lot of enemies. I didn't want to make them your enemies, too." Those enemies were the real reason she wore the burqa, I suspected.

She took another step closer to me. As much as I tried to remember to hate her, I couldn't . . . no matter what she'd done, she was still my mother. She was still the woman who'd held my hair back when I threw up after eating too much Christmas candy, the one who'd cleaned the gravel out of my knee when I fell on the playground, the one who could make me feel safe with one loving look.

And here was that look now. "You're so grown up. The last time I held you, you were just this little thing." She was so close, the gun in my hand was pushing against her heart. "And now look at you. A young woman, doing everything she can to help as many people as she can. I know you and I have different ideas about how to make that happen, but it doesn't mean I'm not so, so proud of you. I love you, Grace. I never stopped loving you, I never stopped thinking about you. Leaving you was the hardest thing I've ever had to do."

And then like a flash, she disarmed me, took a step back, and turned the gun on me. "And this is the second hardest."

10

I stared in disbelief down the barrel of the gun my mother pointed at me. "Mom . . . ?"

Her voice stayed level, sympathetic. "I understand why you could be seduced by these rebel ideas. Freedom is such a tantalizing concept at your age. It's only when you get to be an adult that you realize freedom is merely the opportunity to make the wrong choices, to hurt people, to hurt yourself. I wish we could be free and happy, but we can't. Happiness requires limitations, it requires someone helping us make the right choices. There will always be injustice of one kind or another in this world. We have to choose which injustices we want to live with. Someday, you'll understand that."

I stared at her, trying to process what had just happened. "You're wrong," I said. "If people knew the truth, they never would have picked this world."

"People rarely make decisions that are in their best interest," she dismissed. I wondered about the sins she'd committed. Did she think she deserved to die for them? Was she Punishing the world because she wanted to Punish herself?

She lowered the gun, left it hanging at her side. "You know I won't hurt you, right?"

I couldn't help but snarl back, "More than you already have, you mean?"

Her eyes grew soft. "I'll always protect you. You and your father, both."

"The hospital, in New York," I said as I realized. She nodded, and I felt a weight lift off me. I hadn't hallucinated her after all. "And you're the one who told them to let me go in Israel-Palestine."

"I'm going to get a lot of flak for that one," she said drily. My mother, risking herself to protect me from Joshua. It should have made me happy, but . . .

"Jude almost died because of you, because of the world you created. So did Macy. You can try to protect me, but you can't protect everyone I care about."

My mother shook her head. "You still don't understand. This *is* me protecting the people you care about. They're safer now, trust me."

She was so self-satisfied, it made me wonder. "What happened to the women at the shelter? Are they happier now?"

She seemed surprised by the question. "Yes. Most of them."

Her choice of words made me skeptical. "What about the others? Didn't any of them feel guilty, for subjecting their children to abuse?"

My mother's eyes grew dark for a moment. Just a moment. "On the whole, their lives are better."

Even her own failures wouldn't convince her. She was just as entrenched as my father in her own twisted belief system. There was nothing I could do to sway her from the notion that she was the great hero who had saved our world.

She reached out, took my hand. Her touch felt familiar, like a memory come to life. "It's been a long, strange journey, but now that we've found each other again, I can keep you safe. Maybe we can all be a family again."

I tried to imagine what that would look like, and I couldn't wrap my mind around it. Samantha was looking like a great maternal figure right now. "Or maybe I just leave."

"And go where?" she asked.

I thought of the country Dawn had talked about—a safe haven for people who knew the truth. "I have an idea."

My mother laughed. "You mean Dawn's little rebel country plan? Do you really think we'd give the opposition a base to operate from?"

My heart skipped a beat. "How do you know about that?"

"You've been tapped into our network, we know. But we've been tapped into yours, too. We've been watching you, listening in on your communications. We've overheard enough. You're planning to remove the nanotech from every person in this stadium. Or at least, you would have been able to, if the device in the ventilation room were operable. We disabled it as soon as we learned about your plans."

"Disabled it . . . ?"

"You can enter that code all you want, but it can't create any new material."

So it had all been a waste. Everyone who worked for Dawn

and Mohammed was about to be arrested—maybe tortured, maybe killed. And there was nothing I could do to stop it. Jude, Layla, Irene, and Zack—who'd really joined us at just the wrong moment. "My friends . . . You say you love me—if you really do, save my friends."

"I'm sorry, Grace." And she really did look sorry.

"Stop saying you're sorry and not doing anything!" I shouted.

Before she could respond, the phone rang on the wall. My mother moved toward it, but I was closer, and I grabbed it, staring down the barrel of the gun, daring my mother to pull the trigger. "Hello?"

My mother steadied the gun, voice urgent. "Grace, put it down." But I didn't.

On the phone, Zack was panicked. "Grace, the machine isn't working . . . it's hooked up to the vents, but when I turn it on, nothing happens."

"I know," I interrupted him. "My mom disabled it." And then, I had an idea. "Do you see anything yellow in that room? Like a powder maybe?"

The expression on my mother's face confirmed I was onto something. She moved toward me, yelling now. "I said put the phone down!"

Zack was talking at the same time. "Yeah, there's like a big vat of yellow dust, it's hooked up to the vents already. It looks set to go, I think you just push a button and it all goes whoosh." That yellow dust could be anything. But I had a guess it was the same substance that was in Zack's pills, the same yellow substance that had been left behind when Prophet Joshua gave me his "healing touch."

"Get it into the vents, now," I said. And I dropped the phone and ran for the door.

"Grace!" my mother cried, but I knew she wouldn't shoot me. All my little remnants of memories of her added up to that, at least.

I sprinted out the door, and my mother followed, yelling to nearby guards to restrain me. But I kept running, through souvenir stands and food stalls. I could hear footsteps pounding at my back, but I ignored them.

More guards approached from the opposite direction, blocking my escape. So I veered down an aisle, into the stadium's crowded stands. I raced down set after set of stairs, pushing past gawking conferencegoers until I ran out of steps.

Cornered, I jumped over the fence and onto the field, and I kept running. I could see guards coming after me in all directions—I was running out of places to go.

Desperate, I clambered up onto the stage as the startled band paused in the midst of their uplifting musical number, turning one at a time to see what was happening. Out of breath, I looked around.

I was standing next to Prophet Joshua, who smiled at me—a devilish smile of conquest. "Hello there, Grace."

11

I stared at Joshua, and then I looked out at the ninety thousand assembled faces, all staring back at me. Macy was in that crowd somewhere. I could see my father mere feet away, now finished with his sermon, staring at me with his mouth open, not knowing what to do. And all this was being broadcast across the world, since I doubted Dawn had managed to cut off communication while being held prisoner by Joshua.

"I think we've got you in a corner, don't we?" Joshua whispered to me.

What could I possibly do? My instinct was to pray—that's what I always did in times of desperation. But this time, my head was pounding with the voice of the nanotech. Great Spirit couldn't speak to me now even if He wanted to—there was an impostor living in my brain.

Just give up, the voice was hissing. *There's nothing you can do now.*

"Grace, I'd like you to meet the most pious folks in South Africa!" Prophet Joshua said into his microphone. I waved halfheartedly. Joshua was twisting the knife, but I knew the longer I played along, the longer I had before the guards would escort me off the stage.

This was my last chance. I could attack Prophet Joshua right now if I wanted to, maybe inflict some kind of physical damage. Or . . . I could tell all these people the truth. If Zack had managed to get that yellow dust into the air shafts, if it was healing these people right now, I could reveal the truth without killing them all. I could accomplish Dawn's plan in a different way. A more dangerous way—since, when the uppers wore off, these people might be plagued by the same lingering doubts that had almost killed me six months ago. And even the ones who survived, would be what—condemned to life on an island that was just a larger version of that underground city, with its violent infighting?

But then I had a different thought. A thought that made the intruder in my brain howl and moan. A thought which that intruder begged me not to act on. And that was enough to convince me it was exactly what I should do.

I'd been waiting for Great Spirit to lead me down a path . . . but for the first time I realized, the only path that would ever take me anywhere useful was the path I picked myself. And finally, I knew exactly where I wanted to go.

Inspired, I grabbed a microphone from one of the musicians. "Hello, Johannesburg!" I called out, and the crowd cheered, thinking this was part of the show. Joshua gave me another smirk, enjoying watching me stall for time, and I quelled the urge to punch him in his smug face.

I looked around the stage. I was sure that in addition to the yellow dust in the ducts, all these prophets would be perform-ing one-on-one miracles, which meant they needed to refuel their "healing touches." Taking a stab in the dark, I grabbed the Great Book sitting at Prophet Joshua's side and directed my speech to the nosebleed seats.

"I just started reading this book, have you heard of it?"

The crowd chuckled, used to the cheesy jokes that began sermons. The guards who had been chasing me slowed their approach, not sure whether they should grab me midspeech. Joshua was still coy, assuming that whatever Dawn had planned wouldn't work—that I couldn't tell any of these people the truth without risking killing them, and knowing I was too much of a do-gooder to cause that kind of devastation. But that wasn't my plan at all.

I channeled my father's boisterous preaching style as I con-tinued, "'Our greatest glory is not in never falling, but in ris-ing each time we fall.' That was Confucius, I think. And I like that. We all spend our lives so worried about failing—at least, I know I do. Because we know the consequences are so dire." I gestured to a few Outcast children who were standing near the stage—clearly waiting to be healed by one of the several proph-ets nearby. "These children, whatever they've done . . . do you think they deserved this Punishment? Really, in your heart of hearts, do you think that? *Children*? Because I don't."

I reached down and touched a young Outcast girl on the arm. My guess had been right—this Great Book was covered with the same yellow dust Joshua used to heal people. The girl's appearance morphed instantly, and the crowd began to murmur.

Out of the corner of my eye, I could see Joshua motioning to the guards to intercept me, but they were frozen, in awe of what they'd just seen. No mortal, no nonprophet had ever healed anyone like that before. I barreled forward. "Our leaders have told us to fear Outcasts. But why? Every old religion in this book tells us to embrace our neighbors, to be kind even in the face of hatred. And I know you all have seen it—how many people did we lose in the Revelations who didn't deserve it? How many since? How many Punishments have you witnessed that seemed unjust, but you were too afraid to say anything?

"I'm here to tell you that you're right. Great Spirit never intended us to separate ourselves like this. He thought that those of us who were Forgiven would embrace the Outcasts in our communities. That we would take every opportunity to help them. But we didn't. We ostracized them. And I don't think Great Spirit is happy about that. For the past few days, Great Spirit has been speaking to me. I know many of you have had this experience. Praying, and having your prayers answered. But the things Great Spirit has been saying . . . well, they're different than what I expected."

Joshua nervously spoke into a different mic, trying to cut me off. "I have, too, Grace, and that's what brings us to our sermon tonight . . ."

"No, it doesn't," I interrupted him. "Confucius said something else, too—that our leaders should be humble in word, but exceed in their actions. And Joshua, you've done neither. Everyone here has seen the kind of wealth you parade around with. And you and I both know the sins you've committed behind closed doors." The giant screens broadcasting the ceremony displayed Joshua's in-the-moment reaction to my words for the whole crowd to witness—his deep dread of what I might say next.

And then I saw it—the faces of the remaining Outcast children, morphing before my eyes. Zack had succeeded—the yellow dust was indeed the same chemical as in his pills, and everyone in this stadium was breathing it in right now.

"Cut her mic," I heard Joshua saying to someone behind me.

"I'm here to tell you," I said to the crowd—and then realized my mic had successfully been cut.

Undeterred, I leaned forward and grabbed another mic from the bandleader. "I'm here to tell you that I am your new prophet, Grace Luther. And all of you are Forgiven."

12

I had planned to say more, but this time it wasn't just my mic cutting out. Security finally listened to Joshua and dragged me away. I hoped desperately that my plan had worked, that I'd now have the ultimate bargaining chip to use against Joshua. But the way his security was manhandling me, I was skeptical.

My father reached me when the guards did, following in a panic as they pulled me away from the stage. "Grace, what are you doing?" He leaned in closer, out of earshot of the guards. "I know you're not a prophet. That was a trick, wasn't it? A trick your devil-worshipping friends taught you."

I knew there was nothing I could tell him that would exonerate me, nothing I could say to repair what I'd just broken. I wanted to tell him that my mother was alive, but if he hadn't believed me about any of the other things, he certainly wasn't going to believe me about that. "It wasn't a trick," I said, trying to brush him off.

He ignored me, beside himself. "I thought I was helping you, by not locking you in a mental ward, but now . . ."

I cut him off. "You can't help me, Dad."

"Grace . . ."

"Go home. I'll take care of it," I said sharply, nodding at the security guards, and they resumed taking me away.

"Grace!" my dad called after me in deep despair, but I didn't look back.

Now it was my turn to be thrown into room 20A and handcuffed to the table. I could hear the commotion outside, but I sat alone in panicked silence. I had no idea where Zack was, where Dawn was. Were they alive? Had my actions helped them or endangered them further?

Esther was the first person to enter my prison cell, livid. "What the hell was that?"

I put on a tough front, trying not to let my emotions distract me from my goal. "Promise my friends will be safe, and I'll renounce myself."

My mother was not swayed. "Do you think any of those people really believed you? You looked like a crazy person out there. Joshua's denounced you already, as will the other ten prophets here tonight. Those are the only voices that matter."

My breath was jagged with fear, but I kept on my brave face. "Maybe. Or maybe not."

Her expression was pained. "Do you have any idea how hard it is to protect you now?"

"Forget about me then. Protect Jude, protect Zack, protect the people I've been working with . . ."

"A bunch of terrorists? That's who you're throwing yourself on your sword for?"

"You gave up everything for a cause, but that life was yours to sacrifice," I shot back. "You never would have hurt me, or Dad. I put my friends in danger, and I have to make it right."

My mother shook her head, stoic. "That was your decision. It's too late. The raid is already in progress."

My heart skipped a beat. "Raid?"

Her expression was grim. "The compound in Turkey. It'll be empty in a few hours. You're the one who led us there, didn't Dawn tell you that?"

I stared at her in horror. "How?"

"I suppose she wanted to spare your feelings. The little green card that Samuel gave you has a GPS chip." I remembered how the voice in my head had insisted I take it to Turkey, even though Jude had told me to leave my pockets empty . . . how naïve of me to have forgotten that.

My mind was spinning. "I knew Zack was following me . . ."

"We suspected Zack might be sympathetic toward you, so we called in backup. We've had a twenty-four-hour operation watching you on satellite. We've seen every person you've interacted with, every person who's helped you. And now, every one of them is going to be arrested."

"No!" I cried. "You have to stop them. Jude's there . . ."

"Jude was a sweet boy," my mother remembered aloud. "I wish I could help him."

"You can. Why don't you realize it?"

Her voice shook with passion as she insisted, "If I let these few thousand people live, then millions, maybe billions more could die. These people you've allied yourself with—they're working to destroy everything I've built."

"Because you destroyed everything they had. You killed their families, you almost killed them. You almost killed *me*. Six months ago, I nearly died in our driveway, Punished to death. You came to my school plays, but were you there to see that? Were you there to save me from that?" My mom grew quiet and didn't answer. "Jude was. Jude saved me. Your actions would have killed me, but Jude saved me. And now you'll arrest him? Kill him? I know you wanted to do good, that's why you're here. So go do it. Help them. Please."

My mother stared at me—perhaps I'd gotten through, even just a little bit. But she didn't respond, just walked out the door.

I was left to stew in my own worry. Even if she did save Jude, what about Dawn? What about Zack?

That last question was answered about twenty minutes later, when Zack was thrown into the room and handcuffed to the same table as me. "Nice speech."

"Fat lot of good it did," I muttered.

"I don't know," he said. "You didn't get to see the response."

"What do you mean?"

"When Prophet Joshua started his sermon, people booed. They were chanting your name."

The notion filled me with a strange sort of pride. "I thought all the other prophets disavowed me."

"Not yet, they saw the writing on the wall. Your healing-the-stadium trick seems to have been a winner."

"Joshua didn't just take credit for it?"

"Of course he did, but no one believed him, not after they

saw you heal that girl. And all that stuff about Outcasts . . . I guess you tapped into something." He saw I was still skeptical and added, "Hey, I'm a convert."

I'd wanted to undermine Joshua and save my friends. Those were the only goals I'd had in mind. But the idea of people believing in me, cheering for me? It gave me a rush of excitement I hadn't quite expected.

Before Zack could say anything else, Esther reentered the room. "Prophet Joshua is willing to speak with you," she said, her voice clear of any emotion.

"What does he want?"

"I wish I knew." Esther unlocked my handcuffs and quickly relocked them. "Luckily you don't have quite the same martial arts skills as your boyfriend here." I quickly averted my eyes from Zack—while I'd always imagined what it might be like to introduce a date to my mom, this wasn't quite how I'd pictured it.

As I followed her into the stadium hallway, something very strange happened. The crowds of people we passed suddenly went silent, all staring at me. Some grabbed for their phones, snapping photos, taking videos. I averted my eyes, embarrassed that I was being paraded around in these handcuffs. Though, I remembered, Jesus of Nazareth had been in police custody at some point, so maybe the cuffs didn't undercut my prophet status that much after all.

As we walked, I saw a few news reports playing on phones, and I could hear snippets of the audio: "A new American prophet, popping up in South Africa of all places." "Grace Luther, only eighteen years old, could be your next prophet."

And then there was one particular video that caught my eye—a beautiful teenage girl I didn't recognize, speaking to a reporter. "She is the prophet, it wasn't just a trick on TV. She healed me six months ago."

"Healed you?" the reporter asked.

"I was in the hospital, in Tutelo, that's her hometown. I was dying in the Outcast Ward, and I looked up, and I saw her. She touched my face, and I healed. Instantly. I told people about it, but no one believed me, until now." I remembered her now—she was the girl in the Outcast Ward I'd given a pill to, when I'd gone to the hospital to save Macy. I'd just meant to get rid of it, so I wouldn't be caught with it. I never imagined that someone would say I'd performed a miracle.

Maybe Zack was right. Maybe people were more convinced than my mother had led me to believe.

Prophet Joshua was in his dressing room, flanked by two guards. "Please, sit."

I sat across from him, and he nodded for Esther to leave the room. I could tell she was nervous about leaving me alone, but she did as she was told.

After the door slammed shut, Prophet Joshua moved closer to me. "Cute. Very cute. Trying to sway the crowds in your favor."

"Seems like it worked," I said, trying on a little bravado.

"You excited the media. I wouldn't say you've begun a movement quite yet. No prophet has ever declared herself independently and been taken seriously. I had the support of every existing prophet in the world before I took power. People here believe in one religion. One. You can't start your own."

I ignored his spitting sarcasm and held his gaze. "So what do you want from me?"

"I wanted you to watch." He flipped on a TV screen in the corner, and it showed satellite footage of what looked like an empty piece of land.

"What's that?" I asked.

"Central Turkey," he said. "You've been there, I hear?" The footage zoomed in, and I could see an army, poised around a familiar entrance. The underground city. *Jude was in there.*

"What are you going to do?" I asked, voice trembling.

He relished watching my fear. "I'm considering. There are so many options. I could fill those airways with poison gas, so everyone suffocates slowly. I could send my men in, take everyone out individually, make sure your little friend Jude is good and dead. Or I could leave the whole thing as a smoking hole in the ground. Plant a sign, maybe? 'Grace Luther slept here.' What do you think?"

I was frozen. I had to save Jude, Layla, Irene, Mohammed. I had to save all of them. "What do you want me to do?" I asked quietly.

"I have a speech written up for you. You'll memorize it, and you'll perform it for all those folks out there, just as well as you did your last little song and dance. And if you do it well enough, I'll think about *just* arresting your friends."

I stared him dead in the eye. I knew I had leverage. I knew I'd won over that crowd, and I knew how powerful that crowd was. It could destroy him if I let it, if I could figure out how to wield it . . . but he had me. I wouldn't let my friends die. I was weak in that way, in a way someone like Dawn wasn't. This is why she was a leader, and I was not. I would give up my power in a heartbeat to save the people I loved.

"Think it over," Joshua said. "You've excited a few people, and I'd like to capitalize on that if I can. Worst-case scenario, I think I can find a good story to spin about Grace the martyr."

"I'll do it," I said, ignoring his last threat. "Just tell me what to say."

13

It was a good speech. I had to hand it to whatever prophet's aide had written it so quickly—a draft appeared as soon as I'd agreed to give it. As I rehearsed for Joshua, he instructed me to emote more, to smile at him more, to be more soulful. He enjoyed having me as his puppet, making me dance.

Twenty minutes later, satisfied by my performance, he opened the door. "Let's go."

The guards let me out of my handcuffs, and I followed him into the hallway, adrenaline rising. The moment I spoke these words, I knew I would lose everything. And I would be relying on the word of a man who had no incentive to keep that word. I looked around for my mother—surely she would be on my side, surely she could coerce Joshua into keeping his promises. But she was nowhere to be seen.

As we emerged into the stadium, escorted by an entourage of guards, the rowdy crowd saw us and swarmed, Joshua's security team holding them back. I'd seen this before—Joshua was overrun everywhere he went, by those trying to get just a taste of his healing touch.

But this time was different. People were clamoring to touch *me*. "Prophet Grace! Prophet Grace!"

As much as their adoration filled me with a strange kind of excitement, I kept my eyes down—I knew better than to acquiesce to their wishes. My friends' lives depended on every tiny move I made.

And then the other voices began to echo, to boo. "Hypocrite!" "Liar!" I glanced up and was shocked to realize that those voices were directed at Joshua.

He seemed shocked, too, but out of embarrassment, he ignored them, pushing ahead, confident that my forthcoming speech would set them straight. I began to question my strategy. Was there some way I could use this fervor to my advantage? Regain my edge?

And then I saw it—a balled-up napkin flying through the air, straight at Joshua's head. A guard batted it down and yelled at whoever had just thrown it, but the crowd still cheered. A paper cup now, thrown at Joshua's back, crumpling and spilling its contents down his suit, leaving an ugly brown stain.

"Great Spirit does not take kindly to blasphemers!" Joshua warned the crowd, but the jeers only got louder.

No one was being Punished, I realized. Not a person in the crowd. They were still acting under the protection of the dust. Protection they believed came from me.

And then I saw a bright glint of metal—a knife. Fear barely had time to shoot through me as I spotted the middle-aged man wielding it, his face a mask of fury. Joshua saw him, too, and tensed—realizing we were pinned in by this crowd, with no escape. As the attacker lunged toward us, careening like a wild, unstoppable force, the guard blocking Joshua stepped out of the way, terrified, taking no care to protect the prophet. Startled to be exposed like this, Joshua tried to run, but he only had a moment before the attacker was on top of him, driving his weapon straight into Joshua's spine.

Joshua cried out, then convulsed, wrestling the man off, freeing himself, as time slowed for a moment. I watched the horror on everyone's faces as the blood trickled down Joshua's back. He collapsed to the ground, screaming in agony, as his attacker took a step back, shocked by his own success. There wasn't a trace of Punishment on his face. Attempted murder, with no consequences.

To my absolute revulsion, the crowd cheered again, trembling with animalistic delight as Joshua cursed in pain, blood pooling around him. A few guards rushed to his aid, but the rest stayed back, pulling me away from the fray.

As I was dragged away, I saw the crowd closing in. Still Unpunished. Wild with glee. Tearing into him.

When security finally dispersed the mob, it was clear—Prophet Joshua was dead.

14

Not knowing what else to do, the guards threw me back into room 20A with Zack. I was unhandcuffed, but for once I had no desire to leave—I was terrified to step outside.

Zack was stunned to hear the news. "Could it have been Esther?" he quietly surmised, face pale. I knew what he was implying. Might the CIA, afraid of having two prophets, have taken one out, choosing to protect me in the process?

"Maybe," I said anxiously. It would let me off the hook at least, if someone else was responsible for this. But I felt cold; I couldn't shake that the feeling that it hadn't been Esther—that my speech had riled up those people so much that they were capable of committing murder.

Eventually Esther returned, pulling off her veil. "Are you okay?" she asked, shaken.

"Yeah. Joshua . . . ?"

"He's dead. You need to go." Her urgent tone unnerved me.

"Why?"

"He had a lot of allies. It's hard to tell where loyalties lie. Who might be out for revenge."

"What about Jude, and everyone in Turkey?"

"Safe for now."

I was incredulous. "How?"

She pulled out her phone to show me—the speech I'd given only an hour ago already had millions and millions of views. "Your little sermon made it all the way to Turkey. You managed to turn just enough of Joshua's troops to derail the operation. Right now, the army's in a stalemate. As long as it holds, your friends should stay safe." I wondered how long a detente like that could last . . . and how long the resistance could go without replenishing supplies.

Esther tossed me a second burqa, which I put on, and I followed her as she led Zack out in handcuffs. No guards hassled us while we were with Esther.

"Where are we going?" Zack asked as we walked.

"You'll find out when you get there."

When we arrived outside, a car was waiting for us with Dawn already inside, beaten and bloody from her interrogation. But she smiled at me, glad to be alive. "Great speech."

After taking the handcuffs off Zack, Esther opened the car door for me. "Don't come looking for me again."

"I won't," I said. For once, I knew I'd made a promise I could keep. I'd almost sacrificed everything just trying to see her one more time, and now I never wanted to see her again.

After a moment, I gave in and let her hug me. I hated how

much I still loved her. Her hug was safe and warm, and for a moment, I forgot what year it was, and who she'd become.

"I love you, Grace," my mother whispered.

"Goodbye, Mom." At least, this time, I got to say it.

Zack drove us to the point Esther had marked on the map, where we were to meet our transport out of town. It was near the docks, an unmarked building that appeared abandoned. But as we exited the car, a figure stepped out of the shadows.

"Grace?" It was Samantha, my dad's girlfriend, walking toward us. I *knew* she had her own agenda! "I'm here to help you get to safety."

Dawn and Zack instinctively followed her, but I hung back, suspicious. "Who are you working for?"

Samantha seemed to expect my wariness. "Your mother. She was worried when you got involved in all this. She wanted someone loyal to help keep an eye out and make sure you stayed safe."

I tried to ignore the implications of my mother hiring someone to date my father. "So you *were* spying on me."

"I never would have given the prophet any information that would have hurt you. That's why I was there, to make sure no one did. After you tried to tell your father the truth, I was the one who convinced him not to take his concerns to Walden Manor." I was disappointed to hear my father *had* broken my confidence, at least to Samantha. On the other hand, I'd never been so grateful to have an Evil Stepmother in my life.

As I followed her inside, I asked, "So what now, you disappear and break up with him?"

"No. He's in more danger now than ever before. Because of you." Her tone worried me—I hadn't even thought about what might happen to my father.

"Can you get him to safety, too?"

"I'll try," she said. Though I believed her, the thought of him being watched over by an agent of my mother didn't ease my worries as much as I would have liked.

"You're getting us out of the country, right?" Dawn asked, clearly uncomfortable following a plan that wasn't her own.

"We're going to smuggle you out by boat," Samantha said. "Someone on the other end will let you out." Like everyone else in my mother's organization, she either didn't know or was unwilling to tell us our final destination.

Samantha loaded up the stock of supplies we'd need for the journey—enough food and water and Dramamine to last us weeks. The space belowdecks was cramped, and I knew we'd have to hide there until we got out onto the open sea. But we were safe, and alive, which is more than I could say for Jude and the others in the compound. I prayed that they were safe, prayed to Great Spirit, hoping He could hear me over the rambling voice in my head, hoping He might protect them. Hoping that I'd get to see Jude again.

Once it was safe for us to emerge, the men who sailed the boat were eager to speak to me. They knew exactly who I was, and they were excited to aid my cause. Over the course of our weeks-long trip, they bombarded me with questions. The captain wanted to know, should he propose to his girlfriend? The first mate worried about her father's health—could Great Spirit heal him? I tried my best to answer, realizing just how far out of my depth I was. I had taken no class on how to be a prophet, and it made me nervous to realize just how powerful each and every word I uttered was now. And after witnessing Joshua's death, that power scared me to my core. As did the thought of what would happen if people discovered the truth.

I remembered the conversation I'd had with Irene, Dawn's wife, about religion being a mechanism for control. Assuming she was right, I'd just taken the reins to control a massive number of people . . . and I wasn't sure how I was supposed to feel about it. Especially because, while I could say I believed in Great Spirit, I still couldn't fully define what that meant for myself, much less for the world I'd just created.

I missed that feeling I'd had so briefly, when I'd first been infected with the mind control bugs—that my life had some kind of purpose again. The nanotech had hijacked my brain and convinced me that Great Spirit was leading me somewhere, that my actions looking for my mother were part of some greater plan. And it was a lie, I knew it was.

But in a way, the bugs had given me purpose, if only by accident. If I hadn't been compelled to search for my mother, I never would have ended up in Joshua's office, never would have seen that yellow residue, never would have been able to come up with a plan to stop him. It was simply a series of random events that had led me to this place, I knew that. But if I wanted to, I could create a story out of those random events, a story that gave my choices some kind of meaning. I knew it was a stretch, a selfish attempt to justify my own mistakes as being part of some larger purpose. Maybe that was all the purpose you could get out of life, the meaning you gave to it yourself.

And I knew now, this choice I'd made, this path I was going down—that was all my doing. And whatever came next, it wasn't Great Spirit who would have to answer for the consequences . . . it would be Grace Luther.

After weeks on the open ocean, sun beating down hotter by the day, we saw land again. As we navigated closer to the shore, I saw a small port, flanked by lush trees, sandy beaches—paradise, with a silver city peeking through treetops in the distance. Massing along the shore, there was an immense crowd of people—Outcasts, I realized, as we grew closer, all cheering. They knew we were coming; *they were cheering for me.*

As I exited the boat, they reached for me, all at once, overwhelming. Zack had to step in front of me, acting as my bodyguard. One woman tentatively touched my arm, then shivered with delight. I saw her face change—become more beautiful. I realized, with equal parts astonishment and fear, that I no longer needed any kind of special chemicals to heal people. Just being near me created a powerful spiritual experience inside someone, the kind that Forgave.

"The prophet of the Outcasts! You bless us with your presence," a grotesque man said happily as he embraced me. He identified himself as the mayor of the nearby town and explained that we'd made it all the way to the northeast coast of Brazil, to one of the largest Outcast encampments in the world: Redenção, named for the Portuguese word for "redemption." An Outcast metropolis, it seemed like, from the gleaming skyscrapers I could see not far from shore. The folks assembled here had been camped out for days—these were my most ardent followers. And it was true—Zack couldn't hold back the crowd as they grabbed at my arms, touched my face, healing bit by bit.

"I'm sorry I didn't come sooner." I stumbled over my words, overwhelmed by their response. And though my instinct was to avert my eyes from their mangled faces, I looked on through my disgust and saw their beauty. All these souls who wanted the same things I wanted—love, respect, companionship. I was their prophet now, whether I wanted to be or not.

"What can we do for you?" another woman asked, as she clutched at my sleeve.

I looked at Zack and Dawn, and they nodded at me encouragingly. "We need a place to stay for a little while. Somewhere safe."

The crowd jittered with excitement. "She's staying with us! She chose us!" I heard among the chatter.

The mayor reached out his hand and took mine, pulling me away from the fray. "Welcome home, Prophet Grace."

ACKNOWLEDGMENTS

Six years ago, I sat in my friend Ari's apartment, and together we mapped out post-Revelation Earth—its detailed history, its major players, its future. It was one of those moments that made me realize just how much I loved that friend—what writer doesn't want to date their very favorite collaborator, after all? Since then, Ari, you've read just about everything I've ever written, and I can find your thoughts entangled with mine on pretty much every page. One book dedication doesn't seem like quite enough to thank you for your unflagging emotional support, and how frequently I get to borrow your brilliant creative mind. And I'm even more grateful knowing that this series is just the first of many worlds we'll get to build together.

I also want to extend a massive thank-you to everyone who bought and read and tweeted about and recommended *Sinless* to their friends! I've been overwhelmed by all the love and support from friends and family and colleagues and delightful strangers; your kindness has meant the world to me. And a mega, massive thanks to the whole Harper Voyager marketing and publicity team for all the hard work you've put into this series!

Thanks as always to my amazing agent, Peter Steinberg, for your thoughts and helpful advice throughout this process.

A huge thanks to Priyanka Krishnan for your deft editorial skills, helping to shape this story and shepherd this series—you'll be missed! Tessa Woodward and Elle Keck, thank you for getting this book to the finish line.

And thanks of course to the folks who helped get this series started: Rebecca Lucash, David Pomerico, Randy Kiyan, Claire Londy, Markus Plank, and Eva.

To Julianna Hays at MarVista, who's been supervising the television adaptation—working with you has been such a pleasure, and I'm so excited to see where this journey takes us!

To Silanur Inanoglu, our fabulous sensitivity reader, thank you for all your thoughtful insights!

To everyone else who gave feedback on early drafts: Sarah Hawley, Laura Herb, Becky Ridgeway, Allie Kane, Janet Epperson, Casey Joy Ward, Cathy Hill—I'm so grateful for your wisdom!

To my *Arrow* family, for your support throughout this adventure, as well as all my mentors and creative partners from other projects.

And as always, my amazing parents. I wouldn't be here without you (quite literally, duh), and I'm so grateful to get to share this with you.

ABOUT THE AUTHOR

SARAH TARKOFF currently writes for the CW series *Arrow*. Other TV writing credits include ABC's *Mistresses*, Lifetime's *Witches of East End*, and the animated series *Vixen* and *The Ray*. She graduated from USC with a degree in screenwriting (hence all the screenwriting), and currently lives in Los Angeles. *Sinless*, the first book in the *Eye of the Beholder* trilogy, was her debut novel.

www.sarahtarkoff.com
Twitter: @sarahtarkoff

ALSO BY
SARAH TARKOFF

SINLESS

EYE OF THE BEHOLDER; VOLUME NUMBER 1

"What [begins] as girl-meets-boy escalates to geopolitical intrigue, espionage, daring rescues, and Grace's growing, bittersweet self-awareness of what it really means to be a good person. Clever worldbuilding elevates the story... and the plot is juicy enough to carry readers to the sequel." —*Kirkus Reviews*

With shades of Scott Westerfeld's *Uglies* and Ally Condie's *Matched*, this cinematic dystopian novel—the first in the thrilling Eye of the Beholder series—is set in a near future society in which "right" and "wrong" are manifested by beauty and ugliness.

DISCOVER GREAT AUTHORS, EXCLUSIVE OFFERS, AND MORE AT HC.COM

AVAILABLE WHEREVER BOOKS ARE SOLD